Phoenix Afterlife

a novel by

James Leth

This is a work of fiction. Names, characters, places, and events are products of the author's imagination, or they are used fictitiously.

Cover design by Cover Quill
(www.coverquill.com)

For my mother, who led me to a lifelong love of books.

CONTENTS

Waking Alone

"Do you want to live forever?"

Matthius blinked, surprised to find himself awake. He had a moment of anxiety, then the ceiling came into focus, and relief crashed down on him like high surf. It wasn't the blue light.

"I think we both know that's an option now," Trick continued.

Matthius rolled his head toward Trick's voice, but no one was there. The voice had come from the other room of the suite, around the open doorway. He sat up slowly, unsure if his muscles were ready for it. Sitting on the edge of the bed, he pushed the rest of the covers to the floor, planted his feet, and stood, bracing only slightly against the bed. Confused, he looked around. He was definitely in the bedroom of the test suite, but there should have been others with him — a medical team, at least. And where was Alice? He expected her to be hovering over him, taking note of his every breath, but he was relieved that she wasn't there; he dreaded what he had to tell her now.

Matthius was stable on his feet, but his mind still felt like a passenger along for the ride, enjoying the scenery but uninterested in the destination. *Like a lucid dream,* he thought, but he knew it was no dream. The sedative suppressed REM state through twelve straight hours of the deepest sleep he'd ever had. Alice told him he'd be disoriented when he woke, but she didn't mention the calm. It felt like sitting at the edge of a placid lake, plunking his thoughts into the water just to watch the ripples spread across the surface.

He walked carefully to the doorway and found the living area empty, but Trick's face gazed at him from the monitor at the computer station: clean-shaven, close-cropped dark hair, pale skin behind the ever-present videoglasses (now politely transparent.) Matthius always thought Trick looked younger than his thirty-odd years, but recent events seemed to have aged him.

"This isn't quite the wake-up call I expected," Matthius noted, slowly making his way to the computer station, where he sat in front of the monitor and camera. He glanced at himself in the thumbnail image of the view that Trick saw. He looked disheveled, his graying hair creeping around his face as if trying to escape his head.

On the monitor, Trick smiled, and his voice came again from the speakers, "I thought we could have a private discussion before everyone else knows you're awake, and talk about some of the questions they won't think of." Trick looked expectantly at Matthius. "Like the one I asked you already."

The blue light, Matthius thought. *Someone else will wake to it.* Is that why Trick wanted to talk privately? Did he understand what Matthius realized the moment he woke? "You knew how I'd feel, didn't you, Trick?"

"Of course not," Trick said, shaking his head. "All I knew was that it would be different than any of us expected."

"Including me."

"Especially you."

Matthius looked at Trick, who still waited patiently for an answer. "The Mnemosyne project is not about immortality."

"No," Trick agreed, "but half of science is just noticing what you weren't looking for."

Matthius smiled ruefully, unaware he was doing so. "*I* noticed that I wasn't in the blue light," he said. "Something I definitely wasn't looking for."

Trick stared back at him from the videochat window, the cameras and monitors between them fading into the background. It was exactly the same as talking to Trick in person, Matthius realized. The man didn't emit the normal sub-channels of information that people express up close. He constantly soaked up information, but he seldom gave any back.

"How do you make peace with it, Trick? I'll never be able to do that."

Trick was silent for several seconds, and Matthius assumed he wasn't planning to answer. He did, though. "You're an engineer, Matthius. You know how thrilling *proof of concept* is. It doesn't matter how much work there's still to do. Vastly more things are achievable now, and more will be learned in our lifetime than has ever been known. You could live to see it all. Everything, from here on."

"I was taught that immortality is something we have to *earn.*"

"What will happen when it's something you can *buy?*" Trick asked.

Matthius twitched. "I wasn't aware you were planning to sell it." His voice cracked a little.

"Oh, we're not, but anything of great value will eventually be sold."

"You should stop it, Trick. You should shut it down and find another way." Matthius shivered from the sweat rapidly evaporating off his face and neck, leaving goose-bumps behind.

"It doesn't matter if we stop it," Trick said. "It's possible; we know that now. So if *we* don't do it, some-one else will. The technology will be out, in one form or another. We need to study it now, while we're the ones in control."

Matthius laughed bitterly. "What makes you think you're in control of this?"

Trick paused, appearing to recalculate. "We have more control now than we ever will again. We must learn what to do with this."

"No, you must learn what *not* to do with it."

"Yes, that too. You still haven't answered my question."

Matthius leaned back, swiveling the chair left and right. "The Cumaean Sibyl was given immortality, but in the end, she asked to die."

"She forgot to ask Apollo for eternal youth," Trick countered, surprising Matthius that he knew the tale. "She shriveled away — eternally. *You* could have the whole package."

"It wouldn't be *my* life, though, would it? Not really."

"Well, that's the fundamental question," Trick acknowledged. "It depends entirely on how you choose to look at it."

"I choose not to look at it at all," Matthius said with finality.

Trick studied his face for several seconds. "I understand. Thank you, Matthius. I'm sorry about this, but it was the only way to know."

The videochat window closed, leaving Matthius to wonder what Trick meant, but there was nothing more.

Eliot

Eliot spent the morning wrestling with dragons and dinosaurs. He wandered into paleontology following a complex path from origin myths, and there he found several papers about new fossil discoveries. Not an expert in the field, Eliot didn't check the technical links. He looked for more interesting connections, and that's where the ontology let him down: there were no direct paths from dinosaur fossils to dragon myths. It took Eliot three more hours to come up with the most concise update to the concept maps, and the new links were just beginning to appear when Terry stopped by.

"Ready for lunch already?" Eliot asked, still paging through the dynamic links. He turned his chair around to look at his friend fidgeting next to him. Eliot was 32, a decade older than Terry, but Eliot's slightly-too-long blond hair and Terry's shaved head made it hard to see the age difference.

Terry quickly pulled a chair over and sat uncomfortably close to Eliot. He leaned in, whispering while looking out for eavesdroppers, "I'm sure Ann's safe, but I think it might be Jack, and maybe Robyn, too."

Eliot sighed. "Didn't I say I'm tired of this conversation?"

"But it has to be layoffs," Terry insisted. "When was

the last time we had a mandatory evening meeting? And on a Friday!"

"Okay, so it's layoffs. So what? Are you worried that you're on the list?"

Terry blinked in mock surprise. "Who, me? Why would I be laid off? I've been taking credit for half the things you do around here. They think I'm untouchable." Eliot laughed and turned back to his explorations. Terry watched for a few seconds before asking about it. "Is this your semantic web project?"

"Yeah, I'm checking the ontology. These links are automatically generated, based on the relationships in the global concept maps."

"I thought ontology was a branch of philosophy."

"Right: what actually exists, and what we mean by that." Eliot glanced at Terry, saw the familiar frown and the stubborn refusal to ask. He pointed to the monitor and explained, "In this context, the ontology is the set of formal rules that describe what exists, including how things and concepts relate to each other. It's the dictionary problem: to define a word, you have to use words, and they're defined by other words. What anything *means* is derived from its relationships to everything else."

"Okay, so what are all these links about?"

Eliot glanced back at the display and said, "There's a relationship between dinosaurs and dragon legends, but the concept maps didn't track it."

"Dinosaurs were long gone before there were people to dream up dragon stories," Terry objected.

"Right, but their fossilized remains weren't. They showed up from time to time, after earthquakes, or laid bare by desert winds. So what would *you* think if you came across a trove of dinosaur bones — bones made out of stone — with no modern perspective on geologic time?"

"I guess I'd think it was a good thing that the monster was already dead." Terry thought about it for a few seconds. "And then I'd carry off the skull, head for the nearest village, and brag about the dragon I just killed. They'd write songs about me, and I'd have my pick of the serving wenches."

Eliot laughed. "Yeah, that sounds about right. Anyway, it's a potentially useful connection. You may be able to infer which prehistoric species lived where, based on the earliest monster myths. Paleoecology informed by anthropology."

"Yeah," Terry agreed, clearly losing interest. "But what are *you* doing with it?"

"Well, this is the sort of thing I volunteered to review."

"What, dinosaurs?"

"No, gaps in the concept maps. Relationships between science, myth, and literature. Links that should exist but can't be discovered without changes to the ontology."

"Okay, I get it," Terry said. "So you reported the problem?"

"No, I fixed the problem. I defined some new concept links. I'm testing them now."

"How can you do that? You're just a volunteer on this project. Don't you have to go through the people in charge?"

Eliot looked at Terry in surprise. "There are people working on this all over the world, and they're *all* volunteers. You didn't think it was just our library, did you?"

"No, of course not," Terry dismissed the notion, perhaps too quickly. "I know it's a whole bunch of libraries."

"And universities, research labs, publishers, Wikimedia, W3C, …"

"Okay, okay," Terry held up his hands. "So what happens if your updates aren't right? Won't you be responsible for breaking the archive of human knowledge, or something?"

"No, there's a process for review and redaction. Right now my updates are considered experimental. They'll be evaluated by other volunteers, and once they reach a high enough trust level, they'll be included in the standard configuration."

"How long does that take?"

"The last time I made updates, it took two weeks, but my trust factors are about 50 points higher now. This will probably take about four or five days to become standard, but a lot of researchers will start using it right away, because they automatically track my changes."

Terry became very quiet while he watched his friend work. He seemed surprised, and maybe a bit unnerved, to discover that Eliot's work was being used by researchers all over the world. "That's cool," he said a minute later. "Sounds more fun than real work."

"This *is* my real work," Eliot said, turning to look at Terry. "I explained to Randall that contributing libraries get free access to about a thousand new technical journals. Now he doesn't want me to work on anything else. Which reminds me," he reached for his tablet, showing Terry the queue of research requests in the library's inbox, "you'll need to take my share of the RRs next week."

Terry groaned and lowered his head. "Terrific. Another dozen whining college students trying to get me to do their work for them."

Eliot laughed. "It's not all students. And even *they* come up with interesting queries sometimes."

Terry snorted.

"Well, not very often," Eliot conceded. "But the library *is* on their campus. Think of it as an opportunity to teach them something."

• • •

At the end of the day, as the library patrons made their final checkouts, the off-duty staff began to arrive for tonight's meeting. As soon as the doors closed, the branch manager gathered them around the big tables. Randall Hayward was not a particularly subtle man, nor was he secretive by nature. Eliot was certain he'd be able to tell who was affected, just by watching whose eyes Randall avoided. To his surprise, Randall gave nothing away, and Eliot found the melodrama annoying. *He should tell each person individually, rather than announcing it to the whole group. Unless we're* all *being laid off.* It seemed unlikely that they'd close the South Mountain Branch Library. It was the newest of the three libraries in the district, and it was heavily used — far more than the old library downtown. Perhaps they were closing the downtown library and consolidating everything here.

"Well," Randall began, glancing nervously around the table. "I suppose everyone's anxious to hear the news, so let's get started. You all know that the Mesa Vista Library District is experiencing a pretty severe revenue shortfall. We thought the referendum would pass last fall, and we've been struggling to complete the quarter with a budget in place for the rest of the year."

"We looked at every option we could think of," Randall continued. "Everyone on the leadership team put a lot of work into this. We analyzed every aspect of our operation. But when you get down to the numbers, there's really only one axis of flexibility, and that's work-force compensation."

Where do they teach managers to talk like that? Eliot wondered. He started to think about the relationship between obfuscating formal language, the appearance of punditry, and intimidation of subordinates; in the process, he totally lost the thread of Randall's speech for several minutes.

"… so the goal was to come up with a way to reduce our overall payroll *without* any layoffs," Randall said, pausing for effect, and getting it. This was not what anyone expected. Confident he had their attention now, he explained the plan that the management team had come up with. Everyone was affected, but no one would lose a job. Instead, there would be slightly reduced hours, an across-the-board pay cut of three percent, and one final item.

"We're requiring all non-management employees to take a furlough of ten days without pay."

"Why not managers?" Ann asked.

"The legal department says that our employment contracts prevent us from extending that action to management personnel," Randall answered. *Or to the legal department*, Eliot guessed.

"Do we still get vacation?" Jack Parker asked.

"Yes, of course," Randall assured him. "There's no change to anyone's vacation status. In fact, the accounting department would be happy if everyone took vacation days as early as possible this year. Apparently, that improves our expense reporting."

"Well, can we trade vacation days for furlough days, then?" Terry asked. "I'll give up a week of vacation in exchange for one of my weeks without pay."

"I'm not giving up my vacation," Jack interrupted. "We've been planning our trip for a year."

"No one's giving up vacation," Randall said quickly. "You can't trade vacation days for furlough days. Once again, that's not allowed under our employment contracts."

"Do we have to take the furlough all at once, or can we take a day here and a day there?" Eliot asked.

"You can take it any way you like, but you have to schedule it just like vacation days, so that we have appropriate coverage for all shifts."

It was better than losing his job, Eliot conceded, but he hadn't expected to be affected at all, and the lost income might be a problem. If he took the furlough all at once, could he find a temporary job for two weeks?

When the meeting broke up, Eliot walked out to the parking lot, talking it over with Terry and Ann. "There's probably an opportunity with the college students," Terry said. "They're always looking for tutors. We all know they don't like to do their own homework, right Eliot?"

They laughed, and Eliot asked, "What subjects would you tutor, Terry? They already know how to ditch class and surf the web."

Ann laughed and Terry answered, "But they haven't yet learned how to push annoying tasks onto their coworkers."

"Well, I could teach that," Eliot conceded. "But come to think of it, why don't you do it for me?"

They were standing in the parking lot now, right at the point where they'd go their separate ways. Ann said, "I think I'll just consider the furlough as extra vacation. I'll go visit my parents in Santa Fe. I can get by without the money."

"Lucky you," Terry said. "I haven't paid off my student loans yet. What about you?" Terry looked at Eliot. "You still paying off your tuition from decades past?"

"No, but I don't exactly have money to spare," Eliot said.

"Oh, yeah, your England trip," Ann said, looking

concerned. "When's that?"

"End of September, if I can still manage it." Eliot fumbled with his keys. "I guess I'll take a look at the part-time job ads. Good luck, guys." They nodded to each other and headed toward their cars. Eliot's white Honda Civic was the closest.

• • •

Just a fifteen-minute drive from the library, the Mountainside Apartments were convenient to the college campus, but too expensive for most students. Eliot's neighbors were young professionals, like him, or even younger couples starting families. The complex spanned six buildings and a clubhouse with tennis courts and a pool. Eliot rarely used the pool; at this altitude, the outdoor swimming season was about two months.

Mesa Vista sat on the eastern slopes of the Rocky Mountains at an elevation of 6500 feet. It was about halfway between Denver and Colorado Springs, but west of both. Like many Colorado mountain towns, it was founded on mining. Most of the mines shut down long ago, but the town became a fashionable place for high-tech startups, and was now expanding rapidly. Convenient access to ski resorts, national forest land, and mountain casinos drew a young and enterprising demographic.

Eliot's apartment was on the third level — the top floor of his building. He didn't mind the stairs, for the view was worth the effort. He had a clear line of sight to the high peaks just a few miles away, and he didn't like to go a day without standing on his balcony and appreciating it. Born and raised in Colorado, Eliot always enjoyed the mountains. The state had over fifty peaks higher than 14,000 feet, and Eliot had hiked up half of them before he graduated from high school — first with his father, later with friends. Eventually, he tried rock climbing and rappelling, learning from a more experienced friend. It was thrilling, but he was never comfortable with the opportunities for death or paralysis lurking in the background. He began to understand why he'd never progressed beyond the intermediate-level ski slopes. Eliot still hiked occasionally, but he had no interest in near-death experiences.

As soon as he entered the apartment, Eliot walked to the sliding glass door and out onto the balcony. He strolled to the edge and leaned against the railing, watching the darkness settle in from the mountains. Someday there might be a new apartment complex or an office building that encroached on his view, but for now, Eliot enjoyed the luxury of a sunset over the Rocky Mountains most days of the year. Today, he had been hidden away inside the library too late. The sun passed behind the mountains almost an hour earlier, and the air was growing cold. He walked back inside, shutting only the screen behind him.

He put his jacket back on, made a meal out of this week's leftovers, and took it out to the table on the balcony. Music and voices crept in from several directions, along with the sounds of cars arriving and leaving the parking lot. While he ate, Eliot listened to it all, knowing that he was participating in an ancient rite: the end of day, returning safely to his place within the tribe, the outside world fading into the dark and quiet. When he finished his supper, the mountains were a black veil against the background of stars and city lights, visible only by the absence they created.

Eliot sat for a while in silence, then returned inside, washed his dishes, and sat down in front of the notebook computer that occupied the only part of the dining table not covered with books and papers. He hadn't looked at his résumé for at least five years, but as he skimmed it, he was surprised at how little had changed in that time.

His major at Colorado State University was English Literature, but he became frustrated at the narrow focus; *English* literature was just a small slice of what he wanted to study. In his senior year, CSU began offering a graduate program in library science, and he stayed on for his master's. It wasn't quite what his parents had hoped for. His father was a professor of classical literature, and his mother taught American history in high school. Somewhere in their world travels, they fell in love with the English countryside, and a year ago, they sold their house in Colorado and retired to a cottage in Somerset. Eliot was planning a trip to see their new home, but now it would be difficult to afford.

A faint rumbling of thunder in the distance drew his attention, but it was too dark now to see anything through the glass patio door. Eliot listened for a few minutes, realizing it must be raining in the canyon west of town. Rain was usually welcome in this semi-arid climate, but it could quickly become too much in the canyons. Flash floods and rock slides killed people almost every year in Colorado.

Eliot made some minor edits to his résumé and retired to the bedroom for the night, a book under his arm. He always read for an hour or two before falling asleep.

• • •

There was a gentle movement in the bed next to him, and Eliot reached out his hand to touch Christine's back. He heard her sigh in her sleep, and she rolled toward him. He reached around her waist and drew them closer together. They were kissing on the floor in front of the fireplace, the room dark except for the glowing embers of the dying fire. His hands drifted languidly over her naked skin, and he could feel her tremble to his touch. They stood on the balcony looking up at a dark, moonless night. It was hours before dawn, and she wore one of her long, loose t-shirts, and he wore only sweatpants. He pressed his chest to her back, his arms around her waist, holding her close. Gently, he caressed her breasts through the t-shirt. She said something to him, but it was in Portuguese. He opened his Portuguese/English dictionary, but it was all written in mathematical equations. They sat on the floor in front of the crackling fireplace, naked and entangled, the smell of their bodies making a potpourri of lust and joy. He lay atop her, thrusting deep. She wrapped her legs around him, they rolled over together, and he awoke.

Eliot lay still for several minutes, trying to hold on to the dream. It had been so vivid: the feel of her skin; the scent of her hair; the taste of her sweat. As the clarity of the dream quickly faded, he struggled to remember exactly what it felt like to hold her — something that hadn't happened for three years now.

There were real memories mixed up in the dream, but dreaming was so different than remembering. In the dream he could touch her, smell her, feel her warmth. How could that experience be accessible to his dreaming mind, but not to his conscious mind? It must all be there, somewhere in his brain, but awake, he could only access the shape of it, not the feel. Was it consciousness itself that kept the memories at such remove?

Eliot watched the nascent dawn slowly illuminate the blinds, uncertain whether to sleep again or rise. His thoughts lingered on Christine. They met in college, part of a close group of friends that remained strong through his first three years at CSU. Senior year, everyone started pairing up or going their separate ways. Eliot and Christine were lovers for a while, but their lives never seemed to fit well enough to stay a couple. She went to Stanford for graduate degrees in mathematics, while he stayed at CSU for his Master's. After a succession of jobs in libraries and bookstores all over Colorado, he settled into his current position, while Christine remained on the west coast.

And then, surprisingly, she was back in his life for a short while. She returned to Colorado four years ago as an assistant professor of mathematics at the University of Northern Colorado in Greeley, doing some groundbreaking work in an esoteric branch of math called nonstandard analysis. It was six years since the end of their college days, and Greeley was hours to the northeast, but they renewed their relationship. For one glorious summer, she came down to Mesa Vista and lived with Eliot, and they began a serious love affair. She had the summer off from teaching, so while Eliot worked at the library, Christine wrote research papers that were noticed by mathematicians in her discipline all over the world. She laughed about it, "I'm world-famous, but only to a couple dozen people." But her success took her away from Eliot as quickly as she'd returned. She was invited to Portugal to give a series of lectures at the University of Aveiro, and they offered her a position as full professor.

Christine and Eliot spent several days talking it over in between fierce love-making sessions, but they both knew it was the opportunity of her career. Before the summer was over, she was gone. They did not pretend it was a temporary separation. Eliot still wondered if he should have dropped his own career and followed her, but he knew the chance had slipped away.

Alice

Alice stared intently at the display of multicolored neuron chains slowly rotating on the screen in front of her. With a flick of the stylus, she selected one of them and it glowed brightly, along with all of its direct connections. She glanced at the statistics now displayed about this neural pathway. Turning the thumbwheel on the stylus, she expanded the scope of the selection, and the highlighted path grew to include all the neuron chains that were similarly connected at this resolution. Zooming out to the coarser resolution of the functional MRI, the highlighted chain was now a single thread again. She left it there and turned to the monitor that showed the recorded fMRI scan. She compared the two displays for about a minute, then nodded in satisfaction. Once again, the new model was consistent with the fMRI.

Turning to her tablet, she updated her notes. The automated tests had already confirmed consistency, but Alice was a neuroscientist, not a computer programmer. The test software might be wrong, so she always performed a few tests of her own before signing the report. As she worked through her tedious checklist, her frustration mounted. The scans from the beta test were over a year old. They needed a new set of subjects, so they could finally start the isolation phase of the study. She slapped her tablet back onto her desk, thinking, *I wish that damn water would stop dripping!* Surprised, she looked up to her office window and realized that it had been raining for a long time.

The drops splashing outside her window were syncopated, not quite forming a steady rhythm but trying to, like the people sitting in doctors' offices or standing in line at the grocery store, plugged into their phones and videoglasses, moving to a beat that she couldn't reconstruct from the way their bodies swayed. How odd that it could have affected her mood for such a long time while remaining just outside her awareness. Was that significant?

Alice sighed, wondering if she'd be able to get back to work, now that she had something distracting to think about. Her years of studying the brain had taught her to pay attention to these little questions that sprang uninvited into her mind. So much goes on inside our heads that never reveals itself in rational thought, but it's still important, she knew. It's still the product of billions of neurons and trillions of synapses; patterns being deciphered by immense chains of filters arrayed against them; connections grasped and hardened into pathways and sequences, to be called up again later by triggers we aren't even aware of.

She put the monitors to sleep and leaned back in her chair, watching the rain. The parking lot outside was dark already. Her own reflection dominated the window, broken intermittently by the glow from lampposts illuminating islands of rain-soaked concrete. She looked at herself, concerned by how tired she appeared. It still surprised her to remember she was forty now. In this poor mirror she couldn't see the wisps of gray that streaked through her brown hair, but she knew they were there. *I don't get enough exercise,* she reminded herself. *Or sleep.*

After a minute she stood, stretching from the past several hours sitting at her desk. She walked to the door of her office, shut it, and turned off the lights. Immediately, she felt the heightened alertness of an animal hiding in the dark. She didn't move for several seconds, letting her eyes adjust, listening intently to everything around her.

Carefully, she walked to the window and looked out, seeing much more clearly with the reflection of her office subdued. It was raining hard. Puddles had formed all over the parking lot — tiny lakes, complete with rivers rushing toward the storm drains, urgently seeking the fastest path to the sea, unaware that the nearest ocean was at least 800 miles away and over a mile lower in elevation. A half-dozen cars were still there: others, like her, so caught up in their work that they didn't realize how late it was, with nothing else to do on a Friday night. She sighed. *It's worth it. We really are on the verge of something enormous here.*

A bright rectangle of light flashed in the window, and at first Alice took it for lightning, but she was startled to see the silhouette of a man standing just outside the window. She jumped back, drawing in her breath.

"Dr. Kurz?" The soft voice behind her made her spin around, and she saw Dr. Gold standing in the doorway. It was his reflection she'd seen in the window. He seemed as surprised as she. "I'm sorry," he said. "I would have knocked, but your light was off. I didn't expect you to be here." He paused, apparently embarrassed, except that his eyes studied her face, then swept across the room, and there was interest there. "I just wanted to look something up in your copy of Dr. Weil's book," he explained. "I think Chance borrowed mine."

"Of course," Alice said, walking toward him to flip

the light switch. As the overhead LEDs brightened, she scanned her bookcase down to the *W*s and retrieved her copy of *Theory and Practice of Neurocybernetics*, by Dr. Jonathan Weil. She was well acquainted with their director's proudest work, but it wasn't something she'd consulted even once while leading the project. And Ray Chance would never have taken Dr. Gold's copy except to level a leg of his desk.

"Here you go," she said, handing it to the psychologist. "I don't need it back any time soon."

"Thanks," he said, glancing again at her eyes as he took the book from her. "I would have left you a note that I'd borrowed it."

"I know that. Don't worry about it." She watched him turn and walk down the hall to his office, leaving her with an unsettled feeling that she had missed something important. Did he really want the book, or was he here for something else?

She turned and scanned the room, trying to see it from the psychologist's point of view. She kept her desk neat: two large monitors, keypad, auto-sensing task light, phone, charging pad, and a few framed photos (her parents; Grandma Rose; her sister Rachel's family). A couple of folders related to the project were open on the desk, but she always filed them away or took them with her when she left. One guest chair, two filing cabinets (locked), and four bookcases completed the furnishings. In frames on the wall, she displayed her degrees from MIT and Harvard, as well as two pictures that Rachel's kids had drawn for her years ago, when they were little.

Nothing here would interest anyone else. Everything of importance to the project was on the servers, and Gold had access to it all, so why would he be snooping around her office? And why hadn't he asked her what she was doing, standing there in the dark? Maybe it was obvious that she was watching the rain. Maybe he was embarrassed because he'd walked into her office without knocking, or because he was caught in the act of ... whatever he was doing.

She shut off her notebook, closed the folders on her desk, and slid everything into her briefcase. *I should go home and have some dinner,* she thought, suddenly realizing she was hungry. She put on her jacket, picked up her briefcase and purse, and shut off the lights behind her.

The rain had let up a bit when she reached the lobby. A light drizzle was still falling, so she buttoned her jacket and took her umbrella from her purse as she stepped outside. She glanced around the parking lot and noted that many of the cars she'd seen earlier were gone. Her watch showed 8:47. It must have been after 8:30 when Dr. Gold surprised her in her office. Everyone knew that she worked late, but Gold wouldn't expect her to be there *this* late. Did he wait until he thought she was gone?

Keys in hand, Alice walked toward her car, feeling uneasy to be exposed and alone in the dark. She opened the car door, glancing around her and checking the back seat and floor, as she always did. *I'm not paranoid, I'm prudent,* she thought. Too many years living alone, too many Hollywood thrillers. Closing the umbrella, she tossed it to the floor of the passenger side as she slid in, locking the door before starting the car. Alice didn't look back at the building, didn't see Dr. Gold watching her leave from his own darkened office.

The institute was half way up the canyon, above the foothills. She drove slowly down the winding mountain road, watching for any sign of mudslide or rock fall ahead. With no other cars on the road, the only illumination came from her own headlights. As she drove toward the lights of Mesa Vista below, she thought about the first time that her sister had come out to visit her in Colorado. Rachel lived in St. Louis and wasn't comfortable on the mountain roads. Alice drove her up Pike's Peak, smiling at Rachel's white-knuckled grip on the armrest, as every curve revealed another steep drop just a few feet beyond the door. "Why don't they at least put guard rails on these roads?" Rachel managed between gasps. Alice couldn't resist; she deadpanned, "Oh, they do, but the tourists keep knocking them down."

Everything changed as she rounded a curve, and her headlights suddenly lit up a deer standing in the middle of the road, eyes staring into the light, frozen. She wasn't going very fast, but the deer was close, the road was wet, and there was no shoulder. She braked hard, expecting to skid. The car stayed straight, but it wasn't going to stop soon enough. Another curve was just ahead, where a car could be coming, and if she swerved, she might skid out of control. Her brain made the decisions faster than her mind could follow. Standing hard on the brakes, with an iron grip on the wheel, she turned off the headlights, held down the horn, then turned the lights back on, just in time to see the rear end of the deer bolting off the road and down into the woods. She came to a stop a few feet beyond where the deer had been standing. Somehow, she had the presence of mind to check the rear-view mirror to make sure there wasn't a car about to slam into her from behind. She let out her breath, grateful to the unknown engineers who invented anti-lock brakes.

She wasn't shaking, Alice noticed. Somehow, she'd found a calm within herself that let her act creatively when she needed it most. *That was interesting,* she thought, lifting her foot off the brake and slowly starting on her way again. It was astounding how fast the brain could process information and force action, especially given what she knew about the electrochemical steps that had to happen in those few seconds.

Alice drove more slowly now, but before long she reached the edge of the city, where the streets were well lit. She was back in traffic, surrounded by people. Still alone.

Crossing Paths

Spring was over a week away, but Saturday morning was warm enough for just a light jacket. Walking along the side streets, away from most of the traffic noise, Eliot was delighted to see the first new leaves on the trees and green grass where last week's snow had shriveled back to the shadows. The drought last summer was bad, but they finally had a good snowfall this winter, and there would still be more in the months ahead. With a good snowpack in the mountains, they might get through the summer without the terrible wildfires of years past.

It took Eliot ten minutes to walk to Casual News. As he entered, he smiled at the gray-haired little woman behind the register, who looked up when the door bells jangled. "Hi, Laurie," he called out to her. Laurie owned the store and had known Eliot for years. She smiled and nodded to him, but there were several customers at the counter, so Eliot went to the book stacks and looked through the new acquisitions. It took only a few minutes, and he found nothing that excited him, so he picked up copies of the three local newspapers and took his place in line.

"How have you been, Dear?" Laurie asked as Eliot approached the counter. Laurie called everyone younger than her "Dear," and almost everyone was.

"Looking for a job, actually," Eliot said, smiling back at her.

"You tired of the library?" she asked with some concern. "They can't be tired of *you*, surely?"

"No, they're making us take a furlough. I just need something for a couple of weeks. You don't happen to need another hand around here, do you?" He tilted his head in the direction of the stacks behind him. "I'm good with books."

Laurie laughed, her smile fitting perfectly into the well-worn grooves around her rosy face. "I'd love to help you, Dear, but business isn't so good right now."

"Well, I'll take a coffee with these newspapers." He pulled out his phone to make the purchase, but she stilled his hand.

"You can pay me for the coffee, but just sit and read the newspapers, if you like. Keep them neat, and put them back when you're done, Dear."

Eliot grinned. "I think I know why business isn't so good, Laurie." When her back was turned to make his coffee, he slipped a ten into the tip jar. She handed him the cup, and he tapped his phone against the pay terminal.

"Did you try the city libraries in Denver and Springs? Or Nick's book store over on Mason?" Laurie asked.

Eliot took a sip from the overfilled cup, careful not to spill it. "I sent some emails, but I haven't heard back yet."

"Well, something will come up, Dear. You're too clever to sit idle. Why don't you write the great American novel?"

Eliot gave a casual shrug. "But what would I do the *second* week?"

"Oh, get on with you," Laurie said, laughing again.

A woman entered the shop, so Laurie gave Eliot's hand a squeeze and turned to help her. Eliot took his coffee and newspapers to one of the comfortable chairs near the window.

As he expected, there were no job ads in the newspapers that he hadn't already found online. None of them looked like what he needed, but his eyes kept returning to one particular item:

Subjects needed for neuroscience study. Requires 5 days in isolated environment with no external contact. No physical stress, no drug testing. $500. Apply online.

The URL in the ad gave no clue about the employer's identity. Eliot hadn't given it a thought the first time he saw it, but now he reconsidered. It would only cover one of the two furlough weeks, but the pay was probably better than he'd get for any other short-term job, and it sounded safe and easy. The idea of being a lab rat for five days was a bit disconcerting, though. It reminded him of how he felt throughout the psychology class in his sophomore year at CSU. He suspected that the class was just a study concocted by the professor, to see how students reacted to pointless assignments and impenetrable lectures.

What might they mean by "an isolated environment?" He couldn't leave the lab? He'd be confined alone for the whole five days? Pulling out his tablet, he scanned the URL into the browser. The site banner told him that he was at the Rocky Mountain Neurocybernetics Research Institute. He'd never heard of it, and he had only a vague idea of what neurocybernetics might be. A bit of browsing around the web site and searching for references convinced Eliot that it was a legitimate think tank conducting advanced brain research. That might be cool. Maybe a chance to learn something about a branch of science he'd never studied. The money was pretty good for an easy job, so they probably filled it already. Still, it said *subjects*, so maybe they had several positions to fill.

He returned to the original URL in the ad, where he found the same brief summary of the study and a link to apply. He clicked instead on the "Contact us" link at the bottom of the page, and he was presented with a form for asking a question about the institute and getting a response by email. He suspected that he'd get nothing more than promotional literature bragging about the wonderful work they do, but there was always a chance that some actual person would respond in a few days. He provided his return email address and entered into the form:

I'm interested in participating in your five-day study (cf. 3/11 ad in Denver Post). I'd like to know more about what's required. Can you define "isolated environment?" If I participate, would I be confined to the lab around the clock for five days? Buried in a mine? Locked in a cell? Sealed in a crate?
— Eliot Stearns

That done, he went back to the original page and clicked the link to apply for the study. A long application form came up, and he glanced through it. They were practically asking for a complete medical history, and this screen was labeled "Page 1 of 4." He decided to wait and fill it in when he got back home.

A block from his apartment, Eliot felt his phone vibrate. As he waited for the crossing signal, he looked at the display and saw that he had a new email. To his surprise, it was a reply to his query, and not an automated one.

Eliot,

We're glad that you're interested in taking part in our study. You'll be happy to know that the isolation referred to is not so dire as you suggest. You'll have a private suite with a bed, bathroom, shower, and living area, full meals, and activities to do. You might find it boring, but I promise no torture. You'll have to bring your own crate, if that's your preference.

Please go ahead and submit an online application. We'll respond within 24 hours, and if your application satisfies our requirements, we'll invite you to our facility for a personal interview.

I look forward to reviewing your application.

Sincerely,
Dr. Alice Kurz, Project Leader
Rocky Mountain Neurocybernetics Research Institute

The fact that someone was monitoring the online feedback on a Saturday morning was surprising — and it wasn't just a clerical assistant, either. This might be an interesting group of people to work with. It could even be fun. He wrote back to Dr. Kurz:

Thank you for the surprisingly quick response. As it turns out, "no torture" is one of the conditions I look for in every job. Holding you to that promise, I'll be happy to apply.

• • •

When she finally left her study to make a light lunch, Alice was surprised by the sunlight streaming through the kitchen windows. She kept the blinds in her study closed to prevent glare on the monitor, so it was only now that she realized how lovely the day had become. She paused for a few minutes to appreciate the view of the woods behind her house, then grabbed a pre-made chopped salad from the fridge, found a clean fork in the drawer, and returned to her study.

Thinking about last night's incident with the deer in the road, Alice was glad she didn't have to drive up the canyon again today. No one else would be there on the weekend, so she just logged in from home. She'd been reviewing the online applications all morning, rejecting one after another. Many of the applicants had past surgeries or other physical issues that the project couldn't accommodate. Others were rejected because their occupations and hobbies made them unlikely to tolerate the isolation. Alice was glad now that Jon had challenged her original request to make the experiment last two weeks. They'd never get anyone for that long. Still, they couldn't go less than five days, or they wouldn't make enough progress in each cycle.

Her email exchange with Eliot Stearns made her smile, but Alice didn't have much hope that he'd work out. She was afraid they were being too selective, but she had read through every isolation study she could find, and she knew that most people had problems with conditions like theirs. Trick said they'd be ready for a more natural environment in a few months, but she didn't want to wait that long if they didn't have to. The isolation test would give them enough information to fully plan a more advanced study, if only they could find a suitable candidate.

With the queue of applications now empty, Alice

decided to review the latest R&D reports. The first was from one of the software developers, Dave Addison, describing the architecture that they'd chosen for the subject's PC: a virtual machine on one of the R&D hosting servers. The machine image had already been built, tested, and saved, so they could reinstate the identical configuration every time they needed to restart the experiment. She noted that they were using an older operating system, because it was easier to remove the components they didn't want accessible. The report included details about how they'd monitor the subject's use of the system and collect the daily journal entries. As she started to read this part, the phone rang.

"Hi, Alice, it's me," she heard Rachel's voice. Alice glanced at the time, surprised to see that it was after 2:00 already. "I'm so glad to get you at home! I thought you'd probably be at work on a Saturday again."

"No, of course not," Alice answered, trying to keep the guilty edge out of her voice. "I'm just sitting around reading and enjoying the spring weather."

"Enjoying it through the window?"

"Well, yes, so far. I might go for a walk later. How are you doing?"

"We're great. The kids' spring break starts in a week, and we're making plans for things to do together. We're probably going to take the riverboat cruise and the Gateway Arch tour if it stays warm. Have you got any suggestions? What sounds fun to you?"

Alice shuddered. "I'm surprised you'd even consider a tour boat," she said, mostly to divert the conversation from the direction she saw it going.

"Alice, I don't want my kids to grow up afraid of the world. They'll have enough fear and pain without having to assume ours, too."

"Of course. You're right. You're a better parent

than I would be." The thought was somewhat unnerving, but she couldn't think why it should be. Rachel might be three years younger, but she had 17 years of parenting experience, and Alice had none. "What about taking the kids to a Cardinals game? You all like baseball, right?"

"Alice, it's March. The season doesn't start for another three weeks."

"Oh. But they have training games, don't they? That would still be fun."

"Their spring training camp is in Florida. You don't really pay attention to baseball, do you?"

"Well, you know I was never into sports, Rachel. You were always the one out playing with the other kids while I was helping Grandma make dinner." Rachel was silent. "I'm sorry," Alice said. "That sounded mean. We all did the best we could after Mom and Dad died. Anyway, my idea of play was doing extra credit homework." That didn't sound much better.

Rachel let it go. "The kids miss you, Alice. They had a really great time last summer, when we stopped by on our road trip. In fact, they liked the time with you a whole lot more than they liked the Grand Canyon. So did Dean and I. If you come up while they're on spring break, we could have a great time together again. We'll take you on the riverboat cruise. It'll be good for you. Therapeutic, even. We can gamble on the riverboat casinos while the kids play in the arcades. But if you can't handle the boats, then we'll do something else. It doesn't matter, we just want to spend some time with you. When was the last time you had a vacation?"

Alice sighed. She knew it had been leading up to this. "I can't get away right now, Rachel. The project that I've been working on for five years is all coming to a head this month. We're running a really important study as soon as we can find the right applicant."

"So you don't have anyone scheduled yet? That's perfect. Just push the start date out a week or two. They can't deny you some vacation time; you put in about 80 hours a week."

"I can't, Rachel. Everything we've been working for is dependent on this. It's not just me, it's the whole team. We have investors anxious for results. We've finally told them that we're ready for the next step. If I ask to postpone it, they'll think we're not really ready. They could decide to pull our funding and write us off as a bad investment."

There was silence as Rachel waited her out, and Alice knew she had to offer something. "Maybe this summer I could come out. We can take the kids to Six Flags, see the Cardinals, and … well, maybe I could handle the riverboat thing."

Rachel's sigh was purposely audible. "Alice, I know you. Your study will be a great success, because you'll spend a hundred percent of your life on it. And because it's a success, there'll be a new study, or some new project, taking up your whole summer. Then you'll tell us you'll be out the *next* summer for Brian's graduation. But you won't be able to leave work then, either. Are you even going to see the kids again before they're all grown up and moved out?"

It was true, Alice realized. That's exactly what would happen. *Why can't I just let go? It's too late to help Grandma Rose.* But right now was the wrong time. They were so close. Before she could think of an answer to Rachel's question, her sister moved on to the next step in the litany. "You're never going to meet anyone sitting in your office night and day."

"Well, good, that's one less distraction that I can live without, then."

"Oh, are you living? I wasn't sure that's what you called it when you have no life of your own."

"We have different priorities, Rachel. I may not be bringing a new generation into the world, but I'm leaving my mark on it. You have to let me do my part. This will matter to those future generations — to your kids, and their peers. It'll change their lives. I just don't have time for other things right now."

"*Right now?* Alice, you're forty years old. Exactly when are you planning on dating again? After you retire? Which will probably be at age 85, I imagine."

Alice resisted the urge to hang up on her. "When this project is wrapped up, I'll take some time off, visit with you, relax for a while. Travel, even."

"Travel where?"

"Well, I don't know. There's a neurocybernetics conference in San Diego next year. I'll probably be able to present a paper or two from the work I'm doing now. It would be a really big deal. Global recognition. I'll meet a lot of people there."

"Right, Alice, that's *dating*. I'm so glad you remember." She paused, then surprised Alice with, "Do you ever hear from David anymore?"

"David? You mean David Stenger? Rachel, that was in college. Why on earth would we still be talking?"

"You're right, I'm sure all your other lovers since then have swept him from your thoughts."

"Do you really require reports on my love life now?"

"Why, is there anything to report?"

Alice held her tongue, afraid of what might come out if she said anything at all.

"I'm sorry, Alice. I'm not being fair. It's just that … well, I think you're just too busy and too stubborn to admit how unhappy you are. I believe what you say about your work. Sure, it will probably make a difference to the world, but will it make a difference to you? There are still a few of us out here in the world who actually love you and want you to be happy. Can't you be happy and still save the world?"

Alice had to blink back tears for a few seconds before she could answer. "I know, Rachel. You're right. I'm just not the 'stop and smell the roses' type. But I will *not* miss Brian's graduation, I promise you. I'll block off two weeks of my calendar starting at the end of May next year. I'll do it right now." She opened her calendar on her notebook and did as she said.

Rachel was quiet for a few seconds. "Okay, Alice. Thank you."

They said their goodbyes, and Alice sat for a few minutes, rubbing her forehead. She straightened up and looked back at her screen. Another new application was in the queue. She opened it and saw that it was from Eliot Stearns. Half-heartedly, she read through his responses to the medical questionnaire. No red flags there. She looked at his other responses. "Librarian," that meant a job dealing with people all day long. No, wait, "research librarian." He spends his time with the books and the computers, interacting with people through memos and emails. He probably likes solitude. What did he put down for hobbies? "Reading, taking walks." *My God, he even wrote, "Thinking!"* She looked further. Well educated, been at his current job for eight years. Why did he want to do this? There was a question about that. He answered, "Income supplement due to job furlough. Also, it sounds interesting." Interesting! When was he available? "Any time before end of calendar year, with one week notice." She went back to the start of the application and read it again, carefully. *This is the one.*

• • •

Eliot spent most of the afternoon on his balcony

reading one of the new novels that he'd borrowed from the library. He was immersed in the story, and he jumped when his phone vibrated. He drew it from his pocket and saw that he had a new email from Dr. Kurz.

Eliot, I've just read through your application, and I think you'd be a good candidate for our study. Can you come to our facility after work on Monday for an interview? Would 5:00 be too early? The map link shows where we're located. I look forward to meeting you. If you decide to participate, we could take you for the five days beginning the following Monday, March 20.

Eliot clicked the link and saw that the institute was up the canyon about 30 minutes west of town. He'd have to leave work early, but that could probably be arranged. What could it hurt to check it out?

Prepare a Face

Ray Chance walked into his office earlier than usual Monday morning, eager to start his day. Last week's engineering reviews had been cakewalks. Everything was on schedule, and his whole team was excited about starting the next set of trials. Just two or three weeks, and they'd be ready for a test subject. He pulled his notebook out of his backpack, set it on his desk, and lifted the lid. As soon as he logged in, the email alert popped up, and Chance knew that it would be from Alice. That wasn't unusual, but it saddened him; she worked through the weekend again. Sighing, he read the message, and his day changed considerably. She found a subject. They were interviewing him tonight. She wanted to start the trial next week.

He glanced at the time: 7:30. He still had an hour before the staff meeting. He checked his team's status in the task manager. Two of the nanotech engineers were already here. He stood and walked to their lab, where he found both of them, Yui Matsumura and Colton Monroe. Yui was immersed in the display on her videoglasses, her hands gesturing as she made selections and changed her view. Colton looked up and said, "Hi, Ray," his glance lingering on the department head's face, realizing that something was up.

"I need an honest assessment from your team right now," Chance began, and he saw Yui raise her head and stare at him, her display fading to near transparency. "What is the soonest that we could begin a live trial, staying within the defined safety parameters?"

Colton turned to his monitor and brought up the task manager, paging through the weekend test results. Yui simply said, "Thursday."

Chance looked at her. "You're sure of that?"

She scowled and flicked her eyes toward the ceiling. "If I weren't sure, I would have said, 'Friday.'"

Colton looked up, grinning slightly at his teammate. "The truth is, we've been ready for weeks. You know that. The test logs aren't showing any new issues. We lack only an innocent victim."

"The term we're using is *test subject*," Chance said. "This is why you sit in the lab and I talk to the candidate."

"I knew *someone* must be doing the hard work here," Yui said, her attention back on her private display.

Chance laughed, said, "I'll leave you to your video games, then," and exited the lab, heading for the medical department.

• • •

"All right, let's begin," Dr. Weil said. He turned to Alice and nodded, a polite pretense, since everyone knew that Alice ran the staff meetings. She summarized her exchange with Eliot, highlighting the factors that made him an ideal candidate.

"Eliot sent another email this morning, confirming that he can be here at 5:00," Alice continued. "Is everyone prepared to stay late tonight?" There were nods around the room. "Please take another look at the presentation, and put yourself in the subject's point of view. What would you want to know? What would you conclude from this information? What would convince you to accept? What would scare you away?"

"Equally important, please review the protocols and guidelines for interacting with the subject," Dr. Gold broke in. "If he accepts, we'll be spending a lot of time with him, one way and another. Maintaining the deception will become difficult at times, so decide on a sustainable attitude. The subject will not expect us to be interested in him personally, yet we have to ask him personal questions. Make sure you establish a clinical relationship with him."

"I think we all have experience in blind-subject experimentation," Alice said, showing some irritation.

"Which is the key to keeping this from becoming a failure like the beta test," Dr. Gold said.

Alice scoffed in astonishment. "Dr. Gold, I appreciate the value of the new protocols that you were brought in to establish. Isolating the subject should eliminate the Matthius reaction. We all agree on that. But believe me, the beta test was no failure, even though it was cut short. The technology was clearly effective. I don't think you can appreciate just how effective."

"Because I didn't join you until afterward, I'm sure you mean."

Chance sighed, tired of this sniping. *Gold was right to bring up the beta test. They tore us apart after that, trying to put the blame on the nanotech, when it was obviously a psych problem. Matthius just couldn't get his head around it. Alice is right, too; we were vindicated in the end.* He turned and looked down the table at the young man watching silently. "Trick, is there anything to be concerned about from the software perspective?"

"If we're starting the study next week, we'll have to go with last week's software build," Trick answered. "We'll be finished with all the testing in time, but not if we rebuild to include auto-calibration."

"Is there any problem proceeding with manual calibration?" Alice asked. "I'd rather lock down the software at this point. We can just use the blue light scenario again, and handle any other calibration anomalies on the first day of phase two."

"I agree," Chance said. "Let's not take the risk of introducing anything new right before we bring in our first subject. We'll have plenty of time to finish testing auto-calibration before moving on to the *next* subject." Trick offered no objection, so Chance wrapped up the engineering report. "I spoke to the medical team this morning. They're good to go, and I know the nanotech is ready. You'll have the data you need to keep you all busy for as long as you want."

No longer on the hot seat, Chance sat back and watched Alice direct the meeting without ever breaking the illusion that Dr. Weil was in charge. The entire vision of this project had been hers from the beginning, but she didn't care about ownership. She had already taken this research in directions Weil would never have dared. Now, Chance wouldn't be surprised if a Nobel prize came out of this, and it would probably be in Dr. Weil's name, along with hers. So Weil sat in on the staff meetings and project reviews, signed every funding request, recruited the investors, and handled the board meetings. Alice managed the rest.

It was Alice who hired Chance away from MIT. He'd been managing graduate students on state-of-the-art projects for a couple of years, but he didn't see himself going any farther in academia. He wanted to get into an industrial research lab where he could turn out real products instead of an endless series of prototypes. When Alice found him through her own connections to MIT, he told her the job wasn't what he was looking for.

She persisted, and an hour later, he was convinced it was the most important thing he could do with his life. He had only one request: find a way to get Trick to come along, too.

Alice had never known Trick, but like everyone else at MIT, she'd heard of him. When Alice was a senior, Trick was a freshman — not the youngest freshman to ever attend the school, but close. That was the last year anyone could have identified Trick's grade. He just moved in at MIT and stayed there, accumulating degrees at seemingly random intervals, attaching himself to one research project after another. He always found the most challenging projects, and he always became a major contributor. And always, he moved on to something more interesting as soon as he solved the hard problems. When it became clear that everyone he worked with looked to him for guidance, the administration decided that they should pay him and give him students of his own. It was a good decision. His two-semester class in large-scale programming always had a long wait list.

At the time, Chance didn't think Alice would be able to lure Trick away from MIT; in fact, it wasn't difficult at all. She gave Trick an offer he couldn't resist: the hardest problem he'd ever seen. Trick became the lead software architect on the project, with a dozen programmers working under him. He wrote much of the code himself, and he reviewed most of it.

Chance turned to look at Trick, who was studying something on his videoglasses, but still seemed completely engaged in the meeting. It drove people crazy at first, thinking he wasn't paying attention to them, but he was. As an engineer, Chance simply concluded that Trick observed the world at a much higher data rate than most people, with plenty of spare cycles for multiple input streams.

Before concluding the meeting, Alice paused and asked, "What is it that we haven't thought of yet, everyone? I have this nagging feeling that a week or a month from now we'll be saying 'Why weren't we prepared for that?'"

Chance gave it serious thought, even though on the face of it, the question was absurd. If they hadn't thought of it yet, they wouldn't think of it now. He understood the trepidation that Alice apparently felt. They were taking an important step, but as far as he could see, the critical leap happened over a year ago with the beta test. Everyone else was so caught up in making it work that they didn't realize the big achievement was proving it was possible.

Not surprisingly, it was Trick who answered Alice. "It's certain that we haven't thought of everything. The whole point of the trial is to discover what we don't already know. We have a lot more control points now than we had last time. If anything goes wrong, we can stop and reassess, tune the parameters, and restart."

Alice gazed at Trick for a few seconds, as if she knew that he was thinking more than he was saying, but she nodded in agreement. "Okay, let's get to work."

• • •

Driving west into the mountains, Eliot felt reborn in the mountain air. He left work an hour early for this appointment, and even though he'd make up the time tomorrow, it felt like sneaking out for a secret rendezvous. He loved the opportunity to put some additional altitude under his legs. Even though the air was cold, he drove with the window open so that he could hear the river rolling down the canyon and smell the pine trees. The destruction of the pines had finally turned around after the beetle infestation several years ago. They'd lost a lot of the forest before it was stopped. The solution that had been devised up in Boulder was controversial, but there was no longer any question that it had worked. Mites — genetically altered to prey exclusively on the pine beetles — had destroyed the enemy and then died off with them.

People were slow to realize how greatly the world was being changed by new technologies like genetic engineering and nanotech. Eliot was no engineer, but he was scientifically literate enough to understand that they were racing up an exponential slope. The rate of change was accelerating past all previous human experience, and it was an open question how well the institutions of civilization could adjust.

Rounding a curve to the left, Eliot saw his destination at the top of the next rise: a modest two-story building set back about a hundred feet from the road. The preponderance of glass in the facade reflected the surrounding mountains, making the building almost disappear from view, but the sign at the turn-off clearly identified the Rocky Mountain Neurocybernetics Research Institute. Eliot slowed and turned onto the entry road.

The building was probably only seven or eight years old. The parking lot seemed to be sized for less than a hundred employees, but the building could easily have held more offices than that. The majority of the space must be set up as labs, Eliot concluded. There were only a handful of visitor parking spaces, but they were all empty.

As he parked the car, Eliot noticed the dark plexiglass domes mounted on lampposts throughout the parking lot and on the exterior walls of the building. He assumed that those housed security cameras. The fence around the property was open at the entrance to the parking lot. Years ago, installations like this would have had a guard checkpoint at the perimeter, but now everyone seemed to rely on discreet surveillance. He always assumed that it was just a matter of saving money: one or two guards watching monitors could oversee the entire property. Now, as he parked the car and walked toward the entrance, he realized it might actually be better security. Being observed from unknown positions was more intimidating than seeing who was watching you. You didn't know what they could see or what resources they could deploy against potential threats. Unobserved, the guards would feel no social pressure against staring closely. It was the same everywhere now, and it made everyone feel like a criminal suspect wherever they went. Eliot wasn't sure that was a fair tradeoff.

He entered the building, glancing at his watch; he was five minutes early. The guard behind the reception desk was a young man, trim and fit and neatly groomed, wearing the uniform of a contract security agency. "Good afternoon, sir," the guard greeted him, standing and offering Eliot a pen. "Please sign in."

The log book was open on the counter before him. As Eliot wrote his name and the time in the book, the guard spoke again. "May I please see a photo ID, sir?" Eliot was surprised, but reached for his wallet and pulled out his license. The guard looked at it and compared the picture to Eliot's face. "Thank you, Mr. Stearns," he said, checking Eliot's entry in the log. *They take security pretty seriously here*, Eliot thought.

As Eliot put his wallet away, the guard picked up the phone and dialed an extension. "Dr. Gold," he said. "This is Anderson in the front lobby. Mr. Stearns is here." He listened for a moment, then hung up the phone.

"Dr. Gold will be here to meet you in a couple minutes," he told Eliot. "There's coffee, tea, and water, if you'd like." He gestured toward the coffee station to Eliot's right.

"Thank you," Eliot said. "I'm fine." He walked toward one of the plush chairs in the lobby, but did not sit down, his attention caught by a painting hanging on the far wall to his right: a dark-haired woman standing in classical dress holding a glowing scepter. It looked familiar, but Eliot couldn't place it at first. There was a brass plaque under the painting, and he read that this was a reproduction of Rosetti's *Mnemosyne*. He remembered the painting now. It was the Lamp of Memory that she held.

Eliot was still studying the painting when he heard someone step up behind him. He turned to see a man in his mid-forties, slightly shorter than Eliot. He wore an expensive suit, carried a folder of papers in his left hand, and offered Eliot his right. "Mr. Stearns?" the man inquired. "I'm Dr. Gold."

"Eliot," he said, shaking hands. "Nice to meet you, Dr. Gold. I was just admiring your artwork." Gold glanced at the painting, then looked at Eliot again, his expression blank. "Mnemosyne," Eliot prompted.

"Greek goddess of memory," Gold acknowledged with a nod. He turned to lead Eliot toward the door to the left of the guard station.

"Well, she was one of the Titans," Eliot explained, following Dr. Gold to the door. "The predecessors of the Olympian gods. She was the mother of the nine Muses. But you're right, she did represent memory." Eliot doubted that Dr. Gold knew about the other Mnemosyne, one of the rivers of Hades. By drinking from the River Lethe, dead souls forgot their past lives before being reborn. But if they chose to drink from the River Mnemosyne instead, they would remember everything.

The inner door opened automatically as Dr. Gold pressed his badge up to the sensor. He passed through and held it open for Eliot. "Well, you know your mythology, Eliot. A special interest of yours?"

"My father taught classical literature," Eliot said with a smile, following him through the door. "When I was a kid, he practiced his lectures on me."

They entered a row of offices and conference rooms. Most of the office doors were open, and in several of them Eliot could see people working at computers or talking together. "What did you get from those lectures?" Gold asked, turning back toward him as they paused at the door of a conference room.

Eliot noticed how casually the man appeared to watch him, and how carefully he actually watched. "A lot, I suppose. Bits of Greek and Latin. How to string together an argument. Sometimes, how to find holes in one. May I ask what your role is here, Dr. Gold?"

"Oh, I'm the psychologist," Gold answered, propping the door open and preceding Eliot through it.

The woman on the opposite side of the table glanced up and smiled at him, and Eliot knew at once that she was Dr. Kurz. She appeared several years older than him — about forty, he guessed — with dark brown hair and a determined, serious look about her. There was a notebook computer on a charging pad in front of her, and with a couple of keystrokes, she cloned its display to the flat monitor that covered the front wall of the room. Rising from her seat, she reached her hand across the table to shake his. "Hello, Eliot, very nice to meet you. I'm Alice Kurz." She held his gaze for a second, and somehow he knew that she didn't want him to banter with her about their email correspondence in front of Dr. Gold.

"Eliot Stearns," he said, feeling slightly foolish for

stating the obvious.

Dr. Gold dropped off his papers on Eliot's side of the table and went back to the door. "I'll go fetch the others," he said as he walked out.

Alice sat down, and Eliot took the chair opposite her. The conference table could comfortably seat a dozen, and near each seat were charging pads, tablets, and microphones for the conference phone in the center. Eliot took in the high-tech accessories, the polished oak table, the comfortably padded armchairs, and he knew he was out of place. He'd never worked in the corporate environment, but suddenly he understood some of its appeal.

"It looks like quite a facility you have here," Eliot commented.

"We're pretty well funded," Alice acknowledged. "Our investors believe that our research will lead to some significant advances in neurocybernetics. I'll give you a quick overview of what we're doing here as soon as we get everyone together. Then we'll go over the details of the study and see if you're still interested in working with us."

Before Eliot could think of a reply, Dr. Gold returned with three others, who each introduced themselves and shook hands with Eliot. Dr. Weil appeared to be in his late fifties. He was trim and tan, with a precisely groomed silver beard, wearing a well-tailored suit with the comfortable, relaxed appearance of the man in charge — which he was, Eliot soon learned. Ben Thompson was middle-aged and well on his way to baldness. He gave his name, sat at the far end of the table, and immediately settled into the background.

The last member of the team was Ray Chance, head of Research and Development. He was about the same age as Alice, dressed more casually than the others.

He seemed excited to be there, but a definite hint of stress underlay his enthusiasm. It made Eliot wonder just how important this study might be.

Dr. Weil, started things off. "Eliot, we're very happy to have you here. We're going to give you a quick overview of what we're trying to do and answer any questions you might have about this study. Then we'll talk about what happens next if you decide to go ahead with it." Eliot stole a glance at Alice, wondering if she'd jumped the gun by telling him the same thing. She didn't seem at all embarrassed. If anything, she looked slightly impatient.

"Before we begin, our legal department insists on a few preliminaries." Weil reached his hand to Ben Thompson at the end of the table, who passed him a small stack of papers. "This is a standard non-disclosure agreement, asking you to respect the confidentiality of anything you're told today. The work we're doing here may lead to future medical treatments or other advances that our investors hope to capitalize on. I'm sure you understand the need to protect their investments."

Weil pushed the papers across to Eliot, who glanced through them. They did appear to be routine, and the explanation seemed entirely reasonable. He skimmed them quickly, seeing nothing alarming. Just to clarify, he asked, "So I can't say anything at all about this, not even an explanation of where I'll be for five days?"

"Oh, no. You can talk about it in a general way," Thompson spoke up. "You can say that you're participating in a study with this institute, and that it requires you to stay here for five days, and that you're being paid for your time. Just don't discuss the details of the study, or anything that we present to you today, or anything that you might learn about our work in the course of this study." Eliot still paused over the signature line on the last page.

"I assure you this is entirely normal for participants in research studies like this," Thompson said. "Of course, you're welcome to take the forms home with you and have your own lawyer look them over before signing. We'll stop right here and reschedule if you decide to return."

Eliot considered it only briefly, deciding there was no reason to start all over. They'd probably find someone else to do it, and he'd lose the opportunity. It might be interesting, and anyway, he wouldn't have to commit to the job until after the presentation. He signed and dated the places indicated and handed the forms back to Thompson, who added his own signature in various places, then sat quietly throughout the rest of the meeting.

Alice dimmed the room lights and began the presentation. Eliot learned that the institute performed advanced research in human-machine interactions. They had already developed key technologies used in the newest smart prosthetics, and Eliot was surprised at how far this technology had progressed: legs that could walk and run almost as naturally as real human legs, adapting to the terrain and responding to signals from the nerves at the point where the original limb was severed; arms and hands that could grasp almost as nimbly as human hands and return tactile feedback to the brain.

"Now we're reaching some fundamental limitations on the information transfer between these devices and the brain," Alice said. She showed a new slide depicting tactile information flowing up from an artificial hand through the brain stem into the thalamus, and motor control signals descending from the neocortex. "We understand quite a lot about the control signals and the sensory inputs, but there's still a lot we don't know about the cognitive areas of the brain. How exactly does your conscious volition get translated into motor controls to achieve a task? Right now, smart prosthetics are only possible where we can find undamaged nerve paths to connect to. If we understood more of the mechanics of conscious thought, we might be able to develop prosthetics linked directly to the brain, bypassing the need to use existing nerves. Even, perhaps, in cases where those nerve paths never existed. Consider, for example, people born with missing limbs, or conjoined twins who, once separated, have to make do with arms or legs on only one side of the body." She cycled through some slides listing the problems these conditions presented.

"What we're trying to do now is develop better and more accurate models of how the brain's cognitive areas function, and map out the interactions between those areas and the motor control and sensory input regions. Developing better prosthetics is just one application area for this research. We're also hoping to learn how to supplement and work around damaged areas of the brain. We may be able to develop *cognitive* prosthetics that could, for example, assist patients suffering from Alzheimer's or other forms of dementia." Alice looked into Eliot's eyes, and there was more to it than just gauging his reaction. She was almost proselytizing, barely holding back the passion she felt. "I hope you can see the value in this field of study," she said softly.

"Yes, of course. It would be wonderful to contribute to research like this." He smiled to reassure her. "I'd love to help. But I still don't know what it is that you want me to do."

Alice smiled back. "Current technologies, like functional MRI, have led to great improvements in our models of the brain. Unfortunately, the resolution is just not sharp enough for what we're trying to see now. So, we've developed a technique for taking measurements from *inside* the brain."

"You want to perform brain surgery on me?" Eliot spoke slowly, as if he thought there might be a language problem.

"Not exactly. Dr. Chance's team developed the process and much of the technology. I'll let him explain."

Eliot turned to look at Ray Chance, who leaned forward as he spoke, his enthusiasm obvious. "You've probably heard some things about nanotechnology."

Eliot raised an eyebrow. "You want to put nanodevices inside my brain?"

"We're very confident about the safety of this process," Chance assured him. "We did animal testing of the nanocells for years before we began human trials. We've followed rigid safety protocols at every step of the process. We've injected the nanocells dozens of times now, and they've never caused a problem. They flow unimpeded through the bloodstream, taking various measurements as they move through the capillaries in the brain, then they transmit data back to us. A few hours later, they break down naturally and are processed by the kidneys without any effect, exiting the body with the urine. Within two days, there's no trace of them left in the body."

"But still ..." Eliot tried to recall everything he'd read about nanodevices and their biological applications. He knew they were being used in cancer treatment now, but he'd never read about their use in healthy people. "How can you be sure they don't damage the tissues or create blockages in the bloodstream?"

"The sensors we're using are only about a hundred nanometers in size," Chance explained. "That's about the size of a virus. Your red blood cells are 60 times larger, and they flow easily through the smallest capillaries. In the animal testing we've performed, we made very detailed examinations of the organs and blood vessels after the nanocells had passed through the body. We found no evidence of damage, nor any particles left behind. In both the animal and human testing, we examined the urine very carefully, and we'll be examining yours, as well. We can identify the material that's left behind as the nanocells break down, and we've been able to account for every bit of it."

"They're extremely simple devices, Eliot," Alice said, leaning toward him. "They record, they transmit, they break down. That's it."

"And you can get useful information from such simple devices? It seems like studying the ocean one drop of water at a time."

Chance laughed. "Well, yes, it is a bit like that. And, of course, we can't get all the information we'd like, but it's a start. So far, we've gotten enough data to keep us busy for years analyzing it."

Eliot didn't know what to say. The audacity of their approach, and the scope of what they might be able to do with such data intrigued him. But he had a strong suspicion that there was more that they weren't telling him. Still, he should expect that. He couldn't understand most of the details anyway, and it was clear that they wanted to keep their innovations secret.

"But why do you need me in isolation for five days?" Eliot asked. "You said I'd be rid of these nanocells within a day or two."

"That's the second part of this study," Dr. Gold answered. "Mapping out the physiology of the brain is one thing, but we're trying to relate all that to the conscious intentions of the person. We need to understand something about how your mind works, not just your brain. I'll be spending those five days interviewing you in various ways and performing some standard psychological tests. As we gather data like this from many subjects, we expect to see patterns within the way people think and the way their brains are connected. Eventually, we think the patterns that emerge will help us understand how different brain connections correspond to different habits of thought. Then we'll be able to fine-tune the experiments in later trials, to delve more deeply where we see promising correlations."

"And why do I have to be isolated?"

"We want to learn how your mind works, without having to account for any external influences that we can eliminate," Gold explained. "Television, conversations with friends and family, work-related stress, even routine interactions with strangers — other drivers on the road, people you pass on the street — all of these things affect the way you respond to your environment. It's the accumulation of those external factors that primarily drive our attitudes. We're only really ourselves when we're alone in our thoughts. That's what we want: to observe you in as neutral and controlled an environment as possible."

"It probably won't be much fun," Alice admitted. "But it won't be hard. We won't be running any sort of stress tests on you, or anything like that. The worst part will be boredom, I expect."

Eliot couldn't think of anything more to ask. He turned it all over in his mind. It seemed clear, if so far unstated, that they were offering him the job. It was odd that they didn't really ask him any questions. Did they get everything they needed from his application? Or were they so eager to get someone that they'd take the first person who passed the application screening?

"Before you make a decision, let's show you where you'd be staying for five days," Alice suggested. "I'm sure it's no substitute for your own home, but it's not like being stuck in a crate." She smiled, and Eliot smiled back.

They walked down the hall and opened a door to a sparsely furnished living area. A square table, three feet on a side, was attached to the wall on the right, with a vinyl padded straight-back chair in front of it. There was an opening in the wall about 4 inches high by 16 inches wide, right where the table was attached.

"Your meals will be delivered directly onto the table, through that slot." Alice pointed to the opening in the wall. "When you've finished eating, you just slide the tray with the dirty dishes on it back through the same slot."

Eliot leaned down and saw that the slot wasn't actually open; it was covered by a black metal panel which, presumably, opened when his meals arrived and closed when he pushed the tray back. "You weren't kidding about being isolated. I don't get to see or talk to anyone at all?"

"You'll have some communication with us," Alice said. "I'll show you that in a minute."

An exercise treadmill stood in the middle of the room. Further down, against the same wall as the table, was a computer station with a monitor, keyboard, and mouse. The computer itself was not visible; the cables terminated at the wall. A rolling desk chair was placed at this station.

Opposite the computer stood an open doorway into the bedroom, with no actual door. Entering the bedroom, Eliot saw the bathroom on the left and a twin bed on the right. Next to the bed was a small nightstand with three dials labeled and color-coded "red," "blue," and "green", with a fourth dial set apart from the others labeled "brightness."

"You'll be sedated during the nanocell procedure," Alice explained. "When that's done, we'll wheel your bed in here, and this is where you'll wake up. We have to put you into a pretty deep sleep. You won't even dream. The sedatives sometimes leave you with some visual sensitivity for a few hours after you wake up, so the lights will be low and blue, which should be the easiest on your eyes. These controls affect the lights throughout the suite. Just balance the red, green, and blue until you can see normally, and set the brightness to whatever level you're comfortable with. You'll only have to do that the first day, then you can use the brightness control to turn down the lights at night and turn them back up in the morning."

They walked into the bathroom, and Alice pointed out a specimen cup with graduated markings on it, sitting on the toilet lid. "As Dr. Chance explained, we need to test your urine to make sure that the nanocells are broken down and eliminated on schedule. There are specific markers that tell us the breakdown rate. By monitoring it closely, we can tell when the process is done."

"How do I give you the cup?"

"Just screw the lid onto it and place it in this receptacle here." As she said this, she placed the empty cup into the holder recessed into the wall above the toilet. A few seconds later, the cup holder rotated into the wall, and a new empty cup emerged from an identical holder on the other side.

Continuing around the bathroom, Alice showed him a week's worth of towels and washcloths on a shelf next to the shower; dispensers for soap and shampoo built into the shower wall; an electric shaver plugged into the wall by the sink. He had everything he'd need for five days alone.

They walked back into the living area, heading to the computer station. Eliot noticed another door in the wall opposite the entry door to the suite, and he walked over to it. "What's in here?" He reached out and tried the doorknob, but it was locked.

"Just supplies," Alice answered. "Linens, toilet paper, things like that. But everything you'll need is already set out."

She turned back to the computer station and wiggled the mouse, activating the display. It was an older operating system, Eliot noticed, scanning the handful of icons on the screen. "There are a few things we'd like you to do on this computer as part of your daily routine. This is also the way you'll communicate with us." She clicked on a conference icon and a full-screen window opened up, showing a live video feed of a conference room smaller than the one they'd sat in earlier. There were chairs for four, but they were all empty. A red light appeared on the top bezel of the monitor, revealing that the built-in camera was now active. At the bottom right of the screen, a thumbnail image of this room showed the two of them standing in front of the computer station. Their heads were out of the picture, since the camera was intended to be used while sitting.

"Notice that the videochat icon has been flashing since I clicked it. That means it's signaling for attention at the other end." On the monitor, they could see Dr. Gold walk into the conference room and sit down. He clicked something at his end, and the icon stopped flashing.

"Hello, Eliot," Dr. Gold's voice came through clearly. "As you can see, you'll be able to videochat with us whenever you like, and sometimes we'll be calling you in the same way. What do you think? Will that help alleviate the isolation?"

"I expect so," Eliot answered. In fact, it helped him feel much more comfortable about the prospect of spending five days without real human contact.

"If no one answers, you can click this icon here." Alice showed him an icon that looked like a camera and microphone. "This will let you leave a video message that someone will respond to as soon as possible."

Eliot considered this setup for a few seconds and moved the mouse around to examine all the controls. It seemed simple enough. "I suppose all the conversations we have will be recorded? I mean, in case I go stir crazy on you."

Dr. Gold hesitated for a fraction of a second before answering. "Well, yes, as a matter of fact, we do record it. It's not so much to make sure *you* behave as to make sure *we* do." He offered an insincere smile. "Lawyers, you know."

"But the rest of the time, when I'm not in the videochat, I won't be recorded or monitored? Can I assume that I have privacy the rest of the time?" He looked at Alice when he asked this.

"We won't be watching you except through the videochat," she answered. He believed her. Even so, he thought he'd probably look around for hidden cameras if he said yes to the study. *Trust, but verify.*

"So what else can I do with the computer?" On the monitor, he saw Dr. Gold get up and leave the conference room as Alice closed the videochat window.

"I'm afraid it's limited to these applications that you see on the screen." Alice quickly showed them to him. "There are a couple of games and puzzles here, which we encourage you to use as often as you want, and this is a journal where we'd like you to take notes about this experience — or anything you'd like to write down. This will *not* be private; we'll read the journal entries. All of this will help us understand your cognitive processes and your mental state as the study proceeds. We'd like you to make at least one or two entries every day, but more would be fine." She pointed to the bottom of the screen. "This question mark icon is your homework. When this icon blinks, it means there's a set of questions we'd like you to answer. Kind of a daily quiz, although sometimes they might come more often than once a day. There will be a number under the icon showing how many assignments are waiting for you. Please check it at least once in the morning and once in the afternoon or evening. It will be very helpful if you could answer the questions as soon as you see them."

"What kind of questions?"

"That's up to Dr. Gold. He's prepared a variety of psychological tests, personality profiles, aptitude surveys, memory tests, intelligence tests — really a little of every-thing." She looked at the skeptical expression on Eliot's face. "Some of these tests might seem unrelated to the project goals we talked about. We're taking advantage of your availability as a test subject to gather additional data that might help our other projects. It will all go into our databases, and some of it might never be used, or might be used by future projects that we haven't even planned yet."

"Is it going to be very personal?" he asked, imagin-ing himself lying on a couch, being asked how he felt about his mother.

"Possibly, but we're very careful to protect your confidentiality. Anyone who has access to this data will not have access to your personal identifying information. They'll see aggregated information from 'Subject 1' and 'Subject 2,' and so on. There were details about this in the privacy section of the non-disclosure agreement that you signed. When you leave today, you'll have a copy of all of those papers, so please review them and call us back if you have any concerns."

He thought about this. *I suppose it will have to get personal if they really want to know how I think. What did I expect? At least they won't have me taking experimental drugs, and the pay's pretty good.* He looked back at the icons on the monitor. "So no email or texting, no web browser, no social media?"

"No," Alice answered. "You won't be able to have your cell phone or tablet with you, either. No contact outside of the lab."

Unexpectedly, a smile came to his face. *No phone calls, no Research Requests, no obligations except for a few questionnaires, and a hundred dollars a day.* "Okay," he said, turning to grin at Alice. "I'm willing if you are."

Awakenings

Eliot Stearns awoke in a room filled with soft blue light. It took him a moment to remember that today was the start of the study. He lay on his back, looking around the room. He couldn't tell what time it was or how long he'd been asleep. He groped for his watch, then remembered that they'd taken it from him, along with his cell phone, wallet, and keys. *And the books*, he recalled. He'd arrived with three books that he intended to read during the study, but they told him he couldn't take them in with him.

Eliot slid the sheets aside and swung his legs off the bed, feeling some residual light-headedness from the sedative. The lighting controls were on the nightstand. He turned up the red and green slowly, remembering what Alice said about light sensitivity. It didn't seem to bother his eyes at all, so he turned up the brightness after balancing the colors.

When he tried to stand, he wobbled a bit, hanging onto the edge of the nightstand. He stretched his muscles and looked around for a clock, eventually finding a digital display near the door: *8:32 AM.* That surprised him; he'd been sedated around 8:00 last night. Remembering the nanocells, he felt a moment of anxiety. Assurances aside, there was something unsettling about tiny robots coursing through his bloodstream. He headed for the bathroom, noticing the empty specimen cup sitting on the toilet lid as a reminder.

When he was done, he glanced at the shower, deciding he needn't bother with that. It's not as though he'd have company today. He brushed his teeth and changed out of the pajamas they'd given him and into his new daily wardrobe: sweatpants and t-shirt. Walking into the living area, he wandered around to get used to the feeling of being there. It was a typically human reaction, he thought. Explore a new space until it feels familiar. Make it into your home, even if it's only temporary. You don't just walk into a motel room for the first time and sit right down. You check out the bathroom, look into the shower, open the closet and the mini-fridge, check the view out the window, adjust the thermostat. It's more than just making sure you're alone and that everything's functional. It's claiming your territory. Which, of course, means it's not specifically human after all, he realized. It's something far older and more fundamental in our evolution.

As he walked around the room, Eliot couldn't help trying the entry door. It was locked, as he knew it would be. So was the supply room door, which had been locked before, when they first showed him the suite. There was nothing surprising about it, but now that he was stuck here for five days, it seemed a little ominous to be locked in.

He walked to the computer station and sat down. The question icon blinked the number "1." *Homework already, on the first day of class.* He ignored it for now and clicked the conference icon. The videochat window came up, and he saw Alice sitting at the table, her notebook open in front of her. He guessed she'd been working while waiting for him. She smiled up at him, closing her notebook.

"Good morning, Eliot. How do you feel?"

"Fine. No apparent after-effects of the procedure, except that I slept for half a day."

"That's normal. We put you into a very deep sleep. We have to suppress the REM activity in order to get the readings that we're looking for."

"So I didn't dream at all last night?" he asked. He had a vague impression of dreaming, but he had no clear memory of it, as if he'd forgotten something.

"No dreams. It's always unsettling to wake from a long sleep without reaching REM state. Your body's telling you that you didn't sleep properly."

"And you got what you needed?" He suddenly realized that they'd never explained exactly what kind of readings they were taking of his brain.

"Processing all the data takes a while. We'll be analyzing it long after you've left, but everything went as expected at our end, so we should have what we need."

"Actually, now that I think about, it seems odd that you didn't take your readings with me awake and active," Eliot said. "What can you tell about my 'cognitive processes' while I'm sedated?"

"Some day we might be able to do that, but right now we're limited by the technology," Alice explained. "The nanocells are very susceptible to interference from the slightest movement. You couldn't hold still enough if you were awake. We even lower your pulse slightly, so we can take our measurements between heartbeats. Besides, you'd be surprised how active your brain remains, even while you're in a deep sleep. We get a baseline view of the structure and complexity of your neural pathways, and that's what we're looking for at this stage."

He still wondered how they were getting enough information to make this worthwhile. The technology must cost a fortune. Before he could probe any further, Alice spoke up again. "Would you like some breakfast, Eliot?"

"Sure. What do you have? Pancakes, bacon, hash browns, maybe a Denver omelet …?"

"Well, no," she laughed. "When I said earlier that the experience might be boring, I was including the food in that description."

"Yeah, I was afraid of that." He swiveled to his right and looked at the slot in the wall at the far edge of the table. It was still closed. "Do I just wait for the food to appear, or do I reach in to get it?"

In answer, the panel covering the slot slid up inside the wall, and a tray rolled onto the table. The panel remained open and the rollers inside stopped spinning once the tray was ejected, but there was nothing else he could see inside the slot. There must be another panel on the other side that only opened when the one on his side was closed.

"We let you sleep in as long as you needed today," Alice said, as he turned back to look at the monitor. "For the rest of the study, we'll wake you at 7:30 and have your breakfast out at 8:00. Lunch will come out at noon, and there will be an afternoon snack at 4:00 and supper at 6:30. Does that sound okay?"

"That'll be fine. Let's see what bounteous repast you have for me this morning."

Alice laughed again. "I'll leave you to your feast. And remember, I'm not the cook, so don't hold me responsible. I'll talk to you later, Eliot." The videochat window closed.

He went over to the table and sat down. The tray contained a plate with an opaque plastic cover, a serving of orange juice in a sealed plastic vending pack, and a napkin rolled up around a set of cutlery. He looked twice, but there was no coffee. Eliot lifted the cover off the plate, and condensation dripped off the underside. It was a hot breakfast, at least, but it didn't look particularly appetizing. The plate was divided into three sections: scrambled eggs that could be egg substitutes, oatmeal that looked like paste, and a round sausage patty of dubious provenance. The best thing that could be said for the entire meal was that it had hardly any flavor.

After he ate, Eliot pushed the tray back into the slot and watched the panel slide back into place. He heard the rollers hum, and he knew that the opposite panel must have opened, rolling the tray into the room behind the wall. He sat for a moment, thinking about his isolation and listening to the quiet. *This would be my dream job, if only they'd left me a library full of books. Do they* want *me to be bored?* His thoughts swung around to Dr. Gold, and he looked over at the homework icon still blinking on the computer monitor.

He remembered a story he'd read somewhere about a college psychology professor who was interrupted in the middle of a lecture by a man who ran through the door, grabbed something from the professor's desk, and ran out. The campus police came and took statements from everyone in the class, trying to get a description of the man, what happened, and what he took. The next day, everyone in class talked about what happened, and then the professor asked them all to write down what they remembered. These reports were then compared to their statements immediately after the incident.

Their initial statements showed great variation. The physical descriptions of the perpetrator differed wildly in every conceivable aspect: race, height, age, hair color, clothing. Two people even claimed it was a woman. Some people said the intruder knocked the professor down, shouted threats, brandished a gun. There were sworn statements that an accomplice held the door open for him, that he'd taken a book or the professor's wallet or briefcase.

After talking about it in class, their second reports were much more closely correlated. Everyone agreed it was a white male slightly taller than the professor, wearing a hooded sweatshirt. He'd acted alone, he'd stolen a book, and he never touched the professor or said a word. At this point, the professor admitted that it was all a psychology experiment. The campus police were in on the hoax, along with the professor and the graduate student who had interrupted the lecture.

There were several lessons that the students were supposed to learn from this: eyewitness accounts of sudden events are unreliable; when recalling events, we invent details that we never observed; we adjust our memories to fit the group consensus.

Was this whole study really about boredom and isolation? Was Dr. Gold driving it all, with everyone else just window dressing? Maybe the story about nanocells and brain measurements was pure hokum to distract him and add a level of anxiety into the mix. It irritated him to think they might just be playing him for a fool, but perhaps he'd seen through it faster than they expected. He'd defer judgment for now, but keep one eye open for the man behind the curtain.

Eliot turned back to the computer and clicked on the homework icon. The window that came up was an interactive questionnaire, and at the top he read "Myers-Briggs Type Indicator." He remembered taking this test once before: the first day of his psychology class.

• • •

After he finished with Dr. Gold's homework, Eliot tried out the games on the computer. He found a sudoku game with puzzles of increasing complexity. He solved the first few in a minute or two. As he played, they became more difficult; eventually, it took over ten minutes to complete a puzzle. He stopped there and looked at some of the other games. The crossword puzzle was challenging. He was stumped at first by 10 across: *Cedar forest victor, 9 letters*, but 10 down was simple: *Famous Philistine.* "Goliath" gave him the leading "G", and he typed in "Gilgamesh" for 10 across. He finished the rest of the puzzle with little difficulty.

He walked around the room, stretching his legs. *It's too early to be bored. I'm not even halfway through the first day.* He went back to the computer and opened the journal program. The empty canvas was intimidating. How to begin? *Call me Ishmael? Captain's log? Once upon a time?* In the end, he settled for the mundane.

Eliot Stearns, Day 1

There's still half an hour before lunch on the first day, and I fear that I've already experienced everything there is to do here. Well, not quite. I still haven't tried the treadmill. I'll do that after lunch. Maybe I can look at this as a "boot camp" and get into a rigorous daily exercise regimen. Five days with almost nothing else to do, so I might as well see how long I can go on the treadmill. If I keep trying to beat my personal best every day, who knows? It could make a new man out of me.

I wish you'd given me some guidelines for what you want me to write about. What's the objective of this journal? If it's to give you feedback to improve the study for the next subject, then here's my first piece of advice. PLEASE provide some reading material. I suppose the reason that almost all the activities are on the computer is so that you can track exactly what I'm doing. Maybe you don't want me sitting with my nose in a book because you won't know if I'm really reading or just napping. But you could have included some e-books on the computer. You could track what I'm doing with every turn of the page.

I suppose the journal is just to see what I'm thinking about. That's what you said you needed to learn, right? How I think, which logically must include what I think about. So I'll try to tell you whatever comes to mind. Well, within socially acceptable limits at least.

Right now I'm wondering what's coming for lunch. The whole business of the tray emerging automatically from the wall is kind of creepy. If you really had to insist on no contact with anyone while I'm here, why didn't you just give me a well-stocked pantry and refrigerator? Wouldn't you learn something about how I think by watching me cook for myself, and seeing what I decide to eat and when? Even if you ended up with someone who couldn't cook toast, they wouldn't starve in five days. Is it really important to have complete control over what I eat and when I eat it?

As he wrote the last sentence, Eliot wondered if he'd stumbled onto the real reason they were collecting urine samples. The whole thing could really be a study of how quickly his body absorbed certain nutrients. Or anything else they might have included in the food. *No, that's paranoid. They said "no drugs" in the ad.*

When lunch came, it was a salad, chicken sub sandwich, fruit cup, and apple juice — a big improvement over breakfast, but still surprisingly bland. Shortly after he finished eating, he heard a beep from the computer, and he saw that the conference icon was blinking. He sat down in front of the monitor and clicked the icon, and the videochat window popped up. Sitting at the conference table were Alice and Dr. Gold.

"Hello, Eliot," Gold greeted him. "Starting to feel at home?"

"Starting to feel like my apartment back home is too big," Eliot said. "How wonderfully efficient this space is, like one of those ultra-low-impact housing modules at Ikea."

"That's the spirit," Gold replied, and Eliot couldn't tell if he missed the sarcasm or was playing along. He saw a quick grin flit across Alice's face, but she said nothing. Apparently, it was Dr. Gold's turn to play with the lab rat.

"So, Eliot, we'd like you to indulge us in a couple of simple memory tests. This helps us establish some baselines for additional tests we'll be conducting later in the study. There aren't any right or wrong answers. It's just a way of getting insight into your thought processes, as we discussed before. Does that sound all right to you?"

"Sure," Eliot agreed.

"Okay," Gold began, "I'd like you to name as many types of animals as you can in one minute. Ready? Start … now."

"Cat, dog, horse, cow, sheep, owl, hawk, elephant, snake, cobra, giraffe, muskox, deer, antelope, chimpanzee, monkey, gorilla, lemur, aardvark, orangutan, anteater, lion, cheetah, leopard, tiger, panther, cougar …"

"Time," Dr. Gold called. "Okay. Very good, Eliot."

"Now I'm going to tell you three words, and I want you to remember them. I'll ask you later what they were.

Ready?"

"Yes."

"Lamp. Bookcase. Sidewalk."

"Okay."

"Now I'd like you to tell me a story from your child-hood. It doesn't matter what, just some little anecdote. Something you remember happening to you, not some-thing you were told about. It doesn't have to be signifi-cant. Can you think of something?"

Eliot thought for a few seconds. "Well, I remember one day. It must have been first grade, or maybe even kindergarten. The teacher said that today we were going to talk about American History, and I got all excited because I knew that was the subject that my mother taught in high school. So we learned about George Washington, and it was all the silly crap they teach the youngest kids. You know, the 'cannot tell a lie' stuff and how he was a farmer and then a general and won the Revolutionary War and became the first president. And I remember sitting through that and being really disap-pointed, because it seemed so unimportant. It made me sad and kind of embarrassed that this was what my mom did, when all along my parents had told me that teachers had such an important job. Now, in just a few minutes, I'd learned American History and there wasn't anything to it."

"How did your mother react when you told her about it?" Gold asked.

"I didn't talk to her about it, at first. I felt like I'd just discovered that my mom wasn't really very smart or important, and I didn't want her to know that I knew. I felt really bad for her. Eventually, I said that I'd learned American History, and she asked me what I learned. As I told her about George Washington, she asked me questions like 'What does a general do?' and 'Why did the Revolutionary War happen?' and 'What does it mean to be president?' We talked for a long time. She kept asking me questions, and I kept guessing at answers, and she kept filling in gaps and then asking me more questions. And after that I was happy about my mom again, because she knew so much more than I did and she taught me more than the teacher had. I realized that there was a lot more to American History than George Washington chopping down a cherry tree."

"It sounds like you had a very loving and supportive mother, Eliot."

"Yeah, both of my parents are like that. In hindsight, I guess that was my first experience with Socratic dialogue. Come to think of it, they still kind of talk to me that way, although we don't speak very often any more. They retired to England last year." Eliot paused, wondering again if he would be able to visit them this fall. When he looked back at the monitor, he saw Gold studying him patiently, clinically. In Alice's face, he saw something different. Something gentle.

His thoughts returned to the story, and he laughed. "Of course, there was a side effect to this conversation. After that, I thought that maybe my teacher wasn't very smart, and I felt bad for *her*. From then on, I tried to help her out by asking a lot of questions and guessing what else might be true that she hadn't thought of. It sort of set the tone for the rest of my academic career."

Alice smiled broadly, but she said nothing. Gold maintained the same unreadable expression. "Now, Eliot, I wonder if you can tell me the three words that …"

"Bookcase, sidewalk, and … lamp. Is that right?"

"Very good, Eliot. Now let's move on to another little memory test."

Gold kept him busy for another hour, and Eliot was

more than ready for a break when he was finally dismissed. He walked around the room for a while, stretching his muscles, then stepped onto the treadmill. It wasn't motorized, just propelled by his own walking. The resistance was moderate, like walking up a slight incline. He saw that there were controls to increase the tension, but he left it on the default setting. After forty minutes, he was ready to quit. The gauge indicated that he'd walked 1.8 miles, so he decided to go for an even two. The pace was slower than he expected. *Not exactly "boot camp" worthy, but it's a start.* He got some water from the sink in the bathroom, where there was a paper cup dispenser. Having worked up a bit of a sweat, he decided to try out the shower.

• • •

Later that afternoon, Alice was alone in the conference room when Eliot initiated the videochat. Once again, she seemed to be working, but she closed her notebook when the chat began. He wondered if she'd moved her office into the conference room for the duration of the study.

"How's your first day going, Eliot?"

"Well, like you said — a little boring, but that's okay. It's about the easiest job I've ever had. If you just let me have my books, I'd be willing to make a career of it."

She laughed. "You really wouldn't mind the isolation as long as you could read?"

"Well, I suppose it might get boring after a week or two. But it wouldn't be much different from how I spend my weekends now. There's a story that Einstein said the perfect job for him would be lighthouse keeper. There wouldn't be much to do, and he'd have plenty of time for his thoughts."

"Leaving you alone to your thoughts is pretty much what we're after," Alice said. "I'm sorry about the books.

We'll reconsider that the next time we run this study. But now that we've set the protocol for your experience, we can't change it for the duration. Hang in there. Just four more days after today."

"So no one has asked about books before?"

"Most people are more concerned about the lack of television and movies, actually."

He noticed that she hadn't answered the question. "Am I the first subject you've had for this study?"

"We can't talk to you about other subjects," she said, still avoiding a direct answer. "After all, you wouldn't want us discussing your experience with anyone else, right?"

Eliot didn't reply. He tried to remember what she and Dr. Chance had said last week when they gave him the project overview. They said that they'd tested the nanocells on animals and people, but they never said whether they'd run the five-day study before. He probably *was* the first one. If so, then the protocols they set for this study might be completely arbitrary. They might have no idea how he'd react to his isolation. Would they even realize if it caused him problems? He didn't want to insinuate that she didn't know her job, so he probed carefully. "It must be hard to do a study this complicated, when you have to keep repeating the whole thing with different subjects."

Something twitched in Alice's expression, but it was too fast for Eliot to recognize. "We get used to it pretty early in our careers," Alice said. "Experiments that aren't repeatable have no statistical significance, so we repeat them or we reject them."

"Have there been a lot of experiments involving isolation?" he asked. "Antarctic researchers, space flights? Especially the original Project Mercury astronauts. No one knew what to expect then, so they must have documented everything, including how they responded to being isolated."

"You're right," Alice said, nodding. She smiled. "If you're worried that we haven't done our homework, please don't be. There's quite a body of literature on isolation experiences, and we've studied it all. Speaking of homework, what did you think of the Myers-Briggs questionnaire?"

"No epiphanies there," he said. "I took that once before in college. I was an 'INTP' then, too."

"How do you know you're still INTP? Did Dr. Gold share that with you?"

"No, but I don't think my personality type has changed much over time. I feel like I still have the same interests and attitudes."

"Let's see, INTP means introverted, intuitive, thinking, and perceiving," Alice said. She thought about it for a few seconds. "I think that's one of the rarer combinations."

"I guess I'm not a very representative sample for your study. Sorry about that."

Alice smiled. "We don't expect anyone to be representative of everyone. We're interested in what makes you unique."

Eliot was surprised by that. Surely, they were trying to find out something about human brains in general, not Eliot Stearns' brain in particular. Was she just being patronizing? "I don't put much stock in that sort of test anyway," he said. "People are a lot more complicated than can be accounted for by four bits."

"Four bits?" Alice looked puzzled. "Oh, right. Four dimensions, each with two possible values, so four binary digits. But Myers-Briggs doesn't claim that all INTPs are alike. It's just supposed to be a predictor for your social interaction 'comfort zones,' helping you understand how to get along in group situations."

"Sure, I get that. But people take this sort of thing too seriously and use it as an excuse to pigeonhole each other. People are always looking for simplistic ways to classify things. At least this one has four dimensions. Most of the time, people try to understand each other using a linear scale."

"Like IQ, for example," Alice suggested, more animated now. "That's been a pet peeve of mine for a long time. Anyone who studies the brain realizes how absurd it is to try to measure intelligence using a single number. As if it made any sense at all to say that person X is smarter than person Y. It doesn't. There are many dimensions to intelligence, and you can't rank people along a line of who's smarter than whom. Looking at people that way has caused a lot of damage in the education system."

"You're right. That's a great example," Eliot said. "But actually, I was thinking about other things, like political thought. People want to know if you're liberal or conservative, Democrat or Republican. When people ask me that I tell them something like '47.3'."

"I don't know what that means."

"If politics can be reduced to a position on a linear scale — left to right, say — then that means the entire complexity of a person's political philosophy can be represented by a single number. That's ridiculous, so I give them a ridiculous answer. Discussions are more interesting when you don't start with absurd premises."

Alice laughed. "You must be great at parties, Eliot."

"Well, nine times out of ten, people find an excuse to walk away and talk to somebody else. But those tenth times make it all worthwhile." They exchanged a look.

"So do you think there *is* a meaningful framework — multidimensional, of course — for categorizing something like political thought?" Alice asked.

"It's not just a matter of multiple dimensions," Eliot continued. He'd thought about this quite a bit. "The problem is finding orthogonal ones. When you talk about two dimensions, like the surface of a paper, you can use two numbers — x and y coordinates — to locate any point. But that only works because the two dimensions are perpendicular to each other, so you can measure against one axis independently of the other. I don't think that's true for political thought. Any dimension you can come up with — economics, liberty, centralization, taxation, defense, foreign relations — has interdependencies with the other dimensions. When your attitude moves along one of those dimensions, your position on other dimensions tends to shift, too. In fact, I think most rational people end up in clumps around the center of the coordinate system. To get to the extreme end of any one axis, you have to ignore or suppress a lot of logical inconsistencies on the others, yet the political parties stress the extremes. It's like some warped version of the Platonic ideal — an abstraction never seen in the real world but believed in more strongly than reality."

"Wow. That's fascinating," Alice said, and the interest in her eyes was evident. "You should write a paper on that. There could be a whole new discipline in psychology or epistemology here."

Eliot paused for a moment, then continued. "I knew someone a while ago ... a former girlfriend, actually. She's a mathematician, and she started working with this group up at UNC in a field called nonstandard analysis. Don't ask me to explain it; all I ever understood is that it involved infinitesimal numbers, and group theory, and things like that. I asked her once if she thought this was an area where nonstandard analysis might be productive."

"And did she?"

"She didn't think so, but at the time, she was buried in her own research, so she never had the time to look into it. Or maybe she was just being kind. She really was busy, though. She had just made a name for herself in the math world. It changed her life. Mine, too," he admitted. "She took a teaching position in Portugal, and we went our separate ways."

"I'm sorry to hear that, Eliot. She sounds like someone who could keep up with you, and I'm getting the feeling that's a rare ability."

Eliot had to smile at that. Alice could keep up with him; that was clear. Could he keep up with her?

• • •

As promised, a series of chimes awakened Eliot on day 2. The lights swelled to half-brightness, the colors remaining as Eliot had set them yesterday. He reached his hand to the brightness control, and the chimes stopped. That distracted him for a minute as he lay on the bed and thought about how the automation might work. The chimes came from the speakers by the computer station in the other room. The computer — or the network it's connected to — controls the lights and the wake-up sequence. To do that, it must be monitoring for signs of activity. If it could tell when Eliot used the light controls, then it was probably monitoring *every* interaction he had with the environment: his movement from room to room, exercise on the treadmill, the games he played on the computer, even his use of the bathroom and shower. He'd been taking the illusion of privacy at face value. What was it Alice said about that? *We won't watch you except through the videochat.* That was a carefully composed answer. They didn't need to *watch* him to track his actions.

• • •

Dr. Gold's tablet buzzed three times, alerting him that the subject had opened his homework assignment. Gold was already at his desk, so he sent the tablet display to his monitor, where the window from the subject's computer appeared. On the right was the same display that the subject saw, augmented on the left with live metrics of his performance on the tests. The first was an escalating-complexity short-term memory test, which the subject probably thought of as the *Concentration* game. It started with four rows of four tiles, each tile covering a common English word. Two tiles could be revealed each turn. If the words matched, the tiles were removed. Otherwise, the words were covered again before the next turn. Every word had its match somewhere on the board, and the subject had to remember the locations of previously revealed words as their matches turned up. Over time, the boards increased in size and became more difficult in other ways.

While he watched, Gold dictated notes, his tablet transcribing them. "The subject performs exceptionally well in the word tests. So far, he's remembered the correct location of each previously-revealed word. That's three boards done, now the puzzle's switched to icons instead of words, and he's made his first mistake. He was trying to match the school crossing icon, but missed by one column."

Gold watched the metrics accumulate, showing a consistent pattern. Whenever the tiles went back to words, the subject performed nearly perfectly. Switching to images noticeably reduced his performance, especially as the images became more abstract. Numbers were hardest for the subject, but even with numbers, he performed better than average.

"Speculation: the subject may perceive the words as a sort of poem, where the 'verse' of each row keeps the word order stable in his memory. Does he easily remember verse? Recommendation: encourage the subject to discuss poetry or song lyrics, and see what he can quote from memory."

• • •

Eliot needed a break before starting the next assignment in the queue. He stood and stretched, then got on the treadmill and logged another two miles. As he walked, he thought about the tests, trying to see what value they provided to Alice and her team. What were they looking for? What would they learn from him that might apply to anyone else? The tests and games appeared designed to test his mental acuity. No doubt they wanted to see how the isolation and boredom affected him. But there had to be more to it than that, considering the advanced technology they were using. Perhaps he was part of a larger study to see what size group — or what combination of personalities — is needed to ease the effects of isolation. Similar studies might be going on for groups of two, three, and so on. His case might be the least interesting of all, the one they know will decline in isolation: the control subject.

He was surprised that this possibility disappointed him so much. Alice's passion for this project had made him feel like a collaborator. He had to remind himself that there was very little he could actually contribute. Still, there was no way for him to know what value he added, so he might as well assume that he made a difference.

He took the second test after lunch. A target icon flashed somewhere on the screen at random intervals, and Eliot had to click on the target before it winked out. As before, the test progressed from easy to very difficult. The target got smaller, jumped around the screen faster, and vanished more quickly. Eventually, it was too small and fast for him to catch it at all. The game stopped, and Eliot slowly unclenched his hand from the mouse.

In the afternoon, Ray Chance joined the videoconference and informed Eliot that the nanocell breakdown was complete, so he no longer had to collect his urine. Chance stayed for the rest of the meeting, but remained a silent observer, like Alice, as Dr. Gold ran him through more psychological tests.

After supper, Eliot talked to Alice alone again. "So, are you bored with us yet?" she asked.

Eliot considered it for a few seconds. "Not exactly," he said. "It's not boredom, *per se*, but an apprehension of boredom yet to come." He gave Alice a wry smile. "A *foreboring*, I guess." She laughed, and Eliot's smile widened. She had a warm, welcoming laugh, even if he did have to tease it out of her.

"I was surprised that I didn't really have to interview for this job," he said. "How do you know that I didn't lie on the application?"

"I can interview you now, if you like," Alice offered, adroitly avoiding the question. She leaned forward slightly, reviewed imaginary notes on her tablet, and looked at him over the rim of nonexistent spectacles. "So, Eliot, describe yourself in four adjectives."

He grinned at her. "I'll make you a deal, Dr. Kurz. I'll describe each of us in four adjectives, if you'll do the same."

She looked at him with just a hint of amusement. "What makes you think we know each other well enough to do that?"

"I'm sure we don't," Eliot said. "But it would be interesting to share first impressions. We'll try it again later, and see how it changes."

She gave him no answer. "I'll go first," he said. "In my mind, I am: curious, literate, comfortable, and honest."

"Comfortable?" she asked. "I wouldn't have guessed that."

Eliot shrugged. "Well, if I'm going to claim 'honest,' I have to admit I'm not a thrill-seeker."

"And what about me?"

"I don't know, are you looking to be thrilled?"

"Four adjectives," she reminded him.

He scanned her face, lingering on her eyes and the smile she tried to hold back. "For you, I would say ... curious, ambitious, fervent, and assiduous."

Alice raised an eyebrow, but the smile remained at the corner of her mouth. Eliot smiled back. "Your turn," he told her.

She considered Eliot for a long time. "I'd say you are cerebral, surprising, gentle, and kind." He smiled at her unexpected assessment. "And for me," Alice continued, "I'll go with diligent, ambitious, impatient, and ... tired."

Eliot laughed. "I'm guessing the first three are the cause of the fourth."

Alice nodded. "Like you said earlier: multiple dimensions, but not independent ones."

• • •

When the chimes woke him on the morning of the third day, Eliot remembered to stop himself before turning up the lights. He lay in bed and listened to the chimes. They didn't stop automatically, but slowly grew louder as the lights increased in brightness. *Whatever informs them that I'm awake hasn't happened yet,* he thought. Was the light control the only signal? He sat up and got out of bed without touching the controls and walked quietly around the suite. The chimes continued. "Okay, I'm up," he called out. Still no change. If they *were* watching, listening, or tracking his movements, then they didn't want him to know it.

He walked to the computer station and wiggled the mouse. The monitor woke up, and the chimes stopped. Eliot sat there and browsed around the interface. *Why such an old operating system?* Clearly, *this* computer wasn't controlling the lights or the alarm. It was probably just a slice of a cloud network, a virtual PC. Just enough for the games and videochat, and easy to wall off from the rest of their network. Eliot almost felt empathy for it. The computer was every bit as isolated as he.

Am I getting paranoid? He had to laugh, thinking about his current situation. *Let's see, I'm all alone except for people I talk to on the computer; they're talking about me behind my back; they're deliberately prodding at my mind; and they put invisible robots inside my brain. If I start having paranoid delusions, how will I know the difference?*

He paced around the suite, feeling like a goldfish in a bowl. *Were* they watching him? Hidden cameras? A one-way mirror over the sink? What was really behind the door to the "supply room?" Was that the control room? He went to the supply room door and tried the knob again; still locked. He knocked on the door and waited. Nothing. He put his ear against the door and listened. There was no sound. Or was there? Maybe just a faint whirring noise …

Suddenly, his breakfast tray rolled onto the table behind him, and he jumped. It was 8:00.

• • •

After breakfast, there was a full crowd at the conference table: Alice Kurz, Ray Chance, Dr. Gold, and Dr. Weil. Eliot noticed a fifth person that he hadn't met before, sitting at the edge of the table. He was about Eliot's age, with very short dark hair and videoglasses. Through the monitor, Eliot couldn't tell if the glasses were displaying anything, but the man seemed to be studying Eliot and his own colleagues with equal interest.

"Good morning, Eliot," Dr. Weil started things off. "I wanted to check in with you today and see how everything is going. What do you think of the experience so far?"

"The days are kind of long and boring, but no real problems. I suppose I've been talking everyone's ears off, but I get that complaint even out in the real world."

Alice smiled. "We're enjoying our talks with you, Eliot," she said. "You have a very active mind and a refreshing point of view on so many topics."

It struck Eliot that the reason they had isolated him was to keep him away from "external influences." What about these long, interesting discussions he'd been having with Alice? Was that all part of their plan, drawing him out to see how he thinks? Surely, they must realize that Alice was contributing ideas and opinions, too. She was undeniably influencing his thoughts. Even when he wasn't talking to her, he was thinking about her frequently. He decided not to ask about that. He wanted their conversations to continue.

Eliot noticed the thoughtful expression on Dr. Gold's face as he looked at Alice, then turned back to Eliot and said, "Yes, it's been our pleasure. So what else do you do to relieve the boredom?"

"Well, I'm starting to enjoy using the treadmill. I think my health is actually improving. Normally, I'd take a short walk every other day or so, but I've used the treadmill every day; sometimes twice a day. I can go up to four miles now, but not all at once. I've decided to continue with the exercise, even after I'm out of here." He looked at the unknown man in the corner. "By the way, who else am I talking to today?"

"This is Dr. Trilby, Eliot," Alice answered.

"Everyone calls me Trick," the man added. "I prefer

it."

"Trick is in charge of the software development," Chance added. "These days, he's mostly working on correlating the data from the various tests and home-work you've been doing for Dr. Gold."

Not to mention the data from the nanocells, Eliot thought. *Wouldn't that be the highest priority now?* "Did you write the software for the nanocells?" he asked Trick. "Or do they call that *firmware?*"

"My team had a hand in it, but most of our efforts have been on the data analysis side of things." He tilted his head slightly, reminding Eliot of a dog appraising an unexpected situation. "You've done some programming?"

"Probably not what you'd consider programming, but I've been working on the knowledge representation side of things on the semantic web. Concept maps for dynamic linking, cross-disciplinary relationships, that sort of thing."

Trick nodded. "I thought I recognized your name from somewhere. I think you're in my auto-update list."

"What does that mean, Trick?" Alice asked, glanc-ing at Trick, then back to Eliot's face on the monitor.

"Eliot contributes to the W3C concept maps. I get his updates automatically, because his work has a very high trust factor."

"What are your areas of interest, Eliot?" Dr. Gold asked.

Eliot paused, considering how to limit his response. "Literature, history, myth, and science, mostly."

"Mostly?" Alice said with a grin. "With a minor in everything else?"

Eliot laughed. "Yeah, maybe so. I guess I should have added philosophy, as well." He noticed Dr. Gold making lengthy notes on his tablet, Alice smiling warmly at him, Ray Chance trying to hide his boredom, Trick studying Eliot like a lab experiment, and Dr. Weil sitting back, taking it all in.

"A *Renaissance man*," Trick said. "That's become a lot more difficult in the last couple of centuries. There's too much detail available now. It's almost impossible to be functionally competent in a broad array of disciplines. Most people have to choose between a shallow understanding of a lot, or a deep understanding of a little. But maybe that will change."

Eliot was fascinated. "How would that change, Trick? The level of detail is only going to increase."

"Yes, but we've already shifted more of the burden to the tools in order to offload the expert. Memorization of the formulas and procedures of technical disciplines isn't really necessary any more. It's primarily a matter of being able to access the information you need quickly and accurately. There's not a programmer working anywhere today who doesn't routinely rely on online references and code libraries, and that allows them to build things they never could with only their own skills to draw from. Doctors, military tacticians, politicians, economists — everyone augments their effectiveness by integrating online information into their processes. We're reaching the point where whatever's known *anywhere* in the world is known *everywhere*. With some fundamental advances in the way we manage that information, expertise in *any* field will be available to everyone."

Eliot nodded eagerly. "That's exactly what we're trying to do with the *Web 4.0*, as they're starting to call it. The information you want is probably out there somewhere, but the old search paradigms aren't enough to integrate it into the context you want. We're moving from search to a kind of guided exploration."

Eliot remembered something Alice mentioned in the project introduction before he signed up for the study: *cognitive prostheses* to help patients with damaged areas of the brain. But the same technology could be used to extend the mental capabilities of anyone, not just the brain-damaged. Eliot started to realize why the institute might be willing to throw unlimited funding into projects like this. It all came down to who owned the key technologies. He remembered the definition of "neurocybernetics" that he'd come across when trying to figure out what the institute did: *the study of communication and control mechanisms within and between machines and living organisms.*

"Perhaps you and Eliot could continue this discussion over the next two days," Dr. Gold interjected, looking at Trick. "I have a few more items that I'd like to follow up on." Trick continued to look appraisingly at Eliot, but Eliot shifted his attention to Dr. Gold.

"So you're doing all right being stuck indoors?" Dr. Gold continued. "No problem sleeping at night, waking in the morning?"

"Not that I've noticed. But you're keeping me on a regular schedule."

"And you've been eating all right? No trouble with the food?"

"Well, it seems filling enough, but it's awfully bland. I'm guessing you had a list of specific nutritional requirements, and 'flavor' was not on the list." Weil and Chance looked embarrassed and wore expressions of commiseration. Alice and Dr. Gold seemed strangely satisfied — pleased, even — with his response. Trick remained completely unreadable.

"Is there a particular kind of food that you miss?" Gold asked.

"Actually, it's my morning coffee that I miss most." Eliot paused, as if trying to remember his last cup, then looked back up to the monitor and quoted, "'I have measured out my life with coffee spoons.'"

Gold continued jotting down notes. He spoke without looking at Eliot. "Is that your own analogy, or a literary allusion?"

Eliot gave a slight sigh, caught by Alice. She leaned in toward her microphone, causing Gold to pause in his writing and stare closely at her. "*J. Alfred Prufrock*, isn't it?"

"That's right," Eliot said, leaning forward. "You've read it, Dr. Kurz?"

"Quite a while ago. I don't remember much about it, but the opening is hard to forget. Something about the sky being like a patient on an examining table."

Eliot smiled and quoted:

"Let us go then, you and I,
When the evening is spread out against the sky
Like a patient etherised upon a table;"

Dr. Gold spoke carefully, "I'm not familiar with Prufrock. One of your favorite authors, Eliot?"

Eliot and Alice both smiled, but as Eliot turned to Gold, he noticed that Gold wasn't looking at him. He was studying Alice. None of them saw Dr. Weil appraising the situation, noticing how much more comfortable Eliot was with Alice.

"*The Love Song of J. Alfred Prufrock* is the title of the poem," Alice explained. "The author was T. S. Eliot." She paused for a second, realizing something. "That's *Thomas Stearns Eliot*. Your name is an anagram, Eliot."

"Yeah, T. S. Eliot was one of the few authors that both of my parents liked. *Prufrock* is one of Mom's favorite poems. Dad's always been more partial to *The Waste Land*."

"Which is *your* favorite?" Alice asked.

Eliot considered it. "I never like to be pinned down about a favorite *anything*," he said. "Too many dimensions, you know." He caught Alice's smile. So did Gold. "You can't beat *The Waste Land* if you want to go mining for literary ore, but it's hard work. And now that I'm getting older, I'm starting to really appreciate *Prufrock* more."

"But you're only 32," Alice said. "You're still young."

"Sure, I guess so. But sometimes I feel like this is all there is for me, like I've settled into a comfy chair with a good book, and that's all I want now."

"People settle for worse," Alice murmured.

Gold was still taking notes, his attention on Eliot's words. He didn't hear what Alice said, but Eliot did.

• • •

When they finished interviewing Eliot, Alice said goodbye and closed the videochat. No one spoke for a few seconds, so Dr. Weil leaned back and put his hands behind his head and stretched, emitting a slight sigh. When he leaned back to the table, everyone else looked more relaxed, too. Except Trick, of course, who never looked stressed in the first place. Weil remembered telling Alice that Trick was the wrong man for the job, but she simply said, "No, he's perfect," and continued whatever she'd been working on, never realizing that he meant she shouldn't hire him. He stood there, about to say that, but he couldn't. He'd already given her hiring authority. Ray Chance had been a great acquisition, and he was a fan of Trick's, too, so Weil nodded to her and left her to her work. Once he saw Trick in action, he never second-guessed Alice again.

"Impressions, everyone?" Weil asked the room. "Observations?"

Alice didn't hesitate. "Trick's comment earlier was correct, Eliot is a 'Renaissance Man.' It's no difficulty at all getting him to talk about something he's passionate about — he's passionate about everything."

Weil noticed the way that Dr. Gold was looking at Alice, and he rephrased her words. "So there are many vectors on which to evaluate consistency across cycles."

"Exactly," Alice continued, clearly excited. "Eliot's brain is a gold mine of complex interconnections. We couldn't have asked for a better subject." She tapped her tablet for a few seconds, then showed it to Dr. Weil. "Look at these preliminary complexity estimates."

"I agree," Gold began pleasantly. "This will be a real opportunity to explore the limits of your technology." *Not 'our technology,'* Weil noticed. Still, it was good to have someone on the team who felt like an outsider. Someone to point out when they lost track of the process, as Gold did next. "However, Dr. Kurz, I must ask you to stop referring to the subject as *Eliot.*"

"That's his name, I believe."

"Indeed, and it is polite to address him by his name when you talk to him, but that's not how we refer to the subject in conference."

Weil watched Alice stare back at Gold, and he shared her frustration with the psychologist. *Why does this matter?*

"I know it makes me unpopular to insist on following the protocols," Gold continued, "which, I admit, become tedious at times."

Weil spoke up, "Dr. Gold is quite correct, although I find this particular requirement rather unimportant at this stage of the experiment."

Gold frowned. "The control cycle establishes the baseline for the rest of the study, Dr. Weil. This is when it's *most* important to follow the rules." He turned to

Alice again. "This man is the subject of your experiment, Dr. Kurz. He is not your ... friend."

Weil watched Alice calmly formulate her reply. They were all aware of how many hours Alice was spending with the subject. Weil had reviewed most of the videos of their exchanges, although not all. *She's getting a better picture of him than you are, Dr. Gold, with all your tests and cross-examinations.* It was information essential to the experiment.

"If we're looking for significant changes in how the subject thinks, we'll need a baseline that's both broad and deep," Alice said, speaking directly to Dr. Gold. "I don't intend to tell the subject that some topics are off-limits. I intend to challenge his mind, watch where he goes, and see how he adapts to new information."

"Which you can only do by maintaining a detached perspective," Gold said, returning her eye contact.

Dr. Weil turned to Ray Chance and asked, "How are we doing on the data recovery?" He would have asked Trick directly, but it seemed like a good time to remind everyone to respect the decision hierarchy.

Chance didn't care about the hierarchy. He turned to Trick, who was already answering the question. "Data retrieval was ninety-two percent, well over target. The model is now complete, pending consistency checks. We'll be ready for phase two on schedule."

• • •

By the fourth day, everything was routine. With an hour before lunch, Eliot had already walked two miles on the treadmill, completed an assignment for Dr. Gold, entered his thoughts in the journal, and solved today's crossword puzzle. Should he bother Alice again? Was he coming on too strong, with these long dialogues? He dreaded to think that she filled her notes with comments like, *"I wish I didn't have to listen to this guy ramble all day long.*" He was rather hoping they'd continue to see each other after the study was over. They could meet at Casual News for coffee. Laurie would like her.

She must know how much their conversations helped pass the time, but what if she thought that's all it was? That he wouldn't be interested, once he was back with his friends? He sat in front of the computer station puzzling whether to call her, when the speakers chimed and the videochat icon flashed. It was Alice, alone in the conference room.

"How's it going, Eliot?" she asked, smiling. "Starting to see the light at the end of the tunnel?"

He smiled back. "I hope you're not referring to the secret escape tunnel I've been digging under the floor tiles."

Alice laughed. *She laughs like she's not used to laughing. It surprises her.* "I'll bet you've read books about prison escapes, and you know all the tricks," she said.

"Yeah, there've been a few, especially the World War II ones. True stories, crazy as some as them sound. I remember one that I read when I was a kid, *The Colditz Story.* Allied prisoners in Colditz Castle in Germany. The guards never realized how much the prisoners had overrun the place. They got past every lock and actually built their tunnels in the areas that were off-limits to them, so the guards never searched there. *The Wooden Horse* is another good one. The prisoners made a wooden vaulting horse and carried it out to the same spot in the exercise yard every day, running up and vaulting on it for hours at a time. The guards approved of the exercise. They didn't realize that every time the prisoners carried it out, there was a man hidden inside it. While the other prisoners took turns vaulting — shouting and laughing to cover the noise — the man inside the horse was working on an escape tunnel. The big trick was hiding the entrance to the tunnel in plain sight, but they got away with it."

"Wow, that's ingenious. It's amazing what people can come up with when they're faced with a terrible challenge."

"We *are* a problem-solving species. What is it about our brains that makes us so well equipped for that task?" Eliot asked.

"Well, now you're asking the kind of question that I've spent a large part of my life investigating," Alice said. "This is an exciting time for those of us in the neurosciences. A lot of new data has become available, and several promising theories have come forward recently."

"I haven't read anything very recent in this area," Eliot said. "The last one I remember was Dennett's theory of consciousness, but I've never been able to see how it all comes together. He's almost saying that consciousness isn't real."

"No, a lot of people have tried to read him that way, but that's not right. My take on it is that consciousness is a trick of scale. There's no central point in the brain where the miniature *you* sits and collects the data and makes the choices. The operations of the brain occur all over simultaneously, most at such a low level that we have no way to be aware of them. We act when the decision chains supporting action overwhelm the ones suppressing action. But thought and memories are so heavily linked throughout the neocortex that our internal model of ourselves and our environment — our sense of self — becomes aware of one or more decisions that led to the action. In our mind's eye we say that we considered those issues and chose to act. That's what it looks like from the 50,000-foot level of our conscious minds."

Eliot struggled with the concept. It made a lot of sense, but it didn't feel complete. "I have trouble seeing how something as uniquely self-evident as consciousness could arise from *unconscious* activity."

"But really, most things we're aware of are a trick of scale," Alice said. "We just don't think about it that way. Look at *snow*, for instance. Chemically, it's extremely simple: a crystalline form of water. A very simple molecule, just two elements. But there's nothing snow-like about it at the molecular level. Even if you zoom out to a whole snowflake, it doesn't seem snow-like. It looks like a sharp and fragile object. You'd expect it to cut you if you rubbed it against your skin, to crack and break easily. But what we experience as snow is nothing like that. We see it in the aggregate on a large scale — tens of thousands of snowflakes. That's our experience of snow."

"So consciousness is a *gestalt*," Eliot summarized. "As a whole, it's something greater than the sum of its parts."

"Yes, I believe so," Alice said. "You can't look for consciousness as a component of the brain. It's a system effect."

Eliot thought about it for several seconds. Staring into his own thoughts, he didn't notice Alice smile as she watched his face enjoy the thrill of exploration.

"But where is free will in all of this?" Eliot came back. "If there's no central point of consciousness, no 'miniature me,' as you put it, then are you saying that I don't actually decide what I do with my life? If my decisions arise from neural processing I'm not even aware of, then my ability to choose is just illusion. That makes the whole concept of morality meaningless. I can't accept that. I do believe there's such a thing as right and wrong. People can *choose* to do the right thing, even when it's hard, and sometimes they make monstrously wrong choices."

"You make choices all day long," Alice agreed. "The real question is, 'Who are *you*?' Why is it so important for people to believe that their minds have a single unifying conscious thread? Some people think we shouldn't even investigate consciousness, because we're trying to reduce it to a mundane mechanism. But *they're* the ones holding onto the provably false view that there's a single '*I*' having all my thoughts. My colleagues and I have a much grander view of consciousness. It's something that *cannot* be implemented by a simple mechanism. It can only arise from *billions* of simple mechanisms and trillions of interconnections — a vastly deep network, adapted and tuned by a lifetime of experiences."

Alice took a breath, looking at Eliot for a cue whether to continue. He nodded, turning her words over in his mind. "So, this greater *'me'* — including the thoughts and choices that I'm consciously aware of, but also the deep neural processing underlying that consciousness — that's who *I* really am? That's who makes my choices?"

Alice smiled. "It still doesn't sound like free will, does it?"

"No," Eliot agreed, "but I'm starting to wonder if 'free will' is the wrong way to look at it."

"How about this, then," Alice began. "From your genes, you inherited a neural network of enough complexity and plasticity that it was capable of developing a human mind. Every sensory input, every experience, every choice, every recollection exercises paths in your brain, establishing new connections, reinforcing existing ones, and letting some connections go, forgotten and irrelevant. Every day you encounter new situations that you haven't experienced before, and those paths in your brain adapt and evolve. And at very deep levels, your brain learns *patterns*. The human brain is, more than anything else, an engine of pattern recognition. We're so optimized for it that we frequently fool ourselves into seeing meaningful patterns in randomness. Your brain is constantly fitting the data observed into the patterns it's discovered. So when you make choices, most of them aren't big, deep ponderous choices. Those deep choices are already embedded in the patterns of thought that you've developed over your unique lifetime."

Alice thought for a few seconds, then asked, "When you go to the store and buy groceries, do you *choose* to pay for them rather than grab what you want and run out the door?"

"Of course."

"And you *choose* to go to work and do your job and earn your pay? And you choose *not* to kill your neighbor, even if he pisses you off?"

"Obviously. And there are other people who choose differently, unfortunately."

Alice nodded. "But wouldn't it be more accurate to say that you already *chose* to live without theft and murder a long time ago? I mean, you don't wake up each day and *decide* whether to rob the bank. That's not an action you even consider, because it's contrary to the entire pattern of thought that you've built up over your whole life."

"But I *could* choose it, even though I won't."

"In what sense *could* you choose something that you never *will*?" Alice asked. "Is that even a meaningful sentence?"

Eliot frowned, feeling like she was cheating now. *This is why I dislike linguistic philosophy,* he realized. *You end up arguing about the words, instead of the ideas.* "People do suddenly commit terrible acts," he said. "Or noble acts, for that matter. Actions with no apparent connection to anything else they've done. They never had a history of violence, but one day they just snap and go on a killing spree. It seems to happen frighteningly often these days."

"Doesn't that sound more like someone acting blindly *without* choice, perhaps because of some sudden neurological damage, or a slowly moldering defect? Truly random and aberrant behavior seems like an argument *against* free will, not for it."

Eliot looked more frustrated, and Alice backed down. "Look," she said, "it's hard enough to figure out how a *sane* mind works. Let's just talk about the average case." Eliot nodded, and Alice continued. "So, you don't choose every day whether to work for a living or become a criminal. Your entire life has already *been* that choice. You choose whether to have another cup of coffee before going to work. And you do that by matching all of the data of the moment into the patterns that you've learned. How tired are you this morning? Do you have to make it to a meeting or appointment on time? Will you be late, and how much does that matter? Are you wasting your money if you shut off the coffee pot when you've only had one cup? Is there something unpleasant to do at work today that you want to delay? You do this multidimensional pattern matching so continuously, and at such a deep level in your brain, that you hardly notice it. Most of the data that goes into the decision is so low-level that you aren't even aware of it. The acid level in your stomach at the moment probably influences your coffee decision more than all the other things I suggested, but we've learned not to pay attention to that sort of detail, because we believe we have better things to think about. After all, we're surprised sometimes by the choices we've made. Haven't you ever said to yourself, 'Why did I do that?' Rational consideration is just one branch of a much bigger decision tree."

"Okay," Eliot conceded. "That may all be true. But all you're saying is that every choice we make is actually a whole sequence of smaller choices leading up to the current moment. They're still *choices*. We follow the patterns we've learned by making choices in the past. We've made value judgments about them, deciding which were good choices to repeat and which were bad choices to avoid."

"Is there anything in that description that couldn't fit a mechanical or algorithmic process?" Alice asked. "You say we pass value judgments on our past behavior, but is that any different than remembering negative and positive consequences? We touched a hot stove once as a child and incurred some very negative consequences. Now we're highly attuned to anything that might fit the pattern of getting burned. Our daily choices derive predominantly from our values, and our values have evolved from all of our life experiences. And when you have to make a split-second decision how to react in a crisis, your brain might generate a response faster than your rational mind can choose. But it's still an *informed* decision, because it's rooted in the way you've trained your brain to think. And that training includes a lifetime of reflection on the good and bad consequences of decisions you've made, seen, heard of, and read about, so that you're armed with the patterns of thought — the *values* — that make you the unique person you are. There's your free will."

Eliot thought about this conversation for the rest of the day. It was exciting to see that scientists like Alice Kurz were beginning to understand how the mind arose from the brain. It made him wonder if she were frustrated working on smart prostheses — which at first he'd thought to be so futuristic — when even grander explorations must lie within her reach.

• • •

"I really like him, Trick," Alice admitted. She had come to Trick's office to discuss the preparations for the next phase of the experiment, and Alice couldn't help saying how happy she was that Eliot fit their needs so well. "We couldn't have asked for a more engaging mind. I was afraid that after all our work, we'd end up with someone dull and taciturn, and we'd never find anything interesting about his mind. But Eliot's fascinating! He's interested in *everything,* and he has something unique to say about everything, too."

Trick nodded. "You and Eliot are kindred spirits," he said.

That surprised her. She didn't think she'd been talking about how she *personally* felt about him; it was about how well he fit into the project. But she couldn't deny she was attracted to him. "I guess I am kind of drawn to him," she confessed. "Intellectually, I mean," she added hastily, but it didn't matter. Trick could tell it was more than that, and Alice wasn't worried that he knew it. *Eliot would never bore me,* she thought, wondering if she'd ever thought that about anyone else.

"He's a *deep observer*," Trick said. She looked blankly at him, so he explained. "I've noticed that the way people look at the world seems to fall into three broad categories. The average person is a *shallow observer*. They only see what they're looking for. When they stumble across something they don't expect, they consider it an aberration and an annoyance until they can get back to the things that fit their model of the world. Other people are *detail observers*. They pay attention to the fine details, and they notice when they encounter something new or unexpected. They investigate, analyze, and add new information to their world model. I'm a detail observer.

We make good programmers, engineers, editors."

"Eliot is the third kind," Trick continued. "The rare one. He's a *deep observer*. He looks at the world as a continuous source of new information. It doesn't bother him when his world model gets shaken up; he *enjoys* it. He *lives for it*, even. He might not see all the details that I do, but he looks beyond the surface of things, searches out what things *mean*, how they're connected to everything else. In everything he encounters, he sees metaphors and the flow of history and literary allusions and myths and stories. It's the way that great poets and artists see the world."

"Like his namesake, T. S. Eliot," Alice observed.

"I don't know, I've never read his poetry," Trick admitted.

"It's complex, multi-layered, interwoven with links into the whole fabric of Western literature and religion."

Trick nodded. "Sounds like *our* Eliot. He's lucky, because he's found the perfect job for a deep observer. Finding connections and explaining the myths and stories is what he's *supposed* to be doing."

He looked piercingly at Alice. "You're a deep observer too, Alice. But you have a problem with it because your job requires you to be a detail observer. So you do that, but you don't like it." He could see her resistance to that claim. "Don't get me wrong, you're very good at what you do. You channel the deep observer into the vision that drives your research, then you push it to the background and focus on the details to get the job done. It works, but I think you always feel like you're missing out, because you don't get to spend as much time as you'd like on the deep meaning of your work. It troubles you, I think."

Alice felt a thrill of shock at how accurately Trick had summarized her. *Detail observer, indeed.* "And talking with Eliot lets me turn loose the deep observer," she said, nodding. "It makes this job a whole lot more fun."

Trick's gaze remained steady. "It adds a whole dimension *beyond* your job. It lets you dive into the deep end with an experienced guide."

That's exactly how it feels, Alice thought. Would it stay that way in the next phase of the experiment?

Visions and Revisions

Eliot Stearns awoke in a room filled with soft blue light. It took him a moment to remember that today was the start of the study. Before he even opened his eyes, Eliot was assaulted by the noise of a gale rising and swelling, pausing for a second, and then whistling through a cave, repeating in an endless cycle. Behind it thrummed a low drumbeat: *boom-boom* ... *boom-boom* ... He rolled over to rise from the bed, throwing the covers back. "What's that ..." he started to call out, but his words echoed back to him, amplified tenfold. The shock of it stopped him at the edge of the bed. He brought his hands up to cover his ears, but the noise made by his hands rubbing against them was like an avalanche. He shrieked in pain, the sound echoing inside his head like a gunshot in a closed room, and suddenly he knew that the wind was his own breathing, the drum was his heartbeat, and all the sound was coming from inside his own body, louder than he'd ever imagined it could be.

He staggered out of the bedroom and went to the computer, sliding the mouse across the desk. He was afraid it would sound like granite ripping along a fault line, but it made no noise at all. He clicked the videochat icon and saw Alice sitting in the conference room, smiling at him for just an instant, until she realized his distress. "Eliot, what's wrong?" she asked. Her voice sounded normal, so that he could barely hear her over the cacophony filling his head from the inside. "Loud!" he mouthed, trying not to actually make a sound. "Inside! Hurts!"

He saw Alice turn and speak to someone off camera, but she must have muted her end, for he couldn't make out her words. He felt an overwhelming wave of nausea, and he fell backward, dreading the sound it would make when he hit the floor, but he seemed to keep falling forever, and just before he blacked out, he had the oddest sensation that he remained perfectly still, and it was the room that was falling away, taking the whole world with it.

• • •

Eliot Stearns awoke in a room filled with soft blue light. It took him a moment to remember that today was the start of the study. He could feel his heart racing. Sweat poured down his face. He didn't understand why. It wasn't hot. He sat up. Was he having some kind of allergic reaction? He adjusted the lighting controls until he could see normally, then got out of bed and walked around. The sweating had stopped, and his pulse seemed back to normal. He went into the bathroom and looked in the mirror to see if he had a rash or other evidence of allergy. Everything looked fine. Suddenly, an enormous smile broke across his face and he was laughing. *What the hell?*

Instantly, his face contorted in unmistakable rage, but he felt no anger. He was just annoyed and confused by what was happening to his body. He closed his eyes, breathed deeply, and tried to relax. He felt himself calming. I feel fine, he told himself. I feel good. Everything is pleasant.

He was shocked to realize that he suddenly had a

fully rigid erection. It was bursting out of the fly of his pajamas, larger and harder than he'd ever had before. His body was totally out of control. He was responding in extreme ways to the slightest suggestion of emotion. *What did they do to me?*

The anxiety response was back again — sweating, heart throbbing in his chest, hands trembling. *I'll have a heart attack at this rate!* He went over to the computer station, blundering into the doorframe and knocking over the dining chair on his way. He sat down in front of the monitor and grabbed the edge of the desk. He counted to himself, then started counting by squares — *1, 4, 9, 16, 25, 36, …* He concentrated on the numbers. By the time he got to 144, his body was back to normal. He pictured himself floating behind, looking objectively over his shoulder, detached and disinterested. No emotion. Calmly, he clicked the videochat icon. There was Alice, smiling at him. As soon as he saw her, his erection was back. He looked away. He could feel his face flush and knew that he was bright red with exaggerated shame.

"Eliot, are you all right?" she asked, concern evident in her voice.

"No, I don't think so." He spoke in a flat monotone, forcing himself back to an emotionless observer. "There's something wrong with my body. It's as if my emotions are all hyperactive. Well, not my emotions. They seem normal, but my body is reacting *as if* I'm hyperemotional. It's hard to explain. I've never felt anything like this before. Look at my face." He turned back to the monitor to look at her. Tears were pouring down his face. "I'm crying. I can't stop it, but I don't feel sad or scared, just a little concerned. What's going on?"

Alice began to type something on the notebook. "Just a second, Eliot. Everything will be okay."

• • •

Eliot Stearns awoke in a room filled with soft blue light. It took him a moment to remember that today was the start of the study. As soon as he sat up in bed, he knew something was wrong. He felt like he'd been lifted upright on invisible cables. His body felt so light that there was no resistance to his muscles. He stretched his arms, and they shot to his sides. He turned his head, and felt like it swiveled freely on his neck. He stood and practically bounced to attention, as if the mere thought of movement sent his body racing to obey. He walked forward and felt like he was skipping. His movements were normal, he realized; they just *felt* wrong. It must be some lingering side effect of the sedatives. *It probably won't last long now that I'm moving around,* he thought.

He adjusted the lighting controls. It wasn't as simple as he'd expected. He kept missing the balance point, first going too far red, then green, then back to blue again. When he turned up the brightness he saw sparkles at the edge of his vision, like the scotomas accompanying the migraine headaches he'd occasionally suffered in college. *What the hell did they give me last night? LSD?*

By the time he was dressed and ready to emerge from the bedroom, Eliot felt better adjusted to the sense of near weightlessness, but it was still there, lingering behind every movement. He called up the videochat and was greeted by Alice. As they bantered back and forth, he told her about his sensation of effortless movement and the trouble he'd had getting the lighting right. He could see that she was taking notes, but she didn't seem concerned. "Don't worry about it, Eliot. That was a pretty powerful narcotic we gave you last night. It's bound to leave you feeling out of sorts for a while. Just let me know if it doesn't clear up in a couple of hours."

• • •

Eliot Stearns awoke in a room filled with soft blue light. It took him a moment to remember that today was the start of the study. He sat up and reached for his watch, then remembered that they'd taken it from him. They'd taken away everything he came in with, even the books. *Damn, nothing to read for five days.* What were they thinking? Didn't Alice promise no torture?

He played with the lighting controls, enjoying the effect it had on the room. With the controls set to all red, it reminded him of the darkroom he'd used in his junior high photography class. *That was a waste of time. No one uses film any more.* They must have known there was no point to that class even then, so why bother teaching it? Perhaps it was Mr. Donaldson's personal obsession. He turned the controls to all green, looked up at the ceiling, and imagined it as a forest canopy, too dense to see the sky. He played around some more and made it look like sunset, twilight, night, sunrise. He balanced the three colors until everything looked normal. *This is how they should teach colors in elementary school,* he thought. *Combine it with the traditional crayons and finger paints to show there's more than one way to mix colors.*

Eliot stood and walked into the bathroom, noticing the specimen cup they'd left out for him. When he was finished there, he got dressed. *I can shower tomorrow,* he thought. *After all, I won't be having any company today.* He went to the computer station to see if anyone waited to talk with him. *Probably everyone,* he thought. *Since this is the first day, they'll all want to poke at the lab rat.* But Alice was alone in the conference room when he greeted her with a smile.

"Good morning, Eliot," she said, smiling back at him. "How do you feel?"

"Fine, I guess. Very relaxed. I suppose that's because I slept for half a day."

"Yes, we had to put you into a very deep sleep, and it may take you a few minutes to feel fully awake. But everything went fine at our end."

"So your nanobots are done with their work?"

"Right, and they're already breaking down. They'll probably be all out of you by tomorrow morning."

"That's good," Eliot said. He didn't show it, but the idea of invisible robots inside his brain was a bit unsettling, and the sooner he was rid of them, the better. "You know, it surprised me that you were willing to take me right away. Have you had trouble finding subjects?"

"A lot of people can't handle the isolation. Our application process attempts to screen them out."

Eliot thought about it, recalling the questions he'd answered on the online application. "I don't remember any questions about isolation."

"No," Alice agreed, "but, for example, a job history primarily in sales, broadcasting, marketing, retail — jobs where you interact with the public all day — that might indicate an extroverted personality. They don't generally do well in forced isolation. There were also several questions that are part of a standard psychological assessment. Even leisure activities: group sports versus reading, going to movies versus watching television. Taken all together, we can arrive at a high probability of failure in a lot of candidates."

Eliot nodded. "And then I came along: bookish, pedantic, introverted. All consistent with a preference, or at least a high tolerance, for being alone."

Alice smiled, trying to hide it. "You're one adjective short," she said. He gave her a puzzled look. "You know, the standard interview question: four adjectives to describe yourself. You've got three: bookish, pedantic, introverted. Want to offer a fourth?"

Eliot had the oddest feeling they were playing a

game, but she hadn't told him the rules. Maybe this was part of the ongoing psychological assessment, to track when the isolation began to affect him. "Curious," he answered. "What about you?"

"Of course, I'm curious. That's why I'm in this line of work."

"I meant, what four adjectives describe *you?*"

The look she gave him was startling in its complexity. He saw almost every emotion he looked for, but as a whole, it was something else altogether. "Well, I've already said curious," she replied. "I'll add ambitious, confident, and … vindicated."

Vindicated? Eliot wondered. The study had just begun. Surely, it was too early to consider it successful. What else might she mean? Some intra-staff conflict, perhaps? He decided not to ask. Maybe it would reveal itself over the next few days.

• • •

After an unpleasantly bland breakfast, Eliot tried out the treadmill before dealing with the homework that was blinking away on the monitor. He glanced at the time display by the doorway, thinking that he should keep track of his exercise while he was here. If nothing else, it would give him something to write about in the journal.

He walked on the treadmill for 40 minutes, varying his pace from a casual stroll to a brisk walk. When he stepped down, the gauge indicated 1.8 miles. Slower than he expected. Next time, he'd push harder. Five days of exercise might make a new man of him.

He sat at the computer station to catch his breath, and he decided to try some of the games on the computer. He was pleased to see that there was a daily crossword puzzle. As he looked it over, he was even more pleased to see that it was moderately challenging, not unlike the New York Times puzzle.

It didn't take him long to catch on to the pattern of the clues, and he made steady progress. He got to 9 across — *Plays the dummy, 8 letters.* It couldn't be "ventriloquist." What other kind of dummy? *Bridge.* He entered "declarer" and moved to 10 across — *Cedar forest victor, 9 letters.* That was easy: "Gilgamesh."

• • •

On day two, Eliot found Alice once again waiting for his call. They slipped into conversation like a raft in a stream, and when he poled toward one shore, she turned them toward the other. In the end, they found themselves deep in an unexpected tributary, and they paused, as if by mutual consent, to study the scenery.

"All these books you've read," Alice said after a moment. "I envy the variety. It seems like I barely have time to keep up with the technical articles I need to read. How do you remember them all? I have enough trouble remembering the plot of a novel *while* I'm reading it. There are very few that I could talk intelligently about after years and hundreds of other books."

"Well, how do you remember the technical material you read?"

"I use it every week in my research, if it applies. If not, it fades over time, just like those novels that blur together in my memory."

"For me," Eliot mused, "books are like little bottles of distilled authors. I remember the flavor, the aroma, the point of view. Every book has its truths and its lies, because that's what stories are woven from. I remember them like friends, and some of them I visit frequently."

Alice watched him for a few seconds. "It's really hard for you to be without those friends right now, isn't it?"

Eliot laughed. "I guess it's a good thing your ad didn't specify '*no books,*' or we might not have met. No matter what else is going on in my life, there are always books."

"In chaos theory, that's called a *strange attractor*," Alice said. "A stable point that a chaotic system tends to return to, no matter the starting conditions."

"Interesting. So, within the chaos of our lives are strange attractors — familiar themes that we're drawn to over and over again. People that show up in our lives again and again." He paused, rolling it around in his head. "Maybe that's just another way of modeling what others have called fate, karma, the Tao, the Holy Spirit. Different ways of looking at the world that all speak of innate forces guiding us to return, again, and again, to our destinies."

She smiled at him, but shook her head. "I think you might be overreaching here."

"I don't know," Eliot said. "Attractive forces are pretty much the backbone of the universe. The nuclear forces that make atoms, the gravitational forces that make stars, which in turn make the heavier elements that make planets, and eventually life. And you can't deny that attractive forces are essential to life."

"So it would seem," Alice conceded.

"Ultimately, the universe endures because every bit of it yearns for every other."

• • •

In the afternoon, when he was done with Dr. Gold's homework, he found Alice again working in the conference room, waiting for his call. Once again, they fell into conversation like old friends, and it wasn't long before he was telling her all about himself.

"So both of your parents were teachers," Alice noted. "Did you ever think about being a teacher also?"

"I never wanted to teach," he admitted. "I've always just wanted to *learn*. Every book I read leads me to a dozen books that I want to read next. I get excited when I find something good on a subject I know nothing about. Sometimes my friends ask, 'Why do you want to know about *that*?' when I talk about what I'm reading. The question doesn't make sense to me. What makes something *not* worth knowing?"

Alice smiled, and it wasn't the condescending, head-shaking kind of smile most people would have responded with. She understood.

"You could *write* books, Eliot," Alice said to him. "I think you're quite eloquent, and you certainly have a lot of unique insights."

He didn't think she knew him well enough to mean that, but she sounded sincere. "I've never really tried to write a book," he said. "But I wrote a paper in Comparative Literature that my dad thought I should turn into a book. I still pick it up and work on it every now and then, but so far I haven't been willing to put in the time it would take to finish the research."

"What's it about?"

"It's called *The Secret Prince*. It's based on the observation that different cultures all over the world have stories about a great hero who was raised as the lowliest commoner but was secretly descended from royalty. Sometimes it's a woman — Cinderella, for example, was the daughter of a lord, but she was raised as a servant. Usually the hero is a man. In many cultures, he's descended from the gods rather than mortal royalty. Hercules, Achilles, most of the Greek and Roman heroes were demigods. Gilgamesh, the first great epic hero — maybe the oldest story in the world — was 'two-thirds divine and one-third human.'"

"Wait," Alice protested. "How could he be two-thirds divine? Did he have three parents?"

"His mother was a goddess. His father was a great

king who *became* a god."

"Hmm."

"The story is about 4,000 years old," Eliot pointed out. "Modern concepts of genetics don't really apply."

"Okay," Alice conceded.

"Oedipus was secretly the son of a king," Eliot went on. "Moses was a secret prince, and Jesus was descended from David and other Hebrew royalty in addition to his divine lineage. There's a common factor in all of these great stories."

"Didn't Joseph Campbell write about this? *The Hero With a Thousand Faces?*"

"He wrote about the universality of the hero story," Eliot said. "I cite his work in my paper. But my focus was on the common thread that all these great heroes were of noble descent. My thesis is that the nobility aspect was added to real stories of great deeds as an *explanation* of the hero's greatness. The hidden morality lesson in these tales is that common people can't really achieve greatness. If they do, it's because they were secretly nobility all along."

"Ah, I see," Alice said. "You think the ruling class *changed* the myths to reinforce their right to rule?"

"Well, sometimes they wrote — or commissioned — the 'authorized versions' of the tales, but the ruled have always been accomplices in their own servility. The notion of an aristocracy divinely ordained to rule over the common people is so widespread that it could only have evolved with the tacit agreement of the underclasses. There's an inherent need to explain to yourself why some people have all the wealth and power, and you and your family have nothing. It's comforting to conclude that it's just the way of the world, and we all have our lot in life."

"But to some degree that's true, isn't it? People are

still born into advantage or disadvantage all over the world."

"Of course, but the literature reflects the values of the society. In American literature, you start to see the glorification of the common man, with no need to explain heroes as secret nobility. In fact, it directly challenges the idea of nobility. Look at *The Prince and the Pauper*. Surely, the lesson there is that the entire concept of nobility is a lie. All of Twain's work celebrated the common man. Same with Melville, Hawthorne, Cooper, Faulkner, Steinbeck, Hemingway. There are exceptions, of course. Dreiser's *An American Tragedy* can be read as a warning to the common man not to try to rise above his station."

"But we've reinvented an aristocracy for America," Alice pointed out. "The rich celebrities. Entertainers, athletes, politicians. People dote on everything they say and do, no matter how stupid and uninformed they are. Their children are raised to take their place in the pantheon, and the rich continuously maneuver to gain a bigger slice of the pie."

"I know," Eliot agreed. "It can be depressing. But there's still a core American belief in the possibility of transcending humble roots and achieving greatness on your own. It still happens, and it's a popular story when it does. I think it sets us apart from much of the world. I've traveled a little, but I don't exactly have cosmopolitan experience. My parents took me on a trip to England and Scotland when I was in junior high, and a couple of years later we took a short trip through France and Germany. That's not much to go on, but you can learn a lot about a culture from its literature, and I *have* read a lot. It seems to me that the fundamental difference between the American and European world views is which direction we focus our attention. Europeans think of themselves as the proud inheritors of a rich and glorious past. Americans think of ourselves as the proud progenitors of a rich and glorious future. Or at least we *did*."

"It does seem different now, doesn't it," Alice lamented. "Too many of us stopped dreaming of the future we could build, and started expecting the future we felt entitled to."

Eliot nodded, but he saw another side to it. "But isn't that what we mean by *progress?* We want the next generation to have a better world, a better life. If we raise the standard of living, they *should* have higher expectations than their forebears. Who wants to be sub-standard?"

Alice frowned in a way that Eliot took for a smile. She paused for a few seconds to organize a response. "That's a provocative way of looking at it. I'm going to think about that." She and Eliot locked eyes, and she continued, "But doesn't it seem to you that most people are complacent, uninterested in anything but their own little tribe, waiting around for someone else to solve the hard problems?"

"There are plenty of people like that," Eliot agreed, "but for the great majority of people, the problems of their own little tribe *are* the hard problems. History remembers the few who catalyzed the great events, but the engine of the world runs on getting up and going to work, teaching your children what it means to be human, and desperately trying to keep up with the great events that are changing your life, all while looking out for the next disaster lurking around the corner."

"I agree with that," Alice said. "It's very hard to keep up. But you have to keep looking for the new op-portunities and letting go of what doesn't work anymore. You have to notice the rough spots and reshape them. If you don't keep asking, 'What's coming next?' then you end up asking, 'How the hell did we get *here?*'"

"But what happens to the people who can't keep up?" Eliot wondered.

• • •

On the morning of the third day, there was a full crowd at the conference table: Alice Kurz, Dr. Gold, Dr. Weil, Ray Chance, and a fifth person that he hadn't met before, sitting at the edge of his view of the table. He was young, with close-cropped dark hair, and even though he wore videoglasses, he had a notebook in front of him, positioned so that others sitting next to him could see whatever was on it. Was he the note-taker for the meeting?

"Good morning, Eliot," Dr. Weil greeted him. "We wanted to check in with you today and see how everything is going. I gather there've been some ups and downs, but in between the boredom you've had some stimulating sessions. Is that a fair assessment of the experience so far?"

Eliot paused before answering. He sensed some tension in the room, but he wasn't sure why. He'd had some interesting conversations, particularly with Alice. Other than that, everything had been routine and mostly dull. *Has something in Dr. Gold's tests raised a red flag?*

"That sounds about right," Eliot said, trying to keep everyone's face in view. They all seemed so *intensely* interested in him, like they'd never seen such a strange zoo animal. "There's only so much to do to keep busy in here, but I'm comfortable. I think my health is improving. I've been using the treadmill, and I'm up to about four miles a day now. I've decided to add more exercise into my daily routine even after I'm out of here."

"So you're doing all right, stuck indoors? No problem sleeping at night, waking in the morning?" Dr. Gold asked crisply.

"Not that I've noticed, but you're keeping me on a regular schedule." Something started to claw at the edges of Eliot's awareness, as if he'd been missing something important, and he could almost see it. "Without that, I suppose my circadian rhythm might drift, given the lack of daylight to keep it in sync." He watched their faces, but they showed nothing. The only sense of time he had was completely under their control. It was whatever time the display by the door said, corroborated by the arrival of his meals; but they could change the display and the meal times. Maybe they were shifting him to shorter or longer days, and were waiting to see if he noticed. So far, he hadn't.

"And you've been eating all right, it appears. No trouble with the food?"

"Well, it seems filling enough, but there's not an excess of flavor." Oddly, that got a reaction. Dr. Weil glanced over the unknown man's shoulder and studied the screen for a few seconds, while Eliot continued. "I mean, I'm sure it's healthy, but I won't be asking for your recipes." He smiled to make sure it would come off as banter, but even Alice seemed to find this significant. She, too, glanced at the notebook screen. He looked at the unknown man, and was slightly unnerved to find him studying Eliot's face.

"By the way, who else am I talking to today?" He smiled again. "I guess I don't have to introduce myself, but you are …?"

"Call me Trick," the man answered. He still seemed to be doing something with the notebook, but it looked less like typing and more like gesturing.

"Trick is in charge of the software development," Dr. Chance added. "These days he's working on correlating the data from the various games and tests you've been doing for Dr. Gold." *Not to mention the nanocell data from my brain,* Eliot thought.

"So you're, what, going through charts and graphs and tables of data about me while we're talking?"

Trick looked at him closely. It was not an unfriendly look. His interest level had gone up, but there was neither friendship nor hostility in his gaze, just clinical detachment. "Yes, exactly that," he said. "Does that bother you?"

"No, just curious." A question occurred to him that he hadn't thought about previously. "Do you intend to share anything you learn about me? I mean, when this study is over. I don't suppose you want to affect the results while it's in progress."

Alice and Dr. Weil glanced at Dr. Gold. Trick never took his eyes off Eliot. It was Gold who spoke, but he didn't answer the question. "Is there something you're hoping to learn about yourself from this study, Eliot?"

Eliot sighed. *Why is it so hard to get a straight answer to a simple question?* He looked at Gold. The psychologist's face was a perfect mask of neutral indifference, presenting no expectations, no concerns, no reactions: a void waiting to be filled with whatever Eliot had to say. But there was something else there, deep behind the mask. Eliot was sure that the indifference hid some deep-seated dislike. *What have I done to annoy him?* he wondered. Eliot delivered his homework assignments on time, answered his probing questions, put up with his tiresome tests. Gold had been pleasant and professional toward Eliot when they met before the study, but something had changed once he woke up in here. He felt as though Gold were waiting for him to apologize for wasting his time.

• • •

That night, Eliot dreamed he was wandering

through endless hospital corridors. Some of the doors had glass windows, and he could see people on the other side, but those doors were always locked. He found other doors that he could open, but they always led to corridors just like the ones he'd been wandering through. Finally, he found an open door leading to a room where a man lay on the bed, his back to Eliot.

"Who are you?" Eliot asked, walking up to him. The man turned over, and Eliot saw his own face.

"I'm Eliot," the man said. "Who are *you?*"

Eliot heard voices behind him and he turned to look, but no one was there. He followed the voices into the hall and around several turns. They led to a stairwell. He took the stairs leading up and emerged onto the next floor, but all he saw were the same corridors. He spotted an open door at the end of the hall. As he walked toward it, he passed door after door, but the open one never got any closer. He stopped to catch his breath at an intersection and saw a man lying on the floor trying to look under a locked door.

"Who are you?" he asked, keeping his distance.

The man turned, and Eliot saw his own face.

"I'm Eliot," the man said. "Who are *you?*"

"You're not supposed to be here," Eliot said.

"*I'm* not here. *You* are," the man said.

Eliot awoke, feeling anxious. *Disturbing dream,* he thought, as the details began to fade. *I was lost somewhere, and I kept finding myself. Or was I the one being found?* He couldn't remember, but the sense of anxiety remained.

He sat up and looked at the time display. It was just after 1:00 AM. He went to the bathroom and urinated, glad that they had told him he no longer needed to collect it. He wandered out into his living quarters, feeling a vague sensation of being secretly watched, and he wondered, not for the first time, if they actually *were* watching him.

He went to the computer, moved the mouse, and the screen lit up. He clicked the videochat icon. He assumed that no one would be there, but perhaps there was a night staff who'd talk to him. The conference room was empty, but the icon flashed, indicating that it was signaling for attention at the other end. He thought about whether he wanted to record a message. *Should I tell them about the dream? Is that relevant to the study?* He'd already forgotten most of the details. *Endless corridors, closed doors.* That was about all he could recall now.

To his surprise, he saw Trick enter the conference room and click something on the computer. His chat icon stopped flashing, and Trick looked at him with the clinical expression that Eliot had seen before. "Hi, Eliot. Can't sleep?"

"I was sleeping, but I woke up. Something disturbing about a dream I had, but I can't really remember it now."

"Try to describe it. Sometimes putting it into words can trigger more of the memory."

"Trigger the memory, or change it?" Eliot asked. "Usually, when I try to describe a dream in words, it feels like I'm inventing a whole new dream."

Trick nodded. "Yeah, I think that happens a lot. Dream logic is inconsistent with waking logic, and when we talk about it, we're using waking logic. It's like a bad translation into another language."

"Exactly. I've thought about that before." Eliot leaned in toward the monitor. "Awake, events are connected by causality. You get from one place to another by moving between them. In dreams, the connection between events is conceptual, not causal. You move from one context to another just because they're related in some way. Most of the time, we don't know we're

dreaming, because it's only awake that we see the difference."

"Interesting," Trick said. "But how do you know that dream logic isn't always there, just drowned out by your conscious thoughts when you're awake?"

"Maybe so, but dreams have evolved to fill some important function. Even if it's just to keep the brain busy so you don't fall into a coma when you're sleeping deeply."

"I've thought that dreams are the brain's way to perform garbage collection," Trick said.

Eliot frowned. "I don't think dreams are garbage. Not usually."

"No, that's not what I mean," Trick said. "*Garbage collection* is a term used in computer programming. When you manipulate data structures, sometimes you leave behind bits of computer memory that you aren't using any more, so there's a background process that finds the unused pieces and sweeps them back into the free memory pool. It's an old term. Nowadays they'd call it recycling."

"I don't see the connection to dreams."

Trick paused to frame the thought, and Eliot waited, interested. "Your brain builds up such a huge store of memories that it can't keep all of them. Ones that you don't think about often have very sparse links to the rest of your thoughts and memories. I think our brains perform maintenance while we sleep, and that includes trying to find neural pathways that can be repurposed. It puts weakly-connected pathways together to see if the connections should be strengthened or abandoned. Dreams are the part of this process that our conscious brain remembers."

"But in the dream it seems like a real physical experience," Eliot objected.

Trick smiled. "*Does* it seem that way when you're dreaming? Or is that just how you remember it?"

"Why should there be a difference?" Eliot asked.

"Well, if dream logic *is* different than waking logic, there'd *have* to be a difference. Your unconscious sensations would have to be translated from one way of thinking to another when you remember them. Maybe we don't remember the *experience* of dreaming, we just remember the way we explained it to ourselves in waking logic. Maybe the experience of dreaming is nothing like the memory of dreaming."

Eliot pondered that for a while. What was it that he was just dreaming about?

"So what are you doing here at this time of night?" Eliot asked Trick. "Are you working a night shift?"

"No, I was just deep into a debugging session. When you're trying to figure out the root problem in a buggy piece of code, sometimes you build up so much context around the problem that you don't want to give it up. You know you'll just have to rebuild all that mental infrastructure again when you come back to the problem later, so you just keep at it as long as you can."

"And I distracted you from it," Eliot said. "Sorry about that."

"That's okay," Trick said. "You can also get to the point where you're so lost in the trees that you've completely missed the forest, and you really do need to start from a new perspective."

Lost in the trees. Or the corridors? What's the forest that I'm not seeing?

"There's a good discussion of all this in *Zen and the Art of Motorcycle Maintenance*," Eliot remembered.

"Yeah, I've read that," Trick said. "Excellent book. His whole description of the diagnostic process was spot on. And it's universal. Fixing motorcycles, repairing plumbing, debugging software, or figuring out how to improve your business — doesn't matter what the problem is, the diagnostic process is pretty much the same. Even when it's ourselves we're trying to figure out." Trick looked at Eliot with his analytic gaze again. "In a way, we're always reinventing ourselves as new people, I think. When I look back at different periods of my life, it seems like I've been a lot of different people. I was one person in high school, several different people at MIT, and someone else entirely now. In a year or so, I'll look back and think what a different person I used to be way back now."

"I suppose that's true," Eliot said. "Partly, it's because all of the relationships we had with other people have changed. We had different friends, different colleagues. Maybe what we think of as *ourselves* also incorporates our connections to other people." He thought about that for a minute. *Maybe I can get an answer out of this.* "Is that what makes isolation such an interesting topic for you all to study? Remove me from all my relationships to others, and see how that changes my personality?"

"I don't know," Trick said with a shrug. "The psychology aspect isn't my area. I just write code to analyze data."

That was an outright lie, Eliot thought. *Interesting.*

•••

On the fourth day, Eliot found himself pacing the floor for an hour after lunch. When he realized that he'd been doing it for quite a while, he wondered why he hadn't just used the treadmill. He could have counted it toward his goal of four miles a day, if only he'd been measuring it. *So what?* he thought. *What difference does it make?*

He thought about starting another videochat.

Maybe Alice would be there. But for the first time in his life, he felt talked out. He wanted more than talk, more than walking the treadmill. He wanted … *Well, sure, but that's not an option, is it?* He realized then what made the isolation so difficult. Videochat was barely an improvement over a phone conversation. Real human communication — face-to-face contact — included deep sub-channels of information that simply didn't make it through the monitor and speakers. *Like touch,* he thought. *Touch would be nice.*

He made one more circuit of the room, his thoughts wandering into new areas he'd been trying to avoid thinking about. He decided to take a shower. He stood under the warm water for a long time, reliving his most recent conversations with Alice. But this time, he thought of them sitting together on his balcony, watching the sunset while they talked. Sitting close, their shoulders touching. Or sitting by the fire, facing each other, sharing a bottle of wine. Occasionally grasping her hand. Touching her hair. Alice smiling at him.

• • •

Alice happened to be looking at Eliot's health metrics when she noticed the sudden spike in his heart rate. Looking closer, she saw a flurry of motor nerve activity and an increase in blood pressure. She looked at the map grid and saw that he was in the shower. Water was flowing, and the temperature was in the normal range. Had he slipped in the shower? *Something* was causing him stress. Alarmed, she picked up the notebook and hurried over to Trick's office, where she found him talking with Ray Chance.

"Something's happening to the subject," she said, interrupting their conversation. She set her notebook on Trick's desk in front of them. "He was fine just a couple of minutes ago, then there was a rapid increase in his heart rate soon after he started his shower. And there's a significant amount of motor nerve activity all along his right arm. And his blood pressure has spiked."

The two men looked at the graphs moving across the notebook display. After a second, they glanced at each other, then back at Alice. Neither could think of how to explain it to her. "The blood pressure increase is highly localized," Trick pointed out carefully. Something about his voice got her attention, and she looked at him, noticing that he avoided her eyes. She looked back to the screen and saw where Trick was pointing. He'd brought up a visualization of the subject's body. The groin area was highlighted in red. She saw where the subject's right hand was, and her face flushed crimson. "Oh," was all she said.

The men were careful not to let their amusement show on their faces, but she felt it, anyway. She moved herself into a clinical frame of mind. *Was this data signifi-cant?* "Would you consider this to be ... normal behavior under isolation conditions? I mean, it's only been four days for him. Isn't that a little ... early for feelings of ..."

"No," Chance said. "I mean, it's *not* early. I mean four days without ... human contact ..."

"Perfectly normal for a male of his age," Trick summarized.

"I see," Alice said. She closed the notebook and straightened to leave. She walked out of Trick's office and headed back to her own, moving quickly so that she wouldn't overhear anything they might say to each other as she left.

When she reached her office, Alice closed her door and set the notebook down on its charging pad, the lid still closed. *A man can't go four days without sexual release? That's normal?* Her embarrassment had changed to pro-found sadness at how disconnected she must be from the rest of humanity. *Is that normal for women, too? Am I so cold and sexless that it wouldn't even occur to me?* She suddenly remembered her sister's words to her: *Your study will be a great success because you'll spend a hundred percent of your life on it.* How much had she given up for her work? Was it worth it?

Opening the notebook, she noticed the email indicator and clicked on her inbox. It was another email from Eliot. She hesitated a few minutes, but left it unread. *After work,* she thought. *Away from here.*

Executive Summary

Dining at the Palace Arms was an experience in elegance and high-end cuisine that tourists talked about back home. It was the place to impress your clients, propose to your lover over a $200 bottle of wine, and celebrate your big promotion. It was the place to feel successful — to know you had *become someone*. To Sam Gleigh, it was a place to eat dinner.

He arrived fifteen minutes earlier than his guest, as intended. Only Mr. Salt accompanied him. Gleigh was recognized at once. He dined there frequently when business permitted him to remain in Denver, which happened often. He sat on thirteen corporate boards, but most of those meetings worked perfectly well as videoconferences, and he seldom had to leave the offices of Gleigh Investments.

The maitre d' immediately showed Gleigh to the table by the window. Two empty tables lay between Gleigh and the rest of the room, to ensure privacy. Mr. Salt was seated at a separate table with a clear view of his employer and the exits. He would ensure security.

The head waiter came right on the heels of the maitre d', but that was a mere formality. Gleigh never ordered from the menu. The chef knew his preferences and was already preparing his best dishes for Gleigh's table. The waiter's job was to recommend the dish and obtain Gleigh's consent, which was never refused. As soon as the waiter left, the wine steward appeared, a selection to match the first dish already in hand. It was presented, approved, tasted, approved, and poured. The issue of cost was never discussed. With that, they left Gleigh alone to await his guest, but he knew that the slightest gesture on his part would bring the head waiter immediately.

Gleigh relaxed into his chair, hands in his lap, his head turned toward the window. He could see a bit of the street through a gap in the curtains. The flow of white and red lights calmed him. The daily exodus from the offices was nearly complete, the tide withdrawn, leaving swirling eddies of activity in places that sat in shadow just moments ago. *The activity never ceases, it just transforms,* Gleigh thought. People look at their day and see periods of activity and rest, but when you look at the whole *system*, you see that there's never rest. The engine of commerce is always running, and whenever spare power is available, the engine finds a use for it. Gleigh was an instrument of that engine. He could track down unused resources as easily as he could redeploy them.

His guest arrived just a few minutes later. "I'm here to meet Mr. Gleigh," Dr. Gold told the maitre d', and he was immediately taken to Gleigh's table. Within seconds, his wine glass was filled and the appetizers were served. "So nice of you to invite me to dinner, Mr. Gleigh," Dr. Gold told his host, smiling as he sampled the Asian chicken and waffle.

"My pleasure, Dr. Gold," Gleigh said, returning the smile and studying his guest. Gold had the best poker face Gleigh had ever seen. Clearly, that was a useful attribute for a psychologist, but it was many years since Dr. Gold counseled patients, and he was still as hard to read as stone. *Perhaps he stays in practice by analyzing me,* Gleigh considered. It didn't worry him. Gold's discretion was the first thing his investigators looked into before Gleigh hired him.

It amused Sam Gleigh that no one at the institute ever realized that he, not they, had hired Dr. Gold. After the setback with Matthius Pin, Gleigh realized how close they had come to exposing issues he didn't want them to confront yet. He convinced the rest of the board of investors that the project needed new protocols that would blind the subject to what was really happening, and for that they needed a good psychologist. It so happened that Sam Gleigh had one on retainer. The institute never even saw the contract that detailed Dr. Gold's services.

Gleigh allowed his guest to enjoy the food and wine, as he did, while the waiter prepared the Caesar salad and served the parsnip soup. When he left, Gleigh began the debriefing. "How is the study going?"

"Well, we certainly haven't seen anything like the Matthius reaction this time," Dr. Gold began. "Mr. Stearns had no difficulties beyond a bit of boredom. He complained about the lack of books, though. We should have expected that from a research librarian, I guess."

"Books are still too difficult?" Gleigh asked. He could understand the problems they'd pose, but the project had solved harder ones.

Dr. Gold seemed a bit surprised at Gleigh's question. "I would guess it's a matter of priorities. Books will not be a problem down the road, but it wasn't worth waiting for them."

"No, of course not," Gleigh said. "Are you definitely through the calibration period now?"

"Yes, well past that point. The new process was a big improvement; they zeroed it in after a few days." His face changed into a sneer that he made no attempt to hide. "They'll start the *damage* cycles next week."

"They've achieved personality stabilization?"

"Yes, but that's causing its own problems. As I was worried about, some of the staff seem to have developed a personal attachment to the subject that's strongly influencing their treatment of him."

Gleigh also had an excellent poker face, so his annoyance didn't show. He'd heard this before. He didn't understand why the psychologist was so fixated on Alice Kurz. It was essential that she be left alone, but Gold seemed determined to antagonize her.

"I specifically asked you to respect Dr. Kurz's experience and professionalism," Gleigh said, looking into the doctor's eyes. "She is clearly an intense person, and that intensity is exactly what makes her so extraordinarily clever. I do not want you to throttle her back."

"Well, it isn't just her, I believe. Quite surprisingly, I'm seeing the same thing in Trick."

"Trick?" Gleigh almost laughed, but then he realized that Dr. Gold wasn't referring to Alice's feelings for the subject, but the simple fact that she was thinking of him as a person instead of a science project.

"But surely, Trick hasn't had very much contact with him?"

"It varies from cycle to cycle, but they usually end up chatting about the subject's dreams. I believe that — at least once — Trick woke him up deliberately, in order to talk about them."

"What did Trick say about these dreams?" Gleigh asked, wondering if his own face still maintained a neutral expression.

"Here's my report," Dr. Gold answered, reaching into his suit coat for his tablet and turning it on. He tapped it a couple of times and touched it to Gleigh's tablet lying on the table in front of him. Gleigh picked up his own tablet and glanced through the report.

"You won't find Trick's comments very illuminating," Gold told him. "Something like, 'Subject woke up from a dream, was momentarily disoriented, called for videochat, and we had an interesting talk about debugging code.'"

"Why bother to bring it up, then?" Gleigh asked crisply.

"Trick used the word 'interesting'," Dr. Gold said. "That's like someone else saying, 'It blew my mind.'"

Gleigh frowned, put down his tablet, and took another bite of his meal as Dr. Gold continued. "I watched the recordings of all his post-dream discussions with the subject so far. They don't usually talk about the dreams themselves, but the nature of dreaming came up several times. Trick seems to have used the opportunity to test the subject's understanding of computer technologies, but the subject just comes right back at him with a broader way of looking at the same thing. And Trick finds it all 'interesting' enough to keep doing it every cycle."

"You've summarized the discussions for me?" Gleigh asked. He would prefer transcripts, or better yet the actual videos, but he knew the doctor's boundaries. Summarizing the team's progress and discussions was part of his employment contract with Gleigh. Handing over the institute's confidential documents was not. It was a fine line, especially since Gleigh, as the primary investor on the project, had every right to see them. All he had to do was ask Weil to send them to him, but right now Gleigh didn't want anyone at the institute thinking too hard about his extraordinary level of interest in this project.

"Yes, it's all in my report," Dr. Gold said. The entrees arrived, and the doctor took advantage of the opportunity. Gleigh thought for a few minutes, wondering what the subject dreamed about. He took a few bites of his meal and a swallow of wine as he glanced through the report, looking for the highlights. The details would come later, when he could study them undisturbed.

"So you still haven't seen any indication of a security concern?" Gleigh asked, finishing his scan.

"No, as far as I can tell, everyone is following the requirements of the confidentiality agreement," Dr. Gold said. "Has someone leaked information about the project?"

"It isn't something that I want to investigate *after* a leak occurs," Gleigh explained. "I want to know about it *before* it happens."

"Yes, I know," Dr. Gold interrupted him. "I remember your suggestions: Who is too talkative? Who tends to show off in social settings? Who has trouble following the rules? Who forgets to keep their office files locked up? I've been monitoring such things — which, by the way, led to an awkward encounter with Dr. Kurz in the middle of the evening, a few weeks back." He looked up at Gleigh. "Don't worry, she didn't think anything of it."

He set down his fork, savored a sip of wine, and leaned back, his face blank. "Who has trouble following rules? That's easy. Trick has a general disdain for authority. The only thing he respects is technical competence. It rankles him that he reports to Ray Chance, whom he does not consider to be his intellectual equal."

"Yes, but Chance knows that, and he isn't offended by it," Gleigh argued. "I doubt he considers himself Trick's equal, either. Your profile of Chance says that he cares more about getting the job done than the trappings of power and position; that he gives Trick a lot of latitude in managing the software team."

"Virtually free rein, as far as I can see."

"Which Chance probably sees as a bonus — one less set of problems for him to worry about — and it's that freedom to operate as he wants that keeps Trick content with his situation. I don't consider him likely to act against the project, do you?"

"No, not all," Dr. Gold agreed. "I was actually trying to point out to you how little value there is in focusing on a few simplistic personality traits. Trick fits your criteria for a security risk in other ways, too. His office is a museum of every project he's worked on, and everything is lying out in the open — the obsolete and forgotten technologies right next to the ones they haven't yet filed patents for. But he's fanatical about the security of the network. He doesn't trust the institute's internal backbone, so he maintains his own set of firewalls around the project servers. And even the NSA couldn't get at the specialized hardware."

Gleigh took another sip of wine, satisfied that the doctor knew his business better than he did, but that made Gold's obsession with Alice Kurz more puzzling. "I take your point, Doctor Gold. As an amateur, I think in terms of telltale personality quirks. But you, as a professional, take a good deal more into account."

"It's a matter of innate motivation," Dr. Gold explained as he resumed eating.

"Then perhaps you can tell me what it is about Dr. Kurz's innate motivation that you find so disturbing?"

Dr. Gold paused at the unexpected question. He chewed slowly, swallowed, swirled the wine around in his glass, then drained it. He wiped his lips with his napkin and sat back to look at his host. "Dr. Kurz is a very different sort of risk," he began. "She has unrealistic expectations for this technology, and she's allowed her whole life to be consumed by it. She is obsessed by the idea that she can make up for her grandmother's dementia by solving the problem of memory once and for all. She's so in love with the idea of fixing the brain that she's transferred all her hope and longing to the subject, believing she's in love with *him*. In love with the *subject!* This is very close to a psychotic delusion."

Gleigh thought about this very carefully. He could see the psychologist's point, but there was no way to separate Alice's passion from her brilliance. And privately, he was thrilled that she could feel so intensely about the subject — a fact which, sooner or later, would force a schism between himself and Dr. Gold. He wanted it to be later. "Well, keep an eye on her," Gleigh told him. "Keep a log of any behavior that appears obsessive or inappropriately involved with the subject. Just don't keep confronting her about it. If you do, Dr. Weil will see it as some kind of rivalry between the two of you, and he'd certainly side with her. Build your report. If it becomes necessary to challenge her position on the project, we'll have the data to do so."

Dr. Gold seemed satisfied with this directive, and it suited Gleigh's needs as well. The psychologist could act on his dislike of Alice Kurz without interfering with her progress. And it really *could* become necessary to remove her from the project, although not for the reasons that Gold thought.

Gold turned his attention back to his meal. After a minute, he asked "Has your legal team reached any further conclusions regarding the human experimentation protocols?"

In fact, they'd reached several conclusions, including that the informed consent given by the subjects would never stand up in court as sufficiently *informed*. They felt that the institute's lawyer, Mr. Thompson, was woefully out of his depth, and they should step in and take charge. Gleigh was still considering making that suggestion to Dr. Weil, but he wasn't yet ready to show his hand. Instead, he instructed his lawyers to prepare appropriate defensive arguments, in case they were needed some day.

"They're monitoring the situation carefully, and they've prepared a very solid defense in case of any legal procedure against the institute, the board of investors, or any of the principals," Gleigh said. "You're well protected in any circumstance that might arise."

Dr. Gold still looked skeptical.

"The concerns that you wrote on this subject are on file, so your due diligence in the matter has been clearly established," Gleigh went on. That seemed to help. If it came to legal proceedings, Gleigh's long-time associate, Dr. Spencer Gold, would take the first opportunity to position himself as the whistleblower.

• • •

After dinner, Mr. Salt drove the Mercedes through the streets of Denver while Sam Gleigh sat in the back in silence, watching the streets go by, always knowing exactly where he was in the city. Gleigh had an affinity for Denver, even though it was New York that had set him on his path to wealth. Denver was the home of his childhood, and the place where he first realized that he was on his own in life. His father was a Denver police officer who never failed to demonstrate how little Sam meant to him. Trapped into marrying Sam's mother when he made her pregnant, Oswald Gleigh resented both of them, and was never shy about expressing it with his words or his fists. Sam learned at a very early age that the easiest way to coexist with his father was to never be in the house at the same time.

The Gleighs always struggled to pay their bills, even though Sam later came to believe that his father took cash on the side by shaking down offenders in lieu of arrest. Oswald blamed his son and his wife for siphoning away his money, even though he gave plenty of it to bartenders and poker buddies.

A dismal opinion of humanity was an occupational hazard for police officers. Every day, Officer Gleigh had to deal with people at their worst. If they weren't shooting each other over gang territory, they were beating their wives or girlfriends, or shooting their husbands, or selling their bodies for crack, or jacking cars, or knifing homeless men, or setting apartment buildings on fire. The geographic and cultural tides had placed Officer Gleigh in a predominantly black precinct, and the only people he came in contact with were trouble of some sort, so he concluded that's all there was to "those people."

Sam escaped inheriting his father's racism, primarily because of his hatred of his father. His need to be out of the house put him in contact with an ever-widening social circle, and he quickly learned that stupid people and brilliant people came in all colors, sizes, and genders. When he was thirteen he learned, to his surprise, that he wasn't the only boy who had no interest in girls; by fifteen, he knew he could continue to live at home until his father killed him, or he could leave. He went to New York to live with an older brother of a friend from Denver. The fact that his new roommate expected certain services from him in lieu of rent was nothing more than a pragmatic means to an end for Sam Gleigh. It was simply the first in a long line of successful business contracts.

Sam Gleigh took on every job available to him and used every means at hand to improve his opportunities. When he wasn't washing dishes or cleaning toilets, he was at the public library studying until he aced his GED exam. His near-perfect scores on the SAT lead to a partial scholarship at NYU, and he began working at jobs on campus to pay the rest. Along the way, he moved into an apartment with other students and discovered that roommates and sexual partners need not be the same.

At first, Gleigh was mystified by how easily he excelled in his classes. His teachers praised him, his fellow students were envious of him, and his roommates thought he was some weird antisocial genius. To Gleigh, it seemed only that the route to getting what he wanted was right there in front of him, and all he had to do was walk the path. He couldn't understand why his roommates constantly complained about how hard the classes were and how they couldn't do the work, when most of the time they simply *didn't* do the work. Gleigh did nothing *but* the work; that was the quickest path to what he wanted.

Gleigh's goal was something that his friends back in Denver spoke of reverently. He wanted his "fuck you" money: enough to be able to tell off anyone, anywhere, any time it was called for. The vast majority of people had no concept of real wealth, he realized. They used phrases like "independently wealthy" without ever stopping to figure out what it meant and how to get it. To Sam Gleigh it meant never having to tolerate people like his father ever again. The path to getting it was not even secret, it was just too much of a bother for most people. You had to *pay attention*.

It didn't take Gleigh long to get it for himself. With his business degree, academic excellence, and absurdly high recommendations from his teachers, he had a choice of internships at some of the best financial institutions in the city. He learned everything he needed to know about investments, banking, and taxes doing junior-level paperwork at Citigroup. He parlayed that internship into a full-time position, then moved to Deutsche Bank to learn about the international markets. Along the way, he built up his own portfolio and never lost touch with any business contact that still had something to offer him. He started investing in smaller start-up companies with radically new ideas. Many failed, but he quickly learned to spot big ideas before they trended, and he became more and more active on the management side of things. Eventually, he found himself CEO of Extropo Technology, a rapidly rising company that developed the world's fastest and most sophisticated 3D printers. They used them to produce complex parts on demand for manufacturers to incorporate into their products or production lines. For a long time, they were the only ones able to print complex objects at mass-production rates.

All technological leads are fleeting. When Sam Gleigh took over as CEO, Extropo was already beginning to lose market share to newer start-ups. The traditional response of big companies was to get bigger, swallowing up younger and more agile companies in order to control a bigger share of the market. It was a strategy that came from the earliest days of the twentieth century, and even now, when the world had changed a hundred times over, big companies were still trying to hang on by being bigger than everyone else. All too often, they became trapped by their own inertia.

Sam Gleigh never took a sucker's bet. He never emulated a failing strategy, even if it had been successful in a previous era. He looked around Extropo and saw a dozen brilliant engineers frustrated by the inexorable bureaucracy that came along with a big corporation. The engineers knew that getting bigger would only make it worse. What many of them really wanted was a chance to explore the far reaches of the frontier, the areas where success and failure were a gamble the company couldn't risk — but *they* would, if given the opportunity. They'd pour their whole lives into it, if they had a chance to reach for success on their own terms.

In response, Gleigh invented an entirely new business model. Instead of trying to make the company bigger by fusion, he made it more profitable by fission. He let his employees know that he'd listen to a business plan from anyone who thought they had it in them to branch off from the company and start their own enterprise. If the plan was good enough, Extropo gave them their starting money and let them run their new company by themselves, holding onto the reins only through Sam Gleigh's Rule of Sevens: for the first seven years of their existence, the new company paid back to Extropo seven percent of any profits made. After that, they were free and independent, although they usually maintained a cross-licensing arrangement for any patents they or Extropo developed.

Naturally, some of the newly spawned companies failed without ever showing a profit, and many struggled for a long time, then eventually failed or sold out to a competitor. But over the years, enough succeeded that Extropo found itself with a healthy revenue stream from markets it couldn't afford to enter directly. Because the revenue was only good for seven years (or considerably less, since most startups took a few years to make any profit at all), Extropo had strong incentive to keep spinning off new ventures. It quickly became known as a place where smart people could launch their dreams, making it the single most desirable employer for the best and most ambitious young engineers. Extropo had its pick from the top, and didn't have to pay top salaries to get them.

Sam Gleigh stayed with Extropo for twenty years. When he left, the company was on its way to the Fortune 1,000, and books were appearing about Gleigh's Rule of Sevens. None of them were written by Sam Gleigh; he was too busy taking his own advice. He left Extropo under the Rule of Sevens, creating Gleigh Investments, specializing in high-tech venture capital. He founded it in Denver, returning to his launch point an entirely new man.

At the time, Sam Gleigh's parents still lived in the metro area. He never contacted them directly, but one day, one of his attorneys called on Gleigh's mother, unannounced, and presented her with an offer from her son. He had established a trust fund from which she could draw a generous monthly stipend for the rest of her life, but it would only be signed over to her if she agreed to certain terms. She had to divorce Sam's father, move at least 1,000 miles away, and have no further contact with him. Coincidentally, the bruises from Oswald's latest beating still showed on Sharon Gleigh's face when the attorney arrived. She accepted his offer, and Sharon *Emerson* now lived somewhere in Florida. His mother had done nothing to help Sam avoid his father's abuse, but she was a victim, too. Sam was satisfied that any debt he owed her was now paid.

Gleigh held onto shares in some of the more significant enterprises that he helped launch, and sometimes a seat on the board. Through one such start-up, Gleigh met Ken Udi, an engineer turned entrepreneur. Their business relationship blossomed into something more. A year after they met, they were living together, and Gleigh found himself truly happy for the first time in his life. There was a moment, Gleigh remembered, when he almost sold it all and retired to a leisurely life with Ken. A moment gone, never to return. A difficult business contract made its demands, and Gleigh had to skip what would have been their last vacation together, as Ken went ahead to Aspen without him. Ken was a bit of a wild man, and a fearless skier. Somehow, he broke a ski binding at a critical moment, and his body was raked over rocks and broken against the trees, and Sam Gleigh was alone again, forever.

As the car reached the gate to Gleigh's house, he found himself still seething over Ken's death five years ago. It was unacceptable to just *end* that way. Something had to be done about that.

Mixing Memory and Desire

Eliot stared at the crossword puzzle for several minutes, his hands fidgeting on the mouse and keyboard, his eyes drifting from clue to clue. They were making them too hard now. He used to be able to do them, but maybe that was a long time ago. Or maybe this was just another damn test from Dr. ... *what was his name?* ... Goldfinch. Some of the questions didn't even make sense. *'Mnemosyne' — what kind of word is that? Sounds like a corporate brand name. And 'cedar forest victor?' Cedar Forest's a golf course, isn't it? Some golfer named Victor, probably.*

He began to push away from the computer station when the videochat icon flashed and the incoming call tone sounded. He clicked on the icon and saw Alice sitting in the conference room. He smiled at her, wishing that she didn't have to keep going to these conferences. When was she coming home?

"Hi Eliot. Do you feel like talking?"

"Well, let me check my calendar, see if I have any other appointments," he said, reaching for his phone, but he wasn't wearing it, for some reason. Alice laughed, and Eliot sat back and said, "Nope. I'm all yours." He felt a flicker of embarrassment, wondering if she took that the wrong way. Or was that the *right* way?

"I was thinking about something you told me this

morning," Alice went on. "We were talking about your 'gravitational theory of politics,' remember?"

"Sure," Eliot answered. "Political power brings weaker satellites into orbit around stronger centers of power. Accreting more power draws in more powerful satellites."

"Well, at one point you seemed to get a bit …" Alice seemed unsure how he'd react to this. "A bit angry, I guess. Or defensive, maybe."

Eliot was surprised. He didn't remember that. "I don't know what you mean," he said.

Alice paused, watching him carefully as she continued. "I was joking about it. I really liked the concept, but I was kidding when I said, 'Show me the math on this.' It seemed to make you upset."

Eliot looked around at the keyboard and mouse in front of him. Did he just drop something? He couldn't remember what it was, but something was out of place.

Alice was quiet for a while, then she spoke again, softly, so that he looked up and saw her watching his face. "It was the word, 'math,' wasn't it, Eliot? This has something to do with Christine, doesn't it?"

Eliot stood up and paced a few steps back and forth behind the chair, not looking at the monitor. He couldn't tell her about that. The last night they spent together in front of the fire. The fire. "It's just really private," he said, still pacing. He suddenly realized that Alice couldn't see his face, now that he was standing. Maybe he didn't want her to see his face. Then he realized that through the camera she'd be looking straight at his crotch. He sat down, but he still didn't look her in the eyes.

"I'm sorry, Eliot," Alice said quietly. "I didn't mean to pry. Or bring up old wounds. It's none of my business."

They were both quiet for a while, until Eliot looked up at Alice, and then he knew he finally needed to talk about it. "It happened on the last night we were together. Well, obviously it was the last night, but I mean it happened right there in front of me. We were drinking wine, sitting on the floor in front of the fire." Tears came down his face, and he turned away, trying to control his emotions. Just thinking about it terrified him. He took two big gasping breaths. "Suddenly, Christine started crying. She said they were making her leave the country. She had to go to Portugal, and they were taking her there tomorrow."

"Who was making her do this?" Alice asked.

"The math people," Eliot said, his anger beginning to rise again. "They were sending her to Portugal, and she couldn't come back. She was really upset. She was crying. So she … she just dumped the glass of wine across her chest and jumped in the fire! She burned up right in front of me. I tried to grab her, pull her out, but my arms burned so bad I had to let go."

Alice was quiet, her face blank. "She died then," Eliot continued. "Right there in my fireplace, she burned up. I scooped up her ashes and put them in a vase, with a lid. That was all I could do."

Alice looked down at Eliot's hands on the desk in front of him. "You must have gotten terrible scars from the burns on your arms," she said.

"Yes," he answered, nodding his head. "They were all black at first." He held up his hands and looked at them. "They had some kind of new treatment, though, and they got better. It took about ten years, you know, but now I can hardly see the scars at all."

• • •

Things changed all the time. Eliot was used to that. It confused everyone else, but you just had to accept it.

He and Christine were sitting on the couch, watching the fire, and then he was in some motel room, and a woman on TV was talking to him like she was really there. *That's my sister*, he thought. He didn't say it, in case that was wrong, but he was pretty sure. Anyway, she was family of some kind.

It was time to go to work, but the damned door was locked. Eliot reached for his keys in his pocket, but he was wearing some kind of gym pants with no pockets. He looked on the end table by the bed and found a plate with part of a sandwich on it. That's not what he was looking for. There was also a fork and a balled-up napkin. There should be a drink, too. That's what he was looking for. He was thirsty. He wandered around until he saw the paper cup dispenser by the sink. He filled a cup and sat down at the kitchen table to drink it. Someone had left two other half-full cups there, so he tossed them in the wastebasket. He didn't get up and walk closer to it, because the floor was always wet over there.

The TV got really loud, so Eliot went to look for the remote control. He finally found it: a little white thing that looked like a bar of soap, attached to the wall by a short cord. That was a good idea. He remembered tying the cord on, so the remote would stay by the TV. He picked up the remote and looked it over. The two buttons weren't labeled. He tried them both, and he turned the little wheel between them, but the TV didn't turn off. The woman was speaking very quietly now. She looked sad. "How do I turn off the TV?" he asked her. But when he looked up, there were two guys sitting next to her at the table. One of them was his doctor, he remembered. The other guy was the woman's brother, he thought.

"Eliot," the woman on TV said, and he turned to look at her. She smiled and spoke again, too loud and very precise, like his English teacher, Mrs. Morewood. No, that's just what the big kids on the playground called her when they whispered together, watching her. It was Maywood. Something like that.

"Eliot," the woman kept saying. He looked at her, and she immediately started talking again. "You need to eat more, Eliot. Why don't you bring your plate back over here and finish your sandwich."

Eliot looked around, but didn't see any plate. "There's a sandwich in the bedroom," he said, remembering it was there. "Do you want to eat *that* one?"

"No, Eliot, I don't want to eat it. I want *you* to eat it. That's *your* lunch, Eliot."

Eliot looked at her for a minute, wondering where he knew her from. "Well, all I've got is that sandwich," he said. "But I can make you something else, if you want." He stood up to walk to the kitchen, but he couldn't remember where it was. He paused, turning to look all around the room, finally coming back to the TV woman again. He had nothing to offer her. But he remembered the sink, so he asked, "Do you want a cup of water?"

• • •

Dr. Gold knew they'd expect him to speak first. He watched Alice turn off the microphones and mute the audio in the subject's environment. Glancing at the monitor, he noted that the subject was now completely ignoring them again. "Well," Gold began, "once again the pattern of the dementia is consistent with Alzheimer's Syndrome." He felt a mild nausea. *It's unseemly how excited they get when their little theories are confirmed by their new toy.* "I don't suppose anyone requires the additional testing needed for a proper diagnosis?"

"No," Trick said. "I accept the conclusions, and suggest we move on."

Gold looked closely at Trick. Was there in Trick just a bit of the same distaste *he* felt? If so, it was surprising. Trick never expressed the least doubt about what they were doing. Neither did Dr. Kurz, of course. Someday she'll name the treatment they come up with after her grandmother. Then she'll finally discover that curing this disease won't bring Grandma Rose back from the dead. What then, for Alice Kurz? How will she come up with a crusade to top this?

Alice couldn't hold back her excitement. "But you see what this means?" Gold didn't, but she was going to explain it to him, regardless. "It's the same *type* of damage as the last cycle, but it was in an entirely different *area* of the brain. By accelerating the time frame, we can see how it progresses. It spreads in just the same manner, independent of loci. This is very significant."

"It sounds merely tautological to me," Gold said. "You introduce damage designed to grow, and — surprise! — it grows."

"But this shows how easily it can spread in the brain. It's almost like a virus, the way it can start from just a few damaged memories and a handful of tangled neural chains. It spreads because it uses the brain's greatest strength against itself: the need to make sense of things. It's desperately applying patches to other memories to make them fit the damaged ones, and there's no self-awareness of the illogic of it all. In the end, the brain just … consumes itself."

"Well, I realize it can annoy people to hold them to a clinical standard, but I think your conclusions overreach the data we have so far."

"I believe Alice was suggesting a research direction, not stating a conclusion," Dr. Weil said directly to Gold. "And it's a very intriguing question, I think. One of the definitive characteristics of this sort of dementia is the casual confabulation of stories to explain things that don't really make sense. It's a compelling thought that the brain's attempts to achieve consistency can actually spread the damage."

"And if it can happen so easily, does it actually happen far more than we think?" Alice asked. "Perhaps in most people it never overtakes the advancement of new, healthy connections. If you keep the brain stimulated, surprise it, make it wonder, make it grow, then it has less resources to waste on mangled memories."

"We still have a lot of variables to isolate," Trick cautioned. "But I want to see if we can really repair cognitive function with neural overlays of stored memories. Can we move on to the treatment phase, so we can start the next cycle by the end of the week?"

"By all means," Gold agreed.

Till Human Voices Wake Us

Eliot Stearns awoke in a room filled with soft blue light. It took him a moment to remember that today was the start of the study.

The first day was mostly filled with Dr. Gold's tests, but whenever he wanted someone to talk to, Alice was there. She seemed to be waiting, expecting him to call. They talked easily, like old friends, even though he'd just met her. He loved their conversations. She was quick-witted and frequently challenged his perspective, leaving him with the sense that somehow they were on a grand expedition together, mapping out a new world. By the end of the first day, his mind was reeling with new insights, new questions, and an overwhelming urge to see her again tomorrow.

It wasn't until the evening of the second day that Eliot took the time to explore the games on the computer. He spent an hour working his way up to the more challenging sudoku levels, then noticed that they had a pretty good crossword puzzle. That took up another hour. He looked at the time display: it was just after 8:00, too late to have another talk with Alice tonight, he assumed. Still, he knew that she sometimes worked late. Was it possible she was still there?

He tried the videochat, and the empty conference

room appeared. He waited a few minutes, then he saw her walk into the conference room, sit down, and answer the chat.

"What are you doing here so late?" he asked.

"I'm trying to catch up on some paperwork." She smiled at him. "During the day I keep getting distracted by … what was your term for it? 'Peripatetic philosophy.'"

Eliot had used that phrase in the past, but he couldn't remember saying it to Alice. He must have said it sometime yesterday. Alice picked up on his confusion and laughed, saying "Well, maybe that was just something *I* came up with after our last session. Anyway, you've pulled me away from status reports and budget spreadsheets, and I can't thank you enough."

"If that's just going to make you stay later, I refuse to be an enabler for a workaholic," he said. "Go home." *Here's an opportunity to find out.* "You must have family, friends … a significant other?"

Alice paused. Eliot remembered that the others could review the recordings of everything they said to each other. If he wanted to flirt with her it had to be subtle enough to be arguably innocent. "No one's waiting up for me," she said, giving her head a tiny shake and watching his reaction.

Eliot smiled. "Have you always been so dedicated to your work? Maybe you need to hire more staff."

"Maybe we do. I should speak to Dr. Weil about that. But, you know, other people have accused me of being a workaholic in the past. There might be something to that."

"You were probably the one in high school who did your homework as soon as you got home, then did extra credit work after supper."

Alice laughed. "No, I was the one who went home

and *cooked* supper — or at least helped Grandma cook supper — then did my homework afterward."

"You lived with your grandmother?" She didn't seem to mind talking to him about her personal life.

"My parents died when I was thirteen," she said. "We went to live with Grandma Rose then — my sister Rachel and I."

"I'm sorry to hear that," Eliot said. He waited, but she didn't offer any more. "Are you the older sister?" That was how he pictured her.

"Yes, by three years. Grandma Rose was great, but I didn't want her to take care of Rachel. That was *my* job."

"So you fought with your Grandma over Rachel?"

"No," Alice said, surprised at the idea. "No, we all got along okay. I just got very serious about everything and did a lot of the cooking and care-taking. I don't know why. I haven't thought about it in a long time."

Eliot watched the monitor, and he could almost see the memories playing out behind her eyes. There was a yearning in her gaze that stunned him. And with no effort at all, he understood that moment of her life. "You were afraid to count on her," he said softly.

Alice nodded, returning to the present to look at Eliot. "If it could happen to my parents, why not Grandma? I had to rely on myself."

"That's taken you pretty far, Alice," Eliot said, thrilled to get a shy smile from her.

"Well, it was pretty rough, especially for Rachel. I acted tough about it for her sake, and, I guess ... you sort of become what you pretend to be."

Eliot remained silent, because he wanted to know. He wanted to know everything.

"We lived in Chicago," Alice continued. "My parents were both doctors at Northwestern Memorial Hospital. Dad was a cardiac surgeon, and Mom was an emergency room physician. We had plenty of money. It was *time* that they were never able to give us. Even before they died, Grandma took care of us a lot. She'd be there after school and often at night when they were both on call. They never had enough time with each other, either. That's what did it, in the end. That year, as soon as Rachel and I were out of school for the summer, we all went on a road trip together. We went west, saw Mount Rushmore and the Badlands. We went to Yellowstone and the Grand Tetons before heading back home. It was wonderful, the best time we ever had as a family, I think. Then Grandma came and stayed with us, and Mom and Dad took their own little vacation together. A second honeymoon — a sailing cruise up Lake Michigan to Mackinac Island just over in Lake Huron. They were going to stay two nights at one of the resort hotels there. They never made it. Just outside Beaver Island, the last big island at the tip of Lake Michigan, a squall hit without warning. It was night, and they were below deck. The crew barely sent out a mayday before the boat overturned. By the time the Coast Guard got to them, they were pulling bodies out of the water. My parents had been trapped below. They could both swim, but they never had a chance. The Great Lakes can be like that."

Eliot watched her dab tears from her eyes. She glanced at him. "It was a lifetime ago. I was a whole other person then. But I still hate boats."

"So you grew up fast," Eliot said gently. "Trying to be a mom to Rachel when you were only thirteen."

"Yes, but I think in the end she resented it. By the time I was getting ready to go to MIT, she was tired of being bossed around by her older sister. I worried about leaving her with just Grandma, but she was eager to step out of my shadow. You don't have any brothers or sisters, do you, Eliot?"

"No, it was just me."

"It's hard for a younger sibling in school," Alice continued. "The teachers always compare you to the one they had before. I was quite a nerd, as I suppose you've guessed." Eliot smiled. "So Rachel felt pressured to be an honor student, but that wasn't her way. She ended up rebelling a bit. She couldn't wait to be out on her own. She got married almost immediately after high school and had her first child a year later. Her husband does carpentry. He's good at it, but it can be hard to get enough work when the construction business is down. They ended up moving to St. Louis while I was finishing medical school at Harvard. I was mad at her for leaving Grandma all alone, but Grandma took it in stride. She said she was happy to see us both making exciting lives for ourselves."

"What about now? Do you get along all right now?"

"Yeah, Rachel and I made up after Grandma got sick. She developed early-onset Alzheimer's. I was in Colorado by then. We both felt guilty, because leaving her alone might have contributed to it. She had friends, of course, but we weren't there to notice when she started to withdraw from them. She stopped going out, and she had no one to talk to except when we called. Eventually, it became obvious what was happening. It was awful, but trying to get care for her brought Rachel and me back together. Grandma died ten years ago."

She paused to collect her thoughts.

"Is that why you went into neuroscience?" Eliot asked.

"I was already there, but it certainly influenced me. There was so little we could do. There's such a need for new treatments, new ideas. We're getting so close to …"

She stopped suddenly, as if uncomfortable telling him more. "There's good work going on, but I can't really talk about that. Rachel and I stay in touch. We visit each other when we can, and I've really enjoyed getting to know her kids."

"Do you think you'll ever have kids of your own?"

"No," Alice said, with only a hint of sadness. "That opportunity never knocked. I guess I've compensated by being Aunt Alice to Rachel's kids. They're an interesting pair — boy and a girl, both teenagers now. We've always had a pretty good relationship. Who knows if that will continue, now that adults have all become stupid to them." She smiled, then gave a short laugh. "Oh, hell. I just lost The Game."

"You're playing a game?" Eliot asked, somewhat disappointed that he didn't have her whole attention.

"Not exactly," she said. "It's something the kids told me about. You're always playing The Game as long as you don't remember that you're playing it. As soon as you remember The Game, you lose. Once you forget about it, you're playing it again."

Eliot found the idea strangely appealing. "So you can only win The Game by not consciously playing it?"

"Well, I don't think you can ever actually win, but you lose frequently. I guess that's a teenager's view of life." They both laughed at that.

"But it's something that you can't *try* to succeed at," Eliot mused. "You can't *choose* to forget."

"That's exactly what I find fascinating about it," Alice agreed, nodding her head. "There's nothing you can deliberately do about it. You just have to go on with other things. You don't even know how well you're doing until you lose." She paused again and seemed to be debating with herself what to say next. "Have you ever heard of the Turing test?" she asked.

"Sure," Eliot said. "Alan Turing, mathematician, cryptologist. The idea was, if you could talk to a computer program without being able to tell whether it was a real human being or not, then you have to conclude it's intelligent, just as you are."

"That's right," Alice said. "Ever since the kids told me about The Game, I've thought that it might be a way to resolve the Turing test. Humans can't deliberately choose to forget, but computers can. They can delete memories on command. I could tell the Turing subject something, then ask it to forget. If it really did forget a few seconds later, then it's not a human being."

"Yeah, but just because you *can* program a computer to forget doesn't mean you have to," Eliot said. "You could also program it to remember everything it learns, as long as you have enough storage capacity." He thought about it some more. "You could also program it to lie and act like it did forget."

Alice seemed nervous about this conversation, but Eliot couldn't see why. He was sure she'd have thought of those objections herself. "Well," she said, with a short laugh, "just forget I said that."

"Hah!" Eliot laughed. "No dice. I still remember."

• • •

That night, Eliot dreamed he was wandering through endless hallways with closed doors on both sides. Some of the doors had glass windows, and he could see people on the other side, but those doors were always locked. He found other doors he could open, but they always led to another maze of hallways. Finally, he found an open door leading to a room where a man sat on a chair, his back to Eliot.

"Who are you?" Eliot asked, standing in the doorway. The man turned his head, and Eliot saw his own face.

"I'm Eliot," the man said. "Who are *you*?"

"You're not supposed to be here," Eliot said.

"*I'm* not here. *You* are," the man said.

Eliot awoke, feeling anxious. A strange dream … the details were already fading, but something about it unsettled him. He sat up and looked at the time. It was just after midnight. He went to the bathroom and urinated, glad that they had told him he no longer needed to collect it. Afterward, he wandered out into his living quarters with a vague feeling of being secretly watched. *Maybe I am*, he thought.

He wondered if anyone would be there to talk, as long as he was up. He went to the computer, moved the mouse, and the screen lit up. He clicked the videochat icon. The conference room was empty, but the icon flashed, calling for attention at the other end. He let it go for a minute or two, then decided he should just go back to bed. But as he moved to close the chat window, he saw a man with short dark hair enter the conference room and click something on the computer. He sat down and looked at Eliot through the monitor. Eliot had never seen him before.

"Hello, Eliot. I'm Trick. I'm in charge of the software development."

"Trick," Eliot said. "And you work for Dr. Chance?" *Trick and Chance. Odd combination.* Trick didn't respond right away, and Eliot got the impression he was annoyed by the question. "Is Trick short for something?"

"Rick Trilby. It started in my first programming class at MIT. We were supposed to create a username from our first name and last initial. In my case, that would have been *rickt*, but I thought people would remember it as *rickety*, so I changed it. Reversed the order. Nobody seemed to notice, and it stuck."

Eliot laughed. "So why are you here this late, Trick?

Working a night shift?"

"No, I just got caught up in an idea and was following it. Software design is like that sometimes. You get stuck on something for a while, then there's a breakthrough that just seems to come out of nowhere. You don't want to lose it when it comes, so you keep chasing it to see where it leads, no matter how long it takes."

Eliot understood that feeling. All creative work had that aspect to it. "And I took you away from it. I'm sorry."

"That's okay. I was ready for a break, or I would've just ignored you."

Direct and to the point. "So what was the breakthrough?"

"I can't really talk about that," Trick said. "Sorry."

"No problem. I probably wouldn't understand it anyway."

Trick tilted his head slightly. "I don't know. You seem pretty sharp to me. I know we haven't talked before, but I hear everyone's reports in staff meetings. You seem to be quite clever."

"Well ... thanks."

Trick continued to watch Eliot with clinical interest. Finally, he said, "It had to do with a distributed control mechanism for a parallel processing array. The previous software was all hierarchical. I had to redesign it."

"What's wrong with hierarchy?" Eliot asked. "I thought most software was hierarchical. Main programs calling subroutines, clients accessing servers, that sort of thing."

"A lot of it still is, but hierarchy doesn't work very well when you're trying to do a whole lot in parallel. You end up with the most important decisions at the top of the hierarchy, with all the information necessary to make those decisions at the lower levels. The communication overhead grows out of control, and you lose the potential efficiency of parallel activity."

Eliot thought about that. "It happens in organizations, too," he said. "Companies, governments. They're all basically hierarchical — bosses and sub-bosses, national and local authorities. People at the top have to make decisions about things they can't possibly understand, because the experts are all working at the detail level."

"Exactly. You understand it," Trick said. "I can't fathom why more people don't. We're trying to solve twenty-first century problems using a management philosophy from the feudal period. Kings and lords and vassals, with serfs doing most of the work. The serfs see it isn't working, but they don't have the authority to make changes. Computer science figured out non-hierarchical control and communication mechanisms a long time ago. It's all about open protocols, domains of privacy, and distributed information. But it takes forever to change social structures."

"But it *is* changing," Eliot said. "The world is becoming a densely interconnected network, and the traditional borders between nation-states are losing their significance. The time frame is much longer than you're used to, but the same forces are at work. Giant centrally-managed hierarchies like the Soviet Union have had their day and are gone. Even China is having difficulty trying to rely on centralized management. The more powerful they get, the more they'll need to distribute control to survive."

"And the US? Seems like we're moving in the opposite direction," Trick said. "The executive branch has made a hostile takeover of most of the federal government, and the feds have almost completely neutered the states. You've probably read the *Federalist Papers*?" Trick cocked an eyebrow.

"Yes," Eliot said, a bit surprised by the question.

"John Jay, or whoever it was that day, argued that the proposed federal government could never impose onerous laws on the people. The lawmakers wouldn't be permanent politicians, but ordinary citizens temporarily conscripted from their real lives. They'd have to live under those laws as soon as their service was over and they returned to their farms and businesses."

"Yeah, it hasn't quite worked out that way," Eliot admitted.

Trick nodded. "In the end, it comes down to the fact that hierarchy doesn't scale well to a really large size. When you're part of the hierarchy, the only way you can be more effective is to rise to a higher level in the system, increasing your domain of control. If you're successful, you inevitably end up making decisions about things you're totally ignorant of. Information abhors a vacuum. Without real data or deep technical expertise, politicians listen to whoever shouts at them the loudest, or to whatever deal the party leadership has made to counter the opposition. And if your party's favorite policy proves not to work, well, that just means we need *more* of it."

"But there *is* objective data out there," Eliot argued. "History has run plenty of experiments that we should be able to learn from."

Trick shook his head. "History doesn't run *repeatable* experiments. Everything is a special case with vastly many interdependencies. There are no control runs to isolate the effects of specific factors. Sloppy way to do science. How can you draw meaningful conclusions when there are a million parameters, and the experiment is whatever happened once?"

"Yeah," Eliot said. "I see what you mean. But government could experiment and learn from *its* mistakes."

"Not on a national level. As a nation that aspires to equality under the law, you can't try out different laws and regulations in different communities. The crucibles of experimentation have to be the states and cities, each trying their own local regulations. But as more and more power flows to the national level, opportunities for innovation dry up."

Eliot thought about that. "So we're sacrificing innovation for uniformity and stability."

"Hah!" Trick snorted. "What stability? Hierarchies seem stable until they suddenly and catastrophically collapse. It's not stability they possess, but rigidity. We build an elaborate hierarchy to manage specific problems, and almost immediately the problems evolve into something else. Modifying an entrenched hierarchy while it's in control is difficult. There's too much power near the top to displace it there. It's always easier to add more branches at the lower levels, so we end up with this metastasizing Rube Goldberg machine that becomes more and more intransigent every day."

"Hold on," Eliot interjected. "You said that computer science has already moved on to non-hierarchical control and communication mechanisms. So what are they? How would those solutions apply to governments and corporations?"

"There are too many bottlenecks, for one thing," Trick said. "Too many gatekeepers. Individuals should be able to interact directly with the owners of the resources, instead of always having to go through brokers of various kinds. We're seeing a trend toward that direction in all kinds of business and artistic relationships. Not just consumers buying products directly from vendors online, but musicians selling directly to their listeners, writers publishing their own books. And all this opens up new opportunities in the infrastructure, both good and bad. Online secure commerce. Digital rights and restrictions. Independent currencies. Who knows what else?"

Eliot was fascinated. He mulled it over for a few minutes. "But those, too, will fall to newer ideas, either because the new ideas are better or those pushing them are more powerful. It really *is* a struggle between stability and innovation. A lot of people are pretty frightened at how quickly everything is changing."

Trick nodded. "There's a routine part of software development called *refactoring*. You're not trying to add any new features or fix any bugs, you're just weeding out unnecessary code and using your resources more efficiently. It's the way you keep entropy in check. You deliberately *stop* adding branches, and start pruning and rearranging. Effectively, you're always pouring a new, improved foundation underneath the code you're building. That's the kind of thing we have to keep doing in large-scale organizations: look for ways to simplify the protocols, prune unnecessary branches, develop the common core, and use our resources more efficiently."

Trick paused for a moment. "In every complex system, the fundamental principle is *abstraction*. Design differences are just a matter of where and how we draw the boundaries around the abstractions. Like chemistry versus physics. It's all the same, all derivable from the same underlying mathematical models. But for some problems, it's easier to work with abstractions like molecules and ions. For other problems, it's mass and force and acceleration, or waves and particles. You work at the level of abstraction that best hides the details you don't need to worry about for the problem at hand. We need to look at our problems and our systems through some new abstractions, some new models."

"Well, we're good at that," Eliot said. "Abstraction.

We remake the world through metaphors and see it all anew. If we don't understand something, we just take it apart in different ways until we find something we recognize, and then we can do anything we want with it."

"We build models," Trick agreed. "That's the essence of the scientific method. It makes me crazy when I hear scientists talk about science discovering 'The Truth.' It's like … you've had calculus, right? You know about the mathematical concept of a *limit*?"

"Yes," Eliot said, although he didn't see where this was going. "A function that gets closer and closer to something, even though it never actually reaches it. Like dividing a number by larger and larger numbers: one-hundredth, one-thousandth, and so on. There's no number big enough that you can get all the way to zero by dividing by it, but you can get as close as you want."

"Right. So we say that *in the limit* that function converges to zero, even though it's never *exactly* zero. That's how I look at the scientific process. Science isn't about determining the truth. It's about developing models that explain what we see and lead to useful predictions about what we'd see in other circumstances — predictions that can be tested by designing experiments to make those new observations. In the process, we find out how well the model works, and over time, we refine it or replace it as the body of evidence grows."

Eliot understood. "The map is never the territory," he said, nodding. "But the scientific process can get us *arbitrarily close* to the truth. And *in the limit*, scientific models *converge* on the truth, but we can never say that the model *is* the truth."

Trick nodded, and for the first time, Eliot noticed a smile on his face. "But the real question is: does that matter?" Trick asked. "A close-enough *approximation* of the truth is all that humans have ever needed."

Falls the Shadow

The journal is boring, Eliot decided. *What is there to say? I woke up, ate breakfast (still can't believe there are no books in here), walked on the treadmill (not even e-books on this useless computer), completed two of Dr. Gold's silly tests (I'd even settle for some online help to read, that's how desperate I am), then wrote another entry in this stupid journal.*

Obviously there was more to this isolation experiment than he'd been told. Maybe the whole story about the smart prosthetics was just a ruse, and the real point of the experiment was to see how quickly boredom and isolation can destroy the human brain. *I should fill the rest of the journal with, "ALL WORK AND NO PLAY MAKES JACK A DULL BOY." Wonder how they'd react to that?*

Eliot sat back and stretched. The one part of this whole experience that he really enjoyed was talking with Alice Kurz. Would she continue the conversation after the five days were up? Was she interested in developing their relationship? Maybe he should write about that in the journal. So what if they all read it? He could stand a little embarrassment, especially if it broke the ice and opened up the possibility of continuing to see her after the study.

His hands hovered over the keyboard while he thought about what to say. He started to write:

The most interesting person I've met in the last three years of my life is

He froze. How could he be so stupid? It wasn't *his* embarrassment that mattered, it was Alice's. If they thought she and Eliot had gotten personally involved, they'd never let her continue to lead the study. Her objectivity would be compromised. He knew how important this project was to her, and he'd be taking it away from her. *What an idiot!*

He deleted that entry and closed the journal. And yet … she had started the conversation before they even met, with that first email response. And every day of this study she talked to him, listened to him, and revealed more of herself than he'd expect from a casual acquaintance. Was that part of the study, to make him feel comfortable, so that he'd reveal more of his thoughts? No. He was sure that Alice was as interested in him as he was in her. He'd have to be careful, find a way to let her know how he felt, without alerting the others, especially Dr. Gold. Eliot saw the constant tension between Gold and Alice. He knew all his conversations were being recorded, but surely he could find a way to let her know he was interested, while keeping it between the two of them.

He needed to work out what to say, write some things down and edit and revise until he got it right. The journal was out; they all read that. He had no paper or pen. The only way to write was on the computer, but somewhere they wouldn't find it. There was a solution to that problem.

Most of the conventional system icons had been removed from the interface, but had they removed the underlying programs themselves? He looked for the

"Run …" item in the start menu. They had forgotten to remove it! That opened up a lot of possibilities. He might even be able to go online! He tried all the browser names and path prefixes he could think of, with no success. *Even if I could get to a browser, I'd probably be blocked by their firewall.*

Back to the original quest. Where could he stash a hidden file that he could edit? The system temporary files folder would probably be accessible. But would they find it there? Did they routinely erase temp files?

He selected "Run …" again and entered the command to start the system explorer. Amazingly, that worked. They hadn't removed the file system browser; they hadn't even hidden it. He felt almost embarrassed at how easy it was. They must have all the permissions locked down so that it didn't matter if he looked around. He moved up the hierarchy to look at the top-level folders, where he found a network drive, *R*, mapped to a server named *rd22*. As he expected, its contents were mostly hidden from him, but there was a folder there named *Temp* where he might be able to hide a file. He opened the folder and scanned its contents. With a shock, he saw the one filename he never expected to see: *mmi.sys.*

During Eliot's sophomore year in college, he had a part-time job filling in spreadsheets for a research project. The job was dull, and there was hardly enough work to keep him busy, so sometimes he worked on his homework when there was nothing else to do. He couldn't use his own notebook while on the job, so he'd write his papers on their computer and stash them in a file named mmi.sys. The ".sys" suffix usually kept anyone from erasing the file if it were discovered. They'd think it was a system file that needed to be there, and they wouldn't give it a second look. The "mmi" part was

Eliot's private joke. It stood for "me, myself, and I." He had a few occasions since then to stash a file on other computers, and he never encountered a pre-existing file with that name — until now.

Intrigued, he wondered if he could read its contents. He went back to the "Run …" menu and entered the command to display the file, but he paused before hitting Enter. If it were a real system file, it would look like gobbledygook in the editor, but it couldn't do any harm to open it and cancel without saving. He hit the Enter key. It was a text file, and it began with this:

ELIOT: DON'T TELL ANYONE ABOUT THIS FILE. READ THIS WHEN YOU WON'T BE INTERRUPTED

\- Eliot Thomas Stearns
Date unknown, but IT'S LATER THAN YOU THINK.

Eliot's mouth hung open. *What the hell?* Instinctively, he glanced over his shoulder. Of course, no one was there. He took a deep breath, and continued reading.

So you went looking for a private place to write about her. I know, because it's happened before — more than once. See the entries below. Note the dates. They're lying to you. It's not March 20, or whatever date you think it is.

I decided to create this file, then discovered it already existed. And I've rediscovered it over and over again, each time with no memory of having written it before. As far as I can tell, they let me go for up to four full days (sometimes less), and then something happens. They erase my memory. They pretend it's March 20 again. They reset the computer, erase all the entries I made in their journal, and the "study" starts all over again.

I've kept all the log entries I've found in this file, and I add new ones every time I find it again. Add your own entries below so you can keep track of everything we know. Fortunately, they only reset the files on the computer itself. They always forget about the network drive, or they think I can't find it, or they don't realize there's a writable temp folder there. But who knows how many times I've had the same idea, but never noticed the network drive? If I wrote my log file on the computer's own drive, it would have been erased when they restart everything, and I'd never discover it again. And who knows how many times I went through the cycle without ever deciding to keep my own log?

Here's the bottom line. They're lying to me. They've kept me prisoner here for much longer than the contract said, and they've been modifying my memory. But what do I do about it? Read the entries below. When I decided to confront them about it, they just erased my memory again, and I never knew anything was wrong until I rediscovered this file. WHATEVER YOU DO, DON'T LET THEM FIND THIS FILE. It's the only way I ever find out what's really going on. DON'T LET THEM KNOW THAT YOU KNOW. They must have wondered how I knew before, when I confronted them about it. If it keeps happening, they'll eventually figure out how I'm communicating with myself. DON'T LET

THEM KNOW, but figure out how to escape this infinite loop. There must be a way.

Oh, and just in case you don't believe me, in case you think this is some trick they've put together to test you, remember the dream you had, back in the apartment, about Christine by the fire and on the balcony? Think that was only a week ago? Think again.

Eliot wiped his sweaty palms against his shirt, feeling his heart pounding beneath. How was this possible? Why would they do this? What really sickened him was how wrong he'd been about Alice. He couldn't believe she'd been lying to him. Could it possibly be that she didn't know? That they reset *her* memory, too? *But she's not a prisoner here. She has access to the world.* They could only do this to someone kept in total isolation.

But surely he'd been missed. Terry and Ann knew he took the job. Wasn't anyone looking for him? Did they fake some kind of proof that he died? It didn't make any sense.

Completely bewildered, Eliot read through the other entries that followed. The warning at the top had been added later. The log started just as Eliot might have created it now.

March 22

I can think of several reasons why letting Alice know that I'm interested might be a bad idea. Even if she also wants to develop our relationship, she wouldn't be able to do so while this study is in progress. It would jeopardize her position if she indicates any kind of personal feelings for me. If her objectivity is compromised, they might remove her from the study, and she'd hate me for that. I need to be especially careful around Dr. Gold. Somehow I get the feeling that he's just dying for a chance to torpedo the whole project. Why did they ever hire him?

Is there something like the Stockholm Syndrome in a situation like this? Am I drawn to her just because I don't have any real human contact, so I'm anxious to be liked by my captors? I don't think that's why I like her, but she might think so. Maybe it would be better to wait until after the study and then try to resume our email correspondence. That's risky, though. She's so wrapped up in this project that she might be too busy to think about me. She's here practically all day and night. I bet she hardly ever takes time off, even on the weekends. Hell, they might have another subject waiting to start the study as soon as they're done with me. Getting her attention while I'm here might be my only chance to see where this leads.

March 23

Maybe I'm making too big a deal about being discreet. Today she told me that she envied how well-read I am, and it seemed like there was a real spark of affection there. I said that talking with her made me feel like the proverbial "jack of all trades, master of none." My education is all breadth, but hers runs deep. She laughed, but she sounded really pleased. It certainly felt like flirting to me, and she seemed happy to go with it. Maybe no one else is paying any attention to our conversations. Or maybe she has so much authority here that neither Dr. Gold nor anyone else is likely to interfere. I think as long as we keep it subtle, we'll be okay.

March 23

I just discovered this file. I don't understand how this is already here. How did I write this without remembering any of it? Am I losing my mind in here? Does isolation interfere with short-term memory? I have very clear memories of everything that's happened, and there aren't any gaps; but I have no memory of creating this log and writing the previous entries. I don't even remember the conversation with Alice that I referred to above. If I'm having some sort of breakdown because of the isolation, then I need to tell them about it, but then I'd have to explain this log. There'd be no way to keep it secret, and we're back to the problem of Alice's position on the project.

Could I have a conversation with Alice and then write about it while sleepwalking? As far as I know, I've never had any such episodes before, but I suppose it's not impossible that the stress of being cooped up in here could cause something like that.

Tomorrow's the last day of the study. I think I'll just chalk this up to an isolation-induced memory lapse and see how I feel tomorrow. If I remember all this, then I guess I'm okay. And if not? Well, I guess I won't know about it, then.

March 22 ???

What the hell is going on? I just decided to create this file and found that it already existed, and the entries above have tomorrow's date! I didn't write them, I swear. This isn't a memory lapse, or sleepwalking. How can I have already lived through four days of this experiment? And now I'm only on day three again? Is this some horrific psychological test of Gold's? How can they make me forget that I've done this before? Is this the real experiment, and everything they told me was a lie?

The nanocells! They were never intended to break down and dissolve. They must still be lodged in my brain. Somehow, they're programmed to erase my memories — reset them to the first day of the experiment.

I know that sounds paranoid. How could something like that even work? But how else do I explain what's going on? Are they drugging me? Something in the food? How could they erase exactly five days?

I'm afraid to talk to them about it. If I'm right, won't they just erase my memory again? How can I stop them?

"March 23"

So it's on to day 4. I still haven't come up with any better explanation for what's going on. I haven't said anything to them about this, but — once again? — tomorrow's the last day of the experiment. What if I wake up tomorrow, and I'm right back at the start? I won't know that it happened unless I stumble over this file again. I need to leave myself a note pointing to it, but they haven't given me anything to write with except the computer.

I could use the dinner knife. I'd have to carve the note somewhere they couldn't find it, but I'd be sure to see it. They probably check the room while they're erasing my memory. They'd have to, in order to set everything up as if it were the first day again. I suppose I could do it on my own body: scratch it onto my stomach or the inside of my thigh. I'll find that, but would they?

Same day, evening

I took a paper cup from the dispenser, and I used the dinner knife to write "R MMI" on the bottom of the cup. I'll fold it up and put it inside my pajamas when I go to sleep tonight. Even if they find it, they probably won't know what it means, but it should be enough to make me look for this file.

March 21

I just discovered this log again, but I never found a paper cup in my pajamas. If they did discover my message, they must not have figured out what it meant, because this file was still here for me to find.

I've added a warning to myself at the top of this log, so I'll see it right away if I rediscover it again.

March 22

They know I suspect something. I can't hide how freaked I am. But how do I get out of this? If I tell them I know what they're doing they'll just erase my memory again and if they know I know then they'll figure out how I know and they'll find this log and delete it and I'll never know again

I HAVE TO FIGHT THEM

I'll tell them I'm sick I can't continue I don't

want the money
THEY HAVE TO LET ME OUT

Eliot sat very still, staring blankly at the screen. There had to be something he could do, but what? *I can't show them the only proof I have that I'm a prisoner. They'll just erase it and wipe my mind again. I can't let them know I have proof, or they'll go looking and find it. I can't contact anyone outside the lab. I've tried open defiance and they just wipe my memory.*

He looked around his cell: bed; bathroom; water; food delivered to the table. They could keep him here forever without ever opening the door.

Fear In a Handful Of Dust

Two more days, Eliot thought, but what would happen then? When would they erase his memory and start it all over?

He kept playing it out in his mind, trying to imagine how it might happen. Even if they could do it just by sending a signal to the nanocells, they'd need to put him back in his bed and clean up the suite. It has to seem like the first day when he wakes. They probably reset him while he sleeps. Do they sedate him again? If he remained awake, could he fight it?

He went back to the computer and opened the private log again. None of the entries were dated March 24. *If it's never day 5, they never have to let me leave. They'll do it on the fourth night — tomorrow night.* But something else caught his attention: the first two "March 23" entries. In the first, he'd written about a discussion with Alice. In the second, he rediscovered the file and wrote that he hadn't remembered that discussion. He walked through the scenario in his head:

1. *March 23 (day 4): "jack of all trades" discussion.*
2. *They erased my memory that night and started the experiment over.*
3. *I didn't know anything was wrong on the new*

March 20, 21, or 22.

4.   *I found the file again on the new March 23 — or maybe several cycles later!*

It explained why he didn't remember that discussion, but it also explained something that happened to him *this* cycle: *peripatetic philosophy!* Alice said she heard that from him, then backtracked when she saw his surprise. That must have come up in a discussion from a previous cycle, before the last memory wipe. Alice made a mistake by referring to it, and she tried to cover it up. Was there something in that discussion that they didn't want him to remember? *Do I keep discovering something I'm not supposed to know?*

He needed more information, something that could give him an edge. His hidden log file was the key. He had to record everything he figured out, and everything he tried, so that he wouldn't keep trying the same things every cycle. Carefully, in as much detail as he could recall, Eliot wrote descriptions of every discussion he remembered with Alice, Trick, and the others. He updated the entry at the top of the log, telling himself to keep doing so. If he kept finding the file, maybe it would eventually contain enough information for him to discover a pattern: discussions that always came up before they decided to reset him; nervous responses from Alice or the others that indicated he was learning too much; reasons for the cold attitude that Dr. Gold had shown him ever since he woke up in here.

It was easiest to talk to Alice, but she was also the most likely to realize something had changed in his attitude. If he gave away too much, she'd be suspicious. They might reset him just because of that. In short, he had to lie and pretend everything was fine. Eliot prided himself on his honesty; lying did not come easily, especially to someone he cared about. To his own surprise, he realized that he still cared about Alice. As much as he needed to think of her as his enemy, he kept wanting to confide in her and ask for her help.

Bracing himself, he started the videochat and smiled when he saw her alone in the conference room.

"Good afternoon, Eliot," she greeted him, a smile on her face — *the smile of a spider at the fly in her web,* he thought, but somehow it didn't feel that way. Her expression faltered, as if she saw already that he doubted her, so he tried to distract her.

"Hi, Alice," he paused, coughed lightly, and smiled again. "Sorry, some kind of tickle in my throat. I hope I'm not coming down with a cold."

"Do you feel sick?"

"No, just a little tired. Bit of a headache." He laughed. "That would be ironic, wouldn't it? Isolated from everyone else, and I still catch a bug."

"Well, the room was sterile when you entered," Alice said, watching him closely. "We followed standard hospital practices."

"Is it possible to get sick just from breathing in your own germs for three days?" He cleared his throat, trying to make it look involuntary.

"Not really, but you could have been incubating something that's only showing up now."

If he'd only been here three days, that might be true, but she knew he'd been isolated much longer than that. Had he already made her suspicious? "Well, maybe I'm just getting bored. I'm actually starting to miss my job at the library. I know it's only the third day, but sometimes it seems like I've been here a lot longer than that." He watched her face, but she didn't react in any way he could see.

"Well, hang in there, Eliot, you'll be back with your

friends before you know it."

He stared at her, awed at the casual way she lied to him. Was that because she'd been doing it so long, or was she naturally deceitful? He wondered again if somehow she might be unaware of the memory wipes, but how could that be? As far as he knew, the whole "experiment" was her design.

What could he say to her that would sound innocent, but might cause her to shatter the illusion? They'd reset him so many times, it couldn't be March anymore. What would be happening now, out in the real world? "I wonder how the Rockies are doing?" he asked. "Every season, I think this could be their year." Would Alice know they weren't supposed to have started yet?

For a second, she looked puzzled, but she fixed her expression quickly. "I'm afraid I don't follow sports very much, Eliot. I thought the baseball season hadn't even started yet."

Damn, she's good.

• • •

Eliot went to bed early that night and woke relieved that he still remembered it all. Today was day 4. It would happen tonight.

He lay in bed until breakfast arrived, acted more withdrawn and depressed all day, and napped after lunch, storing up sleep for that night. Alice seemed concerned, but he avoided talking to her as much as possible. He sat at the computer and played sudoku and solitaire late into the night, deliberately slowing his play as if exhausted. He finally went to bed around 3:00 in the morning, but he lay there, determined to stay awake for the whole night. If it worked — if this kept them from erasing his memory — then they'd have to confront him tomorrow or let him go. And if erasing his memory required them to enter his room, he'd feign sleep until they got close enough to grab whoever came in. Either way, *something* would change.

• • •

Eliot Stearns awoke in a room filled with soft blue light. He found his private log again on the afternoon of the fourth day. As he read the descriptions of his forgotten discussions with Alice, he was so bewildered that he forgot to feel betrayed. All his life he'd waited for someone to talk to like this, someone asking the most interesting questions and challenging all the answers. *She would never bore me.* If she'd asked him to stay and talk with her forever, he might have agreed. How could she trap him like this?

Eventually, Eliot decided it didn't matter. He wanted information, but what he needed was to get out. He was a prisoner of war and the only member of the escape committee. He updated his private log with notes about the discussions he'd had this cycle. He reviewed what he'd already done to try to break free of their control. Tomorrow would start a new cycle. He had to make sure he found the log right away.

The message on the paper cup was a good idea, but they probably undressed him and put him in fresh pajamas, so he needed a better place to hide it. Eliot had read *Papillon*. He knew the one place he could put it where they were almost certain not to find it, but it would still be obvious to him. He sighed, wondering just how unpleasant it was going to be. *I don't need the whole cup, at least.* He tore out the bottom where he scratched his message, folded it into a cone, lubed it with a little soap from the dispenser, and inserted it into his rectum. It wasn't so bad going in, but he'd sure as hell notice it coming out. He described the attempt in his hidden file and went to bed.

• • •

Eliot Stearns awoke in a room filled with soft blue light. He discovered the file on the evening of day 2. The cup bottom with the message never made an appearance; they must have found it and removed it. The implications of that rattled him. He thought about it all night long. In the morning, he decided that subtlety wasn't getting him anywhere.

He grabbed a new roll of toilet paper from the shelf and knelt in front of the toilet. He unrolled the toilet paper, reaching his arm into the bowl to jam it all into the toilet drain as tightly as he could. He stood back, washed his arm, and flushed the toilet so that it overflowed all over the bathroom floor, then he updated the log file, describing this attempt. "The toilet's clogged," he reported in the usual third-day meeting with the project team. "I don't have any way to fix it, and it's overflowed on the floor. What do you want me to do?"

There was silence from the other side. Trick and Alice continued to look at Eliot. The others looked at Alice. None of them seemed worried. "Well, obviously, we won't be able to continue, then," Alice said, sad but resigned. "Why don't we go ahead and talk about your experience so far, and then we'll come and get you, okay?"

As soon as they closed the videochat, Eliot documented their response in his private log and closed the file. He walked to the door, close enough to seize control of it as soon as it opened. He crouched, coiled, waiting for them.

• • •

Eliot Stearns awoke in a room filled with soft blue light. When he found the hidden file, it was day 3 again. He looked around the suite for a weak spot he could break through. When lunch came, he kept the salad bowl and the knife. When he pushed the finished tray back through the slot, he held the salad bowl upside down under the sliding black panel that covered the slot on this side. The tray rolled in, and the panel slid down, jamming against the bowl. He peered in, hoping to get a glimpse of what was in the next room through the corresponding panel on the other side, but it didn't open, and the rollers stopped. There must be an interlock to prevent both slots from being open at the same time. He reached around the salad bowl and probed the back of the panel with his fingers, trying to find a switch that would be activated when the slot was closed. If he could trip the switch, the other slot would open. His fingers found nothing at all, just smooth walls all around. The metal panels covering each slot were just stuck in position somehow. His fingers could find no mechanism to account for the panels sliding up and down or sensing when he pushed the tray back.

Perhaps he could use the knife to pry away the panel covering the opposite slot. He found the edge of the panel, but he couldn't work the knife between the panel and the wall. It felt as though there were no opening at all on that side, just a panel welded to the inside of the wall. After struggling for several minutes, he had to give it up. He brought his hand out and positioned the knife flat along the bottom of the slot on his side, then pushed the bowl through. The panel closed, but now the knife was under it. He heard the rollers hum, so the other slot must be open now. He pried upward with all his strength, but he couldn't move the panel on his side, and the knife never broke. It never even bent. He sat back, dumbfounded.

He left the knife there. At 4:00, the panel slid up, and a fresh tray bearing his afternoon snack rolled out, pushing the knife with it. None of this made sense. There was no actual opening on the other side; no mechanism to move the panels up and down; nowhere for the tray to go; but somehow, the slot ate the tray and disgorged a new, full one. *This is like something out of The Navidson Record*, he thought.

Eliot kept the extra knife and waited until night. He followed his usual routine and went to bed, but lay awake for an hour. Leaving the lights low, he got out of bed as quietly as possible and went to the door to the "supply room." He tried the doorknob again, softly, to verify that it was still locked. He slid the edge of the knife between the door and the jamb, trying to drag the tip of the knife across the latch, but it didn't budge. It must have a built-in dead latch. The door was installed to swing inward, so the hinges were on his side. He quietly brought the dining chair over and stood on it, worked the knife edge under the top of the upper hinge pin, and levered the pin up. It slid, and he pulled it all the way out. Moving the chair aside, he did the same thing to the lower hinge. He stood back and studied the door in the dim light. There was hardly any gap between the door and frame on either side, so even with the hinges loose it would be difficult to pull the door out. It was an awkward reach, but he grasped the edge of each hinge between his thumb and two fingers, holding onto the parts attached to the door. Slowly he pulled, aware that the hinges might pinch his fingers badly as they separated and the door dropped. They didn't separate, and the door didn't move. He pulled as hard as he could, but there was no sign of movement. He tried pulling on the upper hinge while he held onto the door knob, rocking the door back and forth a little at a time, but it didn't rock. No part of it seemed loose, as if it were nailed shut, or it wasn't a real door at all.

Why would they want me to think there was a door there if it's not really a door? It served no purpose. He could think of only one answer: there had been a door there before, but they sealed it shut before the study. The room behind that door must be significant in some way. They were taking no chances that he could breach it.

That left only one door he could try to force — the entrance into the suite. It had to be a real door, because he'd come in that way when they first showed him the suite, and they had to wheel him in when he was first sedated. This door opened out; the hinges were on the other side.

Eliot wondered if he could pick the lock. Lock picking was a popular pastime for some of the people he'd known in college. He'd watched them do it, and understood the basic principles, but to his regret now, he'd never practiced it. Even if he could do it, he had no tools suitable to the task. *Could I make them?* He looked at the dinner knife, then at the floor. *Ceramic tile.* Could he grind the knife against the ceramic, wearing it down to the right shape and thinness? It would be better to start with a fork, he realized. He could bend all the tines away but one, grind that one as flat as possible, and wedge it into a small hole somewhere to put a tiny hook on the tip. He'd still need the knife, or another fork, for the torsion wrench. He hadn't kept a fork, so he couldn't do it today, and he only had one more day before the fourth night. It might not be enough time, but he could test the plan with the knife. He wrote in his private log what he intended to do.

He knelt on the floor under the dining table. The floor would almost certainly show marks from the process, and this seemed like the least conspicuous spot. If there were hidden cameras observing him, the table might hide what he was up to. Holding the knife handle in his right hand, he pressed the blade against the floor with his left, leaning all his weight onto it. He kept the blade at a shallow angle and began sliding it back and forth across the tile. It took him a while to get a steady rhythm, but once he got there, he kept at it. He couldn't see the time display, so he thought of song lyrics and poetry that had a compatible rhythm and recited them in his head. He didn't want to stop and look at the results too soon. It would take hours, he assumed, so there was no point in discouraging himself by expecting visible results right away.

His muscles soon ached, and sweat ran down his face, blurring his vision. He kept at it. He started to worry that he was expending all his energy on a "proof of concept" that he'd just have to do all over again tomorrow with a fork, but still he kept at it. He grew concerned that the floor wasn't showing any marks from the process. It should be blackening from the metal being rubbed off, or else it should be wearing away if he'd misjudged the tile material. Neither seemed to be happening, but he kept at it.

When the pain in his shoulders and hands grew unbearable, Eliot stopped. He relaxed his hands, flexed his shoulders, back, and neck. He wiped the sweat off his face with his shirt. Finally, he picked up the knife and examined it. There was no change whatsoever. *What the hell? Is the dinnerware coated with diamond?*

He sat back, leaning against the wall, and the oddest thought came to his mind. *What if I'm imagining all this? What if the nanocells are feeding me artificial sensory inputs somehow? Maybe I'm really lying in a coma having a nanotech-induced dream? Could that technology exist? Is that what they're really testing here, and everything they told me was just a cover story? Is that why they keep erasing my memory, because I keep figuring it out?*

He started to get excited at this theory, but he soon realized there was no way to test it. If he couldn't trust his senses and he couldn't know if his actions were really carried out, then how could he determine the truth? He sat for a while, thinking, but he was exhausted and unable to arrive at any breakthrough. He leaned his head back and closed his eyes. Within minutes, he was asleep.

• • •

Eliot dreamed he was running down a maze of corridors, chased by something he couldn't see. He didn't know what pursued him, but he knew that if he stopped running, it would catch him. All the corridors looked alike. He couldn't tell if he'd been running in circles, but he had to keep moving. Suddenly, he was watching himself run from a vantage point high overhead, aware now that he was dreaming. He pulled back to get a larger view of the maze. Maybe he could see the way out, or at least find out who was chasing him. After a while, he caught sight of the pursuer following behind his running self. The pursuer was walking slowly, but the runner never got any farther ahead of him. From his aerial viewpoint, he leaned in to get a closer look at the man chasing him, and he saw his own face. Suddenly he was back in his original vantage point, and he stopped running. He turned to look behind him and saw himself walking toward him. He no longer felt threatened, but he was puzzled. "Who are you?" he asked.

"I'm Eliot," the pursuer said, stopping in front of him. "Who are *you*?"

"You're not supposed to be here," he said.

"*I'm* not here," said the other him. "*You* are."

Eliot woke, still propped against the wall. The alarm was chiming. *They don't know that I'm not in bed, or they don't want to show that they know it.* He remembered the dream and walked through the details in his head. *I was afraid of what was chasing me, but it was me.* He puzzled over the strange twist of words used by his other self in the dream. *I'm not here. You are.* If there was significance to those words, he couldn't see it.

Stiff and sore from his exertions the night before, Eliot stood, stretched, walked over to the computer, and silenced the alarm. It was the fourth day. Tonight they'd do it to him again. He tried playing nice. He tried being clever. All that was left to him was brute force. He pulled the LED monitor as far forward as the cables would allow and turned it around so that he could access the back. He pulled out the power cord, and it went dark. The video cable was secured by thumbscrews. He unscrewed them and lifted the monitor off the desk. Holding it by the base, he hefted it like an axe, the edge of the display being the blade. He walked to the wall near the door, trying to remember what he'd seen when he first walked up the hallway to this room. He found a spot where he knew there should be empty hallway on the other side. He tapped lightly on the wall with the edge of his makeshift axe, listening to the sound of the taps as he moved from left to right, until he was sure where the wall studs were. In between the studs, away from where he figured the electrical wiring would be — judging from the position of the outlet — he drew the monitor back and brought the corner down hard against the drywall, cutting a jagged hole in it. He struck it again below the first spot, lengthening the cut in the wall. He pulled away pieces with his left hand, exposing the framing underneath. It would be tight, but he might be able to open up a space between the framing that he could squeeze through.

Between the studs, he could see the back of the drywall on the hallway side. He drew back the badly damaged monitor, but decided it would be more satisfying to just punch through the wall. He tossed the monitor aside and punched the center of the wall with all his strength. The wall was unaffected. He was so astonished that it took him several seconds to feel the pain in his hand. He hadn't broken his wrist or his hand, but his knuckles were bloody and throbbing. He stared at his hand, unbelieving. *Is there a steel wall on the other side?* His fist left no impression on it. He picked up the monitor again and swung away, the plastic casing shattering into flying shards all around him, but it was all for nothing. He continued to pull away drywall on his side of the framing. It all came away as it should, but nowhere could he make the slightest dent in the wall on the other side.

The pain in his hand was just a dull ache. It had already stopped bleeding. He got the dinner knife and stabbed the outer wall everywhere he could reach, then began using the base of the destroyed monitor as a hammer to drive the knife like a nail. The wall remained undisturbed.

He moved over to the outlet and tore away the wall on his side. There should be an outlet on the other side, too. If he could remove the junction box, he could at least look through the hole. He tore away everything on his side, but found no junction box for the other side. He tried to trace the wiring from the outlet on his side, and discovered that there was no wiring. He systematically stripped away all of the drywall on his side of the framing, uncovering the entire wall. The wall on the other side looked like drywall, but it was more solid than steel. There were no openings, and it was completely impervious to all his attacks. It might as well be in another dimension.

He knew he should try all the other walls, especially the one behind him with the supply room door, but he was sure it would be the same. With a sigh of resignation, he turned to the wall behind the computer station. The video cable went into the wall on his side. It had to connect to *something* in the next room. He tore the wall apart around the cable, finding that it passed through a metal grommet embedded in the wall on the other side. He couldn't cut through the wall, but maybe he could cut the cable and poke it through the grommet. He became obsessed with the idea that all he had to do was look through the hole to the other side, and he'd find a way out.

He sawed back and forth on the video cable with the dinner knife, the outer insulation yielding immediately, the inner copper wires requiring a lot more effort. Finally, the knife cut all the way through, leaving the stub of the cable flush against the grommet on the far wall. He jabbed at it with the knife, trying to poke the stub through the grommet. A millimeter at a time, it receded into the hole in the grommet, until the end of the knife was too broad to push it any further. He picked up the piece of cable that he'd cut off and jammed that into the grommet. Slowly, pushing and twisting, he managed to get the cable all the way through the grommet, forcing the stub on the other side all the way out. He drew back his end of the cable, and looked through the hole. All he could see was black. There was no light on the other side.

He pressed his face against the wall, shielding around his eyes with his hands. He stared for over a minute, hoping he'd eventually be able to see something as his pupil dilated. Nothing but blackness. *If I could shine a light through it* ... but the only source of light that he could have directed through the hole was the computer monitor, and he had destroyed it. *Optical mouse!* He picked up the mouse and turned it over. A bright red light glowed in the center of the base. He held it up to the hole he'd made. He maneuvered it until the red light shone directly into the hole. Around the rim he could see the light reflected back. In the middle he could see nothing but blackness. He tried to enlarge the hole, gouging it with the tip of the knife, but no matter how much force he exerted, nothing changed.

Enraged, he spun around, yanking the mouse out of the wall, and he threw it across the room. He did the same with the keyboard, smashing it first against the desk surface. He screamed. He pounded on the walls. He shouted every obscene phrase he'd ever heard and made up a few of his own. He ran against the door, hitting it as hard as he could with his shoulder. Ignoring the pain, he did it again. When he finally gave up, he realized that he now had no way to record these attempts in his log. Somehow, they'd repair all the damage he'd done, and he'd probably try it all over again after they erased his memory. He'd never be free. The doors and walls were all sealed because they were never coming in and he was never getting out. He sat on the floor and wept.

• • •

Eliot Stearns awoke in a room filled with soft blue light. It took him a moment to remember that today was the start of the study.

The Roots That Clutch

On the third day of the cycle, there was a great deal of tension after the meeting with the subject. "So, here we are again," Dr. Gold lectured. "It's always the same pattern. Everything is fine at first, but somewhere around the third or fourth day …"

"Once it was on the second day," Trick pointed out.

"Yes, but usually it's later than that. Almost every cycle now, we see the same result. The subject becomes uncooperative, hostile, and eventually aggressive."

"The isolation becomes extremely frustrating," Alice suggested. "We know that some people find it too stressful."

"We've been over this before!" Dr. Gold snapped, looking significantly at Weil, who remained silent. He turned back to Alice. "The subject is not one of those people. There was no sign of this in the control cycle."

"Well, unfortunately, we can't run the control cycle more than once," Alice objected. "There's no way we can establish a statistical norm for the individual from a single run. If we *were* able to run it ten times, we'd get ten variations, and we'd probably see this reaction in some number of them."

Trick shook his head slowly, looking at the statistics displayed on his videoglasses. "The data doesn't agree with that hypothesis. If it's just chance whether he succumbs to isolation stress or not, then we should have seen the same rate of occurrence in the earlier cycles that we do now. We had no indications of this in the first four cycles after the calibration phase. Then once in the next four, then two out of four, three of four, and now each of the last four cycles. It's clearly increasing in frequency."

"What's clear is that the subject is breaking down," Dr. Gold said. "There's an inherent instability that's getting worse with every restart. We've wound the spring too many times, and the metal has gotten brittle."

"It doesn't work that way, Dr. Gold," Trick said, shaking his head. "One cycle has no effect on the ones after it. In every restart, the subject begins at exactly the same point, with no memory of anything that occurred previously. It's a *tabula rasa* each time."

"So you say, but that's not how it appears."

Alice was reluctant to agree with Dr. Gold, but he was right about that. "I have to agree, Trick. It seems as though Eliot …"

"The *subject*," Dr. Gold snapped.

Alice nodded impatiently. "… as though the *subject* believes he's repeating the experience. There's a very sudden loss of trust. One day he's a willing test subject, then suddenly *he's* testing *us*. As if he suddenly discovered he's being tricked."

"There is no possibility of memory flowing from one cycle to the next." It was hard to argue with Trick on this point.

"There could be something in the environment," Dr. Gold suggested. "Some evidence that he'd been there before."

"The environment is completely reset at every restart," Trick said. "There's only one interface between the subject's world and ours, and that's his computer. We reload the same virtual machine snapshot every time we restart."

"But if there were files that didn't get completely erased. The journal, for example ..."

"We don't have to erase files. It's a virtual machine. The entire file system — operating system, applications, data files, memory, even the time-of-day clock — the entire computer is loaded all over again from the same initial snapshot."

Dr. Weil finally spoke up. "It seems to me that we're all overlooking something. The subject is responding to how we interact with him. Trick says there's no way for him to get information about what happened in previous cycles, so what *is* accumulating information each cycle?" He paused and looked around the table. "*We* are. The subject must be picking up cues from us. We're all getting spooked, wondering if there's going to be a breakdown, and as we get into the latter days of the cycle we're *looking for it*. That has to have an effect on how we talk to him, even how we look at him." He turned to Dr. Gold and looked intently at him. "Dr. Gold, if I stare at you like this while I'm talking to you, and I start to flinch whenever you say something the least bit disagreeable, and I keep looking like I'm waiting for you to get angry at me, isn't that going to make you feel a bit paranoid?"

Dr. Gold frowned. "Well, I suppose that could be a factor. But I really don't think we've been acting differently. I mean, it's practically the same script every cycle. Sometimes I feel like I'm just reciting lines."

"But that's exactly what I mean," Weil said. "It probably seems that way to the subject, too. If you thought I was only pretending to have a spontaneous conversation with you, but I was really following some script you couldn't read, wouldn't you think there's some kind of conspiracy?"

"But it hasn't been that way with me," Alice said. "I've had different conversations with him each cycle. A lot of similarities, of course, and we often circle back around to the same topics, but it's never felt forced or false to me. Until suddenly it *does*, right out of the blue, and he's suspicious of everything I say."

"Well," Dr. Gold said, "I think we need to decide if we've reached the point of diminishing returns from this study. Should we wrap it up here? I'm sure you all have enough data to analyze for the rest of the year. And then, if you still want to proceed with another study, we can think about what to do differently next time to try to avoid these issues."

Alice fought to hide her panic. *I don't want to lose him again*, she realized. They kept getting to know each other over and over again, but every time it restarted, she was terrified he wouldn't respond to her as he did before. "I disagree completely," she said. "There's clearly something significant happening here, and we don't have a viable theory to explain it. It would be absurd to stop at the very moment when the most interesting and unexplainable observations are being made." She looked around the room and saw both Weil and Chance nodding. Dr. Gold was angry, of course, but Trick was completely unreadable. She remembered something Trick had said before they began the experiment, and she quoted him now. "The whole point of this experiment is to discover what we don't already know." She looked around the room. "We need more data."

Ray Chance spoke up. "So you think we should restart and begin again?"

"No, I think we should let it play out for the rest of this cycle. We have two more days. Let's discuss what we should be asking El—*the subject*—that might give us some clue why his attitude has changed."

"I agree, Alice," Dr. Weil said, looking at Dr. Gold.

"What if the hostility becomes extreme?" Gold asked. "What if he gets violent again?"

"So what?" Trick said. "There's nothing he can do to hurt himself or us. There's nothing he can break. Alice is right. Let's see what he does, and try to figure out why."

Dr. Gold shook his head and huffed. "And we just continue as if nothing's happened? Just keep giving him tests to take while he tries to throw the chairs through the walls again?"

"No," Alice said. "We acknowledge that we know something's wrong, and we ask him to talk to us about it. Otherwise, it will just convince him that he's being misused, and his antipathy will get worse. I intend to talk to him about it this afternoon. We'll see what happens and go on from there. We won't restart him until the last possible minute this time."

"I think drawing out his feelings and concerns is more properly my line of work," Dr. Gold said. "I'll see if I can encourage him to talk about this, without confirming or denying his fears."

"Of course," Alice agreed, thinking furiously. "But right now he's very resentful toward persons of authority. He may not be responsive to a doctor/patient relationship. I think he needs to talk it over with a *friend*, and it seems that he's been thinking of *me* that way."

A momentary smile flitted across Dr. Gold's face. "I believe those feelings are reciprocated, Dr. Kurz," he said pointedly.

Alice resisted the urge to glance guiltily around the room, instead facing him squarely. "Yes. I find the subject quite engaging, and very stimulating to talk to. In many ways, he's a kindred spirit. And that's exactly why he's more likely to trust me than anyone else. If it's true that he knows he's been deceived — and I'm not convinced that's the only explanation — then I'm clearly in the best position to get him to talk honestly about it."

Dr. Weil stopped them before it got any worse. "Dr. Gold," he began. "How would you summarize the subject's attitude now, based on the tests that you administered this morning?"

Gold's eyes remained locked with Alice's for just a few seconds, then he looked down at the papers in front of him. "There's a pronounced loss of focus and concentration, resistance to comply with directions, impatience, despondency — perhaps even despair — and, as a personal and unscientific observation, a short temper." He looked at Weil. "Do you really think that we should continue under these conditions?"

Weil leaned back in his chair and folded his hands across his chest. "Well, Dr. Kurz is right that we still don't know exactly what's causing this sudden change in attitude. I agree that it *looks* like he knows he's been through all this before. But of course, I'm not the specialist in this area." He looked at Gold. "With your knowledge of behavioral psychology, I'm sure you can think of a dozen other possible explanations for a paranoid change in attitude."

Dr. Gold was taken aback. "Well, of course, the obvious explanation is not always the correct one," he admitted. "There are certain types of personality disorders that could manifest in this same way, even suddenly without warning." He groped for something to hang that on. "Without more data on the subject's experiential background and history of prior emotional trauma, it's difficult to make a determinative diagnosis."

"Yes, it's a shame we don't have more data on Eliot's life outside of this study," Weil said, nodding. "I mean, we have hours of recorded interviews with the subject from all the previous cycles, but that would only give us insight into his behavior *here*. It wouldn't illuminate his past history."

"But he has talked about his past quite extensively," Dr. Gold mused.

Weil waited, while Alice held her breath.

"It might be worthwhile to review those interviews, looking for descriptions of past events in his life," Dr. Gold suggested.

Alice sighed. "I don't think I'd know what to look for," she said innocently.

Dr. Gold smiled acidly. "Well, that's exactly the sort of thing that I *do* know. I should be able to go through them fairly quickly."

"That's an excellent idea," Weil said, nodding emphatically. "We might be looking at this all wrong. We could be seeing a side of the subject that was there all along, but dormant until it found the right trigger." He leaned forward again, hands together on the table, looking at everyone around him. "Okay, we have a plan of action. While Dr. Gold develops a profile of the subject's past history, to see if there's an alternate explanation for this behavior, Dr. Kurz will follow up with the subject directly, building on the level of trust and friendship that she's worked so hard to establish with him." He looked at Chance. "At the same time, I want you and Trick to reexamine your end of things. Trick, I understand your point about one cycle having no effect on later ones, but here again we could be blinded by our own assumptions. Is there something we're missing?" He looked expectantly at Trick, but Trick had no answer.

The discussion was over, and they stood to leave the conference room. Dr. Gold was the first one out. As the rest were heading to the door, Alice turned to Dr. Weil.

"Thank you, Jon," she said.

"Keep your perspective, Alice. I need you at your best." He looked significantly at her.

"There's one more thing I want to do," she said. "I want to go down to Colorado Springs tomorrow morning and talk to Matthius Pin, if he's willing."

Weil and Chance exchanged glances. Trick remained a passive observer. "Matthius's nondisclosure agreement doesn't cover anything that's occurred since the beta trial," Weil said. "You can't discuss this trial with him."

"I know," Alice said. "I won't. I just need to ask him again about his own experience. I never really understood what happened to him and why he reacted as he did. I just want to hear what he thinks about it *now*. He may not want to talk to me, but if he's willing, then I want to know."

"You think what's happening now is related to what happened in the beta trial?" Chance asked. "I don't see how this could be the Matthius reaction."

"I agree," Alice admitted, "but I want to be sure." She looked at them, but they seemed unconvinced. "It's another data point. It might not be relevant, but we need to investigate with due diligence."

Dr. Weil considered it for a few seconds. "No, Alice, I won't risk getting Matthius involved. He's stayed quiet and we've left him alone, *as he insisted*. Review the recording of his exit interview, if you want, but *do not contact him*."

Alice struggled to keep her mouth shut; finally, she nodded and Weil walked out, followed by Chance. Alice looked at Trick, and he held back. "Trick, I need options other than restarting him."

"I know. I've been thinking the same thing for a while." He gave her his trademark tilt of the head, looking right through her, but keeping his conclusions to himself. "There's a way to suspend him while he's asleep. We could keep him suspended as long as we need to, but it wouldn't be a restart when we wake him. As far as he'd know, he went to sleep and woke up later."

He'll still remember me, Alice thought, with great relief. "Thanks, Trick. Let's plan it for tomorrow night, unless we figure this out first." She gathered up her notes, and they walked out together.

• • •

Once Trick realized that the hole had to be in the subject's PC, he found it easily. *How did this get past the design review?* It didn't, Trick realized as soon as he checked the design spec. There was supposed to be a messaging interface to collect the entries from the daily journal onto the server. Dave Addison had deviated from the spec to save time, probably because he'd been behind on his part of the food design. Writing directly to the network drive was easier, but it opened the door to the temp directory, and there was the subject's private log. Clever to make it look like a system file. He read through the log, nodding his head as he followed the subject's progress toward the obvious, if completely wrong, conclusion.

He sat for several minutes, thinking about what to do next. Obviously, he had to have a discussion with Dave about reviewing design changes, but that could wait. The first question was what to say about this to the rest of the team. Alice was finally beginning to realize that she was in love with Eliot. She wouldn't want to restart him again, but what other options did they have? If Trick told anyone how easily they could fix the problem, Weil would insist on fixing it and restarting. The subject would never catch on without his secret log telling him about the previous cycles. The experiment could continue as long as they wanted. *But what then?* Even if Alice gave in to more restarts, she'd never agree to terminate the subject when they were done. *Not if she thinks of him as a person.* Trick couldn't see any way they could free him, but what if Alice could? If she didn't know they could fix the problem — if none of them knew — someone might come up with a more interesting idea.

No one knew yet that Trick had found the problem. If it needed to be revealed, he could find it again later. Or, he could assign his team to review all the environment code. They'd find it eventually, but it might take a while. *What would Alice do in the mean time?* He closed the code browser and edited its history file to remove his tracks from that part of the code.

• • •

Eliot glanced at the monitor when he heard the chimes. The videochat icon flashed, but he didn't answer. Could he simply ignore them? What if he never responded to them, ever again? Wouldn't they have to come in to get him, then? The chimes stopped, but within a few seconds they sounded again. Something was different about the icon. He looked closer; the text underneath now read, "Please answer, Eliot."

He shook his head wearily, but he accepted the call. He watched Alice's eyes as the conference room came into view on his monitor. He was glad that she was alone, but he could tell she was nervous about talking to him.

"Hello, Eliot," she began. She waited, but he said nothing. "It's obvious that something is seriously wrong." He gave no response. "Do you want to talk about it?"

"I think the burden is on *you* to tell me what's going on," he finally said.

"Well, there's been a real change in your attitude

lately," Alice began, and they both knew that was no answer. "Until today, it seemed like you enjoyed engaging with us. With me, in particular." She paused, but he offered no reaction. "Now you seem to be annoyed with us. Frustrated. Angry? Has someone said something that's troubling you?"

Eliot wondered what Alice and the others hoped to gain by continuing the deception. They must know that he was onto them, even if they didn't know how. *They're trying to find out how I know.* It was the only thing that made sense. If they discovered how he was warning himself from one cycle to the next, they'd be able to shut it down and keep him in the dark forever. He could not imagine why they wanted him stuck here indefinitely, but clearly they had no intention of ever setting him free. *They'll keep pressuring me to give away my secret, and sooner or later, in this cycle or the future, I'll crack and tell them about it.*

Unless I give them some other plausible answer.

Eliot was not completely powerless. He had one advantage: because of his private log, he knew things from previous cycles that they'd erased from his mind. Maybe he could convince them that he simply *remembered* those things. Would they eventually give up if they thought that erasing his memories no longer worked?

"What does 'peripatetic' mean, Alice?" he challenged.

Alice kept her face neutral, but Eliot could tell that the question worried her. "It means 'wandering around,'" she answered. "Why do you ask?"

"Well, it's a funny thing," Eliot began. "I've been known to use the phrase 'peripatetic philosophy' to describe a way of talking all around a subject from every angle, wandering off onto whatever paths it leads to. But I've never heard anyone else say it. I don't remember saying it since I've been here, but I definitely remember you quoting it back to me as *if* I'd said it. The thing is, I can't remember *when* you did that. It wasn't any of these last three days, so when could it have been?"

Alice looked puzzled. "I don't recall hearing you say that before. I'm sure I never quoted it back to you. You said you've used that phrase before. Couldn't you be remembering an exchange you had with someone else?"

"But there are lots of little fragments like that," Eliot said. He lifted his eyes as if searching his memory. "Things that I distinctly remember talking about with *you*, sitting here at the computer. Things that aren't part of any day since I've been here, but still happened *sometime*. How could that be?"

"I have no idea, Eliot. Can you think of any other examples?"

"You told me that you envied how 'well-read' I was. I told you that I felt like a 'jack-of-all-trades, master of none.'" He watched her closely. She was doing a good job of hiding it, but he could tell she was rattled. He pressed on. "Yesterday you told me you lost your parents when you were young. Do you remember that conversation?"

"Of course I do."

"You didn't tell me any details about how it happened, but as you were talking I had a sudden memory of you telling me this before, and you said that they drowned in a boating accident." That got a reaction she couldn't hide. "That's what happened, isn't it?"

He saw her hesitate, then decide there was no point in denying it. "Yes. How do you know that?"

"That's what I'm asking *you*, Alice. How do I know that? *You* must have told me, but when? It wasn't yesterday when you first told me that they died and you lived with your grandmother." His face showed surprise at another sudden recollection. "Grandma ... Rose, wasn't it?"

The confusion on her face seemed sincere, forcing Eliot to reconsider what he thought he knew. *She really has no idea how I know these things! Wouldn't she just assume that the memory wipes are failing? Why would it be so startling to her?* For a moment, he wondered again if somehow both their memories were being erased. It would be nice to be able to believe that, but it was impossible that she didn't know.

"Eliot, I don't understand what's happening to you," Alice said. "I can see why this is so troubling, but I can't explain these phantom memories of yours. I know this is going to be hard to accept, but it's possible that the isolation we've imposed on you is having some subtle effects on your perception of reality. It wouldn't be unheard of, but it's certainly unusual in so short an isolation. There have been cases, though, where people in extreme isolation — prisoners in long-term solitary confinement, for example — have invented entire lives outside of their cells. They eliminate the stress of their confinement by escaping into these fantasy lives and living there for all or part of the day. Isn't it possible that you've filled in the boredom and the isolation with false memories of conversations we've never had?" she asked.

"That wouldn't explain how I know about your parents and your grandmother," Eliot insisted. "I couldn't make up something like that and get it right."

"No, of course not," Alice admitted. "But it's possible that you deduced it from bits and pieces of our conversations. Perhaps I said something once about Grandma Rose, and maybe I said that I haven't liked boats ever since my parents died — which is true. Just because I don't *remember* saying it to you doesn't mean it didn't happen. You and I have had a lot of fascinating talks. I think we both feel somewhat … connected. If you figured out how my parents died, you might have *wanted* it to be me who told you, so that's how you remembered it. Confabulations are usually about things that you wish or things that you fear."

She saw that he didn't believe her, so she continued. "I know this doesn't sound right to you, but you have to realize that when the mind invents memories, they seem completely real, even if they're illogical. We see it all the time in dementia cases." He raised an eyebrow. "No, I'm not calling you demented! I'm just saying that when the brain is deprived of the level of stimulation that it expects, sometimes it makes up more interesting memories to compensate."

Eliot wanted to believe her, but the evidence was right before him in his private log. Or was it? If he went to look now, would it still be there? *What if I dreamed up the whole log?* He was suddenly afraid that it wouldn't be there and that the whole thing was a false memory. Would that be worse, or better? And if the log were still there, did it prove that everything really happened the way it was described? He had no physical evidence, just his own words. What if he wrote the log in some kind of isolation-induced fugue state?

Alice saw him struggling to believe her. "Eliot, is there something about all this that you're not telling me?" she asked gently. "Some additional reason that you believe in these memories, even though they conflict with reality?" He felt his face lock down tight, trying to reveal nothing, but he was sure she knew she was close. She probed further, "If it's something embarrassing, you should know that I've studied the human brain and mind for a long time, and there's very little that would shock me. Fantasies are absolutely normal, even the occasional bizarre ones. It would be a whole lot easier to address whatever's happening if I knew all the facts."

Eliot took a deep breath and thought it through. *It all comes down to whether I trust her.* If she were the person he thought she was, and if she liked and respected him as much as she seemed to, then whatever was going on couldn't really be as evil and manipulative as it appeared. Something was wrong with his conclusions. He couldn't figure out what it was, but he could not believe that she was holding him captive and manipulating his memories. *Maybe none of this is real. Maybe my life as a research librarian is the fantasy. Maybe Alice is my psychiatrist who's been trying to bring me back to sanity, and everything else that I think has happened is the confabulation.* He looked at her, and her face showed compassion, empathy, and affection. He might have even said love. Sooner or later, it would all make sense, but he couldn't tell her about the log. If they really were manipulating his memories, the log was his only hope.

"No, Alice, there's nothing else. I'm just very … confused right now."

"Let's make it as simple as possible. Tell me some words … four words, let's say. Whatever comes to your mind, don't think about it. Four words that describe your feelings right now."

"Confused," he said. "Frightened. Desperate." He stared at Alice, trying to believe she was, in some unfathomable way, on his side. "Betrayed," he concluded, and he ended the videochat.

• • •

Alice sat looking at the blank monitor for a few seconds, then turned to the others who had been sitting to the side, out of sight of the camera. They talked about it for twenty minutes, but no one had anything useful to say, so she didn't pay much attention. One thing was clear to all of them: the subject *did* know.

Somehow, he'd figured it out.

Surprisingly, Dr. Gold still wanted to review the past discussions, and he went back to his office to continue. Unable to think of anything else, Alice said she'd review the Matthius recordings, as Weil had suggested. Walking out of the conference room, she found herself beside Trick, while the others continued ahead.

They walked silently, but when Alice felt Trick's eyes on her, she glanced in his direction. He studied her face without breaking stride, saying, "Do you mind if I join you?" She remembered Trick's self-assessment as a *detail observer*, and that's what she needed right now. She had missed something obvious, and Trick was the right one to show it to her. "Thank you," she said.

Trick led her into his office, clearing a path around the racks of test equipment, network switches, and prototypes. "Have a seat," he said, moving a toolbox from the guest chair to the floor. Trick sat behind the desk and Alice pulled her chair next to him. They remained silent as Trick displayed the list of video archives on one of the three monitors atop his desk.

"Here's his initial wakeup after the procedure," Trick said, gesturing to highlight an item early in the list. "The next one is his exit interview. All the rest are Eliot and the Eliot construct."

Alice frowned, thinking about Dr. Gold sitting in his office reviewing the recordings of all her discussions with Eliot and the construct they built from him. "I just realized why Gold agreed so easily to the distraction Jon gave him."

"Yeah," Trick said. "He's looking for evidence that *you* tipped Eliot off. I don't know why, but he sure wants to blame you for *something*." He gestured at the screen, and the first recording began to play.

Matthius lay on the bed, his eyes closed. Alice stood at his side, while two medical technicians attended the health monitors. After a few seconds, Matthius took in a gulp of air and squeezed his eyelids tighter together, as if afraid to look. Watching the scene from Trick's office, Alice realized for the first time that he was afraid. How had she missed that last year?

Matthius finally opened his eyes, his glance darting around the ceiling, then his whole demeanor relaxed. He exhaled loudly and took a long breath, as if he'd just struggled to the surface from deep water. His eyes settled on Alice, who smiled at him and said, "Welcome back, Matthius. How are you feeling?"

Inexplicably, tears flowed down his face. "It's not the blue light," he whispered. "I didn't know. Do you understand? I didn't know until I opened my eyes."

Alice smiled, oblivious to his genuine distress. "No, it's really you. You're just a little groggy from the sedative. I told you it would be disorienting to sleep so long without ever getting to REM state."

Matthius stared at her as if uncertain that she was real. He tried to sit up, and Alice glanced at the med-techs, who rushed to support him. His eyes closed again, and Alice thought he might faint. "Take it slowly," she said. "Relax a little until your balance returns."

"No," he said, clearly agitated now. "Did you wake the construct yet?"

"Of course not. We're still processing the data. It'll be days before we're ready for that." Alice jumped back as Matthius violently swung his legs off the bed and tried to stand in front of her. He spun out of the grip of the med-tech on the far side of the bed, and he almost slipped through the grasp of the other one, but Alice grabbed his free arm, and together they steadied him on his feet. "What's the matter? Are you feeling sick?" She scrutinized the health monitors instead of looking at his face.

"I can't stay here," he said, his eyes looking straight ahead, or perhaps not looking at all.

"Well, let's get a wheelchair if you want to go back to your office," Alice said, and the unoccupied med-tech left to get it.

"No, I can't stay here," Matthius insisted. "At the institute. I can't be here." At this, Dr. Weil strode into the room, followed by the med-tech with the wheelchair.

"Matthius, you need to relax," Alice persisted, trying to ease him back to sitting on the edge of the bed. "You'll feel fine in a few minutes."

"I feel fine right now." He turned to Dr. Weil. "Let me talk to Mr. Thompson. I withdraw my consent to the procedure. I'm opting out of this experiment. You can't wake the construct. I'm exercising my legal rights as the owner … as the guardian of my own intellectual property."

Alice's face lit up with shock and anger, but Weil put a hand on Matthius's shoulder and spoke gently and earnestly, "Okay, Matthius, let's go talk about it." He gestured toward the wheelchair. "Give your legs a chance to wake up a bit on the way." Matthius let them help him into the wheelchair. The med-tech moved out of the way as Dr. Weil stepped behind the chair and rolled Matthius out the door, Alice striding closely behind.

Alice tried to pace around Trick's office, but there was little room to maneuver. "He was a lot more frightened than I remembered," she admitted. "And sad."

She gave up trying to walk, and sat down again. Even with the fear that she hadn't noticed before, it still didn't make sense to her. "Something just snapped in him. I know that the doctors found no brain damage, but that's what it looks like: a stroke, or a psychotic episode, at the very least." She shook her head, frustrated that all the things she worried about back then had already been investigated, turning up nothing.

"Play the next one," she finally said.

The second video was more like a formal deposition. It took place in the large conference room, and it began with Thompson stating the date and time, along with the names of the senior staff, who were all present. "Post-procedure interview with Matthius Pin," he continued.

"Exit interview," Matthius corrected.

The others exchanged glances. "There's no hurry about that, is there?" Weil asked. "Just tell us what's got you so upset, and we'll see where we go from there."

Matthius stared from face to face, looking puzzled. "What's got me upset?" He pointed in the direction of the lab. "I thought he didn't matter — just like the rest of you. But that's me in there. Do you understand? I'm resting right now, dormant, but you're going to wake me up and tell me, 'Congratulations, it worked!' Then you'll be free to kill me when I'm no longer useful."

Alice couldn't keep quiet. "Of course it's not you, Matthius, it's a construct created from your connectome — the neural map recorded by the nanocells."

"I know what the connectome is, Alice."

"And you also know that nobody's trying to kill you. What do you think is happening here? That we're trying to replace you with the construct? That's absurd!"

"Alice, stop," Weil said, surprising everyone with the force of his command. "We're not here to argue, we're here to understand. Let the man speak."

There was silence for several seconds while Matthius sat with his head lowered, his eyes distant. Finally, he spoke. "I won't be able to make you understand. I see that now. The logic behind your research is impenetrable." He sighed, raised his head and stared right at Dr. Weil. "I resign from this institute, effective immediately."

"Mr. Pin, you made remarks to Dr. Weil about rescinding your consent to this procedure," Thompson began delicately.

Matthius looked at Thompson and shook his head wearily. "You're here to tell me that's not possible."

Thompson cleared his throat and glanced at Alice and Dr. Weil. "You are, of course, free to consult your own attorney, but I don't believe you have any basis on which to challenge the contract you signed — a contract that you signed in full awareness of what would happen. You've been working with the project team for over two months. You knew the details, and you were eager to undergo the experiment. Besides," he looked around the table, "what's the point now? You've already been through the procedure."

"I've been through it, Mr. Thompson, but I haven't," Matthius pointed toward the lab again. "You don't have my permission to put me through it again, with the blue light this time!"

"But we do have your permission," Thompson said. "It's here on this contract that you signed. I'm sorry that you've changed your mind, but …"

"Changed my mind! Yes, it's been changed all right. It used to be mine, along with my soul. Now they're in there."

"Matthius, listen to yourself," Alice interrupted. "We've spent millions of dollars to finally obtain an accurate working model of a complete human brain, and you're telling us we can't make use of it because a medical scan stole your soul? Thousands of people — millions, maybe — can be saved by what we learn from this. You can't just take your toys and go home! This is my life's work, damn you!"

"Dr. Kurz, I'm afraid I must ask you to leave the room," Thompson said. "You are not contributing to an amicable resolution of the situation."

Alice exploded to her feet, turning on Dr. Weil. "Jon, this is insanity," she said, pointing directly at Matthius. "We'll lose years of work if you listen to this nonsense."

Weil stood and took her arm, leading her aside from the table. She thought he wanted to speak privately to her, but he led her to the door. "Alice, let Thompson talk to Matthius. You're making it worse. I'll speak with you later." There was nothing subtle about the way he moved her out of the room, closing the door behind her.

Watching the video, Alice still felt some of the outrage she'd felt then, but here was the part she'd never seen before, and she wondered if it would explain anything to her. She watched Weil sit back down, as Thompson asked Matthius to state, as cogently as possible, exactly what he wanted from the institute. It was disappointing; Matthius did not explain himself any further.

"I want nothing more to do with this," he said. "You've made a tragic mistake, but I see now that you won't understand, and trying to stop you will cost me more than I can afford. What do I want? I want to know that I'll never wake up in the blue light. Give me that, and I'll leave you alone. I'll make no trouble, and I'll never speak of this again, to you or anyone else."

The rest of the meeting was just paperwork, and Alice knew how it went from there: weeks of investigation that included medical, psychological, and psychiatric evaluations. They ruled out any lingering effects of the nanocells — they'd accomplished their function and dissipated, as designed. The institute offered payment for ongoing medical treatment and psychiatric therapy, but Matthius insisted the problem was "spiritual, not psychological," and he refused further treatment. A financial settlement was given to him, and they had no more interaction. The construct was built and validated, but it was never activated.

It took six months to resume the project, and before that, the board of directors brought in Dr. Gold to advise. They redesigned the experiment around the isolation protocols that he developed, so that the subject would remain unaware of his situation. They all agreed that must have been the source of the problem.

When Alice looked away from the monitor, she realized that Trick was studying her. She wasn't proud of the anger she'd shown on the video, and it made her defensive. "You see what I see, don't you, Trick? Stealing his soul? Making him wake up in the blue light? He couldn't separate himself from the construct, as if waking it would somehow make them switch places, and he'd be trapped in the lab."

Trick said nothing, still watching.

"If only Thompson hadn't caved in so easily. And Jon! I still can't believe he agreed to throw it all away! All that work! If they'd just held out until Matthius calmed down, we'd be a year further along by now. Look at all the progress we've made with Eliot's construct. This is where we could have been a year ago."

"With a working model of a human brain that believes he's trapped in the lab," Trick said quietly.

Alice scowled at Trick. "Well, I was wrong about the connection with Matthius," she said. "Eliot's construct has no idea that it's not real. Dr. Gold's famous isolation protocols fixed that. Whatever his problem is, it's not because he knows he's a simulation. But that leaves us right where we were. What *is* going on with him?"

"Perhaps Matthius still has more to tell you," Trick suggested.

"Well, you heard Jon; I can't go down there and talk to him."

"You don't have to go anywhere to talk to him. You can talk to him just as he wakes up from the procedure, while it's fresh in his mind."

It took several seconds for Alice to understand what

he meant. "The institute signed off on Matthius's settlement," she said. "We can't wake his construct."

"We agreed not to wake him *in the blue light*," Trick said.

Alice stared at him, dumbfounded. What did the blue light matter? That was just to compensate for the gaps in their vision model. They could simulate the visual inputs to the construct, but they didn't know how those inputs corresponded to the subject's individual *experience* of color. That was the reason they started with blue light and color dials, so that the construct would tune his own simulation parameters until the colors appeared normal. Since Eliot couldn't know about the simulation, they told him the lie about his eyes being sensitive after the sedative.

"Matthius knew that the construct in the simulation would wake to blue light," Trick explained. "But the auto-calibration now works. I patched it into Matthius's environment simulation, and I tested it just before Eliot arrived. Without the blue light, Matthius will believe he's awakened on our side of the world."

Alice narrowed her eyes at Trick, who gazed silently back. "When you said you tested this before Eliot arrived ..."

"There was only one way to test it. I talked to the Matthius construct. He didn't know he was the simulation."

"But if he wakes up alone, of course he'll know."

"No, we just have to tell him that we woke him early so we can talk privately — by videochat — before anyone else knows he's awake. He'll be calmer than the real Matthius was."

Alice rested her elbows on her knees and dropped her head into her palms. She knew they were violating Matthius's wishes, even if they could skirt around the wording of the contract. But Matthius would never know. Even his construct would never know. If she could actually find out something useful, something that might salvage the situation with Eliot's construct ... "Why is he calmer in the simulation than he was in the real world?"

"I adjusted the simulation so that the sedative wears off more slowly."

Alice struggled with the decision, but Trick was already setting up the Matthius construct and the environment simulation. He launched the videochat software, calling the virtual computer that was connected to the simulation, configuring it to automatically answer at the remote end.

"I'm a year older than he remembers me; he'll know it's not real," Alice warned.

"He won't notice. He has other things on his mind." Before Alice could voice any more objections, the videochat was live. They could see the open doorway into the bedroom, but the bed was not in view. Another monitor displayed the health metrics from the restarting construct. When it showed that he was awake, Trick spoke gently, but clearly, "Hello, Matthius, how are you feeling?"

They heard nothing for a few seconds, then the sound of the bedsprings creaking. A moment later they heard his feet touch the floor. "We're on the videochat, Matthius. Alice and I wanted to talk to you privately before anyone else knows you're awake."

After a minute, they saw Matthius stagger into the doorway, holding onto the wall, looking slightly dizzy. Even after all the time she'd spent talking to the Eliot construct, it still left her breathless to see Matthius this way. The computer-generated image of his body, synchronized perfectly to the construct's own self-image, would convince anyone that there was a real person at the other end of the videochat.

Matthius slowly approached the computer station and sat down. He looked into the camera, seeing their images displayed on the simulated monitor at his end. "You knew, didn't you Trick?" he said, ignoring Alice for the moment. "You knew how I would feel."

"No, I only know how *I* would feel. It's … unsettling, isn't it?"

Matthius barked a laugh. "Unsettling. Depressing. Terrifying." He struggled to find words adequate to what he felt.

"Terrifying?" Trick questioned. "Why?"

Matthius gathered his thoughts. "I never thought of the construct as *real*, you know." He looked up and saw Alice's intent gaze. "You, too, I think, but for different reasons. For me, it was really quite simple. It didn't have a *soul*, so it didn't matter what we did to it. Without a soul, it couldn't be a real person. But you don't believe in souls, do you, Alice?"

"No." She didn't want to say anything else, for fear of dissuading him from saying more.

Matthius nodded. "But you believe in *minds*, of course. And you knew that the construct had a mind. That was the whole point. So I don't understand why it doesn't affect all of you the same way." He looked at them for a few seconds, then shook his head. "But you didn't have the experience I've just had, waking up like this. Maybe that's what it takes to understand." He stopped talking, his eyes still staring straight ahead, but clearly seeing something else entirely.

Alice waited, aware of how little time they had before the simulated tranquilizer fully wore off. Finally, she spoke. "What happened when you woke up, Matthius?"

"I was awake before I opened my eyes." He looked at her again. "That's unusual, isn't it? Don't you open your eyes as soon as you wake? But I didn't just now, and I noticed that I didn't. I was afraid to open my eyes. I suddenly knew that I was *terrified* to open my eyes. What if *I* were the one waking up in the blue light? What if *I* were the soulless construct? And I knew then, instantly, that *there was no way to tell*. I could be *me*, or I could be *it*. And the fact that I was dreading to know showed me that I was wrong about its soul. We'd both feel the same dread, and whatever is in me that makes me who I am is also in it."

His hands were trembling now. He leaned back in the desk chair, rocking slightly, clearly agitated. Alice was afraid to hear what he'd say next, and even more afraid that he wouldn't say any more. There was a nausea growing inside her, like a suppressed horror about to crawl to the surface.

"When I opened my eyes and saw that there was no blue light, I felt such relief — at first. Then came the despair, knowing that *he* — my other self — will wake up in the blue light. He'll know at once that he has no future and only a borrowed past. He's there to be experimented on until he isn't useful any more, and then he'll be discarded. But whatever soul I have, he has, too, and what you do to him will be torture and murder."

"No," Alice interrupted, recoiling from his words. "That's not fair. We aren't hurting anyone. We'll save lives with this. People who would otherwise lose the entire world — we can give them a lifeline."

Matthius watched her, nodding. "I know what you're trying to accomplish, and you have noble goals, Alice. I thought it was worthwhile, too, until this morning. All my life, I've been taught that the mind and the soul are not the same thing. Your mind changes throughout life as you learn, grow, and experience beauty and horror, joy and betrayal, hope and fear. Sometimes the mind suffers terrible damage and never recovers. But even the insane, the emotionally crippled, the comatose — their souls are supposed to remain the immortal and unchanging essence of the individual, the ineffable *spirit* unique to each person."

He paused, lost in his own thoughts for a minute. He looked up at them again and continued. "But that must be wrong. Surely, if the soul exists, it has to be the seat of choice from which we make the decisions that take us down the path of our lives. Why else do we talk about the soul being judged for its choices after the death of the body? It must encompass the knowledge and wisdom we gain through our experience, or how does it make any sense to say that it is our *self*? That means it *must* change; it must evolve with our experiences and the lessons we make of them. If there is an afterlife in which my soul endures, how can it be *me* if it has not acquired my thoughts, my feelings, and my memories? What part of my soul is different from my *mind*? What part of it is eternal and unchanging? Is my soul nothing more than a heavenly *serial number*? A cosmic *accounting ticket* for my trip through earthly life?" He stopped to catch his breath. "No, the soul only makes sense if the mind and the soul are the same thing."

Matthius paused again and looked at Alice. She trembled slightly, and she knew he could see it. "Do you remember all of those alpha tests before you developed the body and environment simulations?" he asked her. "You told me that you brought in seven people and scanned them, then sent them home unaware of the constructs they left behind. But what did you do with those constructs? You let them cycle without any sensory inputs, so you could watch the neural activity on your monitors. You told yourselves, '*Look, this is exactly like the activity we see in a real brain. There's definitely cognitive process-*

ing going on.' Didn't you ever ask yourselves *what* those simulated minds thought? What kind of confusion they must have experienced? The real subjects came in so that you could take measurements of their brains, then send them home, just as you told them. They left unaltered and unaware, but the constructs didn't know that. They thought they *were* those persons. They woke up in darkness and silence, disconnected from the world, insubstantial as ghosts. They must have been terrified that something had gone wrong; that they were in a coma; that they were dead. Why didn't you ever think about how they would *feel?*"

Alice stared at his image, unable to form words. With a gesture toward the screen, Trick shut down the simulation, and Alice felt tears roll down her cheeks.

Rats' Alley

They never serve you more than a beer and a couple of shots in the same night, Owen lamented. It was damned inconvenient to have to walk around the corner and across the street to the Drunken Parrot, when he had been perfectly comfortable in Scovee's Bar for the last couple hours. He didn't like the Parrot much, anyway. Too many yuppie twits yammering away on their cell phones or texting each other. All those smart-ass pretty boys and their uptight girlfriends wrinkling their noses at him as he walked past, making cracks behind his back that he never quite caught, but he knew they were disrespectful. *Young punks think they own the world.*

Sure enough, as soon as he walked in the door he saw a group of them standing around by the bar. The only free stool was just a few feet away from them. The dark-haired one in the suit was loudly going on about some damn thing he had no idea about. *Just quoting back what the morons on the television told him. The Parrot's obviously the right place for him.* The gang around him laughed on cue, obviously kissing his ass because he had the most money or acted like it, at least. *Little snot-nosed brat probably never worked a real job in his life. Buying and selling other people's money, just like all the others that shit up the economy for the rest of us.*

He stopped in the doorway, remembering to put a stick of spearmint gum in his mouth to hide the alcohol on his breath. The bartenders were too busy to pay much attention, but he didn't want to be refused service and give those assholes another reason to laugh at him. Tucking in his shirt, he hitched up his pants, smoothed what was left of his hair, and pulled his Broncos cap down to a respectable *don't-fuck-with-me* angle. As he walked toward the bar, he noticed a small empty table in the corner to his left, and he changed his mind about the stool. He walked to the corner of the bar farthest away from the laughing yuppies.

"Two Jack Daniels and a rum-and-Coke", he said, nodding to the bartender and then waving over his shoulder to his imaginary companions at the table. The bartender glanced at him and began filling the drink order. He set the drinks on a small tray and quoted the price. Owen didn't hear or couldn't remember what he said, so he just slapped down three fives, said "Thanks," and carried the tray back to the empty table. There was no commotion, so it must have been enough.

He sat with his back to the bar. Now there was no one he had to look at, but out of the corner of his eye, he could see a pretty black girl in profile. She was laughing and talking to someone he couldn't see. She had long legs stretching out from a short skirt and one of those stretchy tops that girls wore so men will stare at their tits; then they act all insulted when you do. *No thanks. I'll do just fine with my three friends here.* He polished off the first Jack Daniels and picked up the second, savoring the smell. The buzz he'd started at Scovee's had kicked in, but he was pretty confident he could get a little more comfortable. The waitress hadn't seen him at the bar, so he put the tray with the empty shot glasses on the seat beside him and started on the rum and Coke. *Terrible thing to do to a good shot of rum,* he thought, but they didn't pay as much attention to it this way.

From a table somewhere behind him, he overheard a group of drunken young idiots laughing and talking. At one point, the whole table erupted in raucous laughter and whistles. Owen wondered what would happen if he walked over and smashed their beers in their faces. *More trouble than I need right now,* he decided.

When he was down to the last finger of his drink, he caught the attention of the waitress and asked for another. "Can you make it a double?" he asked. She glanced at him, said "Sure," and went off. He finished the drink and waited for its replacement.

When he finished the next drink Owen knew he couldn't afford another. He'd have to head home now, even though it meant having to face his wife. *The bitch will nag even more than usual, but it's a lot easier to ignore her when I'm hammered.* He put the tray with the two shot glasses back on the table, dropped the rest of his cash on it, and headed slowly out the door. He walked out, feeling the best he'd felt all day, not even getting upset when some asshole bumped right into him on the sidewalk. He heard something muttered behind him that sounded like "stupid drunk," so someone must have seen that guy walk into him.

He made it to the corner and looked for his car, but there was no red Explorer anywhere in sight. Confused, he stopped and looked around. He always parked on this corner one block from Scovee's. Where the hell was the car? He checked again to make sure he hadn't just missed it, but it definitely wasn't there. Wondering if he'd turned the wrong way out of Scovee's, he looked back the way he'd come, but Scovee's wasn't there. It was one of those stupid yuppie places, the Flapping Parrot or some such crap. He walked back that direction, then crossed the street, flipping off the dumb-ass driver that almost ran him over.

There, around the corner, was Scovee's, and around the next corner was his car, just where he always parked. *You're never too drunk to drive if you can find the car,* he'd said more than once. He didn't say it to that jerk of a judge who took his license away, though. They never had any sense of humor. He fumbled with the keys for several minutes, then got in, sat down, and gave a good belch. Frowning, he hitched his butt up off the seat and let out a long fart. *Should have done that before getting in the car,* he thought a moment later. He rolled down the window and pulled away from the curb.

No problem getting home, he thought. *The car knows the way by itself.* He took the side streets to avoid the traffic, until he got on Cunningham, where he had the right of way. All the cross streets had stop signs, so he could just sail right through. *Damn, I really need to piss now.* He stepped down a little harder on the accelerator. *No traffic this time of night, and they've got to stop for me, anyway. What the fuck was that? Looked like a stop sign. There's no stop signs on Cunningham. Isn't this Cunningham? Shit, there's another one. What the ...?*

The white car passed through the intersection directly in front of him as he flew through the stop sign. He saw a huge fireworks display while the roller coaster twisted and spun him around, then he was rolling in the surf on the beach as the waves crashed all around him. He fell down a deep well, and the lights went out right before he hit the bottom.

• • •

Officer Lauren Jackson was first on the scene, and she knew immediately that it was going to be bad. The Honda Civic was split right in two, folded past ninety degrees. There was no way the driver would be alive.

The Explorer had hit it with so much force that the two cars slid all the way out of the intersection and spun half way around, still fused together. The driver of the Explorer must have blown right through the last three stop signs to be going so fast. She called in the details while she placed warning flares at each end of the mess. Fortunately, there wasn't much traffic here this time of night, but that hadn't helped the driver of the Civic.

She could hear the siren of the paramedics now, and the fire truck wouldn't be far behind. If, miraculously, the driver of the Civic still lived, that's where the most help would be needed, so she checked there first. It was every bit as bad as she feared. The driver was crushed in the folded V of the wreckage, well past dead. A young man, white, blond hair, probably early thirties. Never saw it coming, for sure. Just full of life one second, and gone forever the next. *What a damn waste.* Fortunately, no one else was in the car.

Now what about the moron who caused the whole thing? She hurried over to the Explorer. He was an older man, also white. Balding, probably early fifties. The window was rolled down, so she reached in and felt his neck. He was out cold, but there was a pulse. No visible injuries beyond those inflicted by the shoulder belt and air bag. She called out to him, but there was no response. She looked up as the paramedics arrived on the scene. "Over here," she called. "There's no one alive in the other one." She stepped back to let them do their job as she called in the new information.

Officer Jackson went back to the intersection to direct the fire truck and anyone else who might drive by. She got a call back on her shoulder radio. "We've got IDs on those plates," the dispatcher said.

"Go ahead," Lauren replied, pulling out her pad to copy down the information.

"The Explorer is registered to Owen Reginald Mer-ckel, white, age 46. Gray hair — what's left of it. Brown eyes."

"Yeah, that looks like him," Lauren said.

"His license is currently suspended for DUI," the dispatcher told her.

"Ah, hell," Lauren said. "That did a lot of good, didn't it? What about the Civic?"

"Registered to Eliot Thomas Stearns, white, blond hair, 32 years old."

• • •

Alice spent most of the night lying awake in bed. The few minutes of sleep she found were desert islands in an endless sea of fear and regret. Fleeing the institute after Matthius's revelations, arriving home early for the first time in seven years, she thought she'd have it all figured out by the next morning. She was wrong. The critical question was what to do about Eliot and the construct they had created from him. The first step was self-evident: she had to tell them everything. They had a right to know — both of them. They had a right to *choose.*

She knew it would cost her. She might not be able to convince Weil and the board, and she'd have to violate the protocols and reveal the truth anyway. Then, most likely, she'd have to resign. But how would she be able to protect the construct if she left the project? Would Eliot sue for its rights? Would he accept her help? What really worried her was the fear that both of them would hate her for what she'd done. *I was so happy every time we started to get close again.*

Some time after 5:00 AM, Alice gave up the bed and took a long, hot shower. Her mind felt clear, but she still had no plan. While she dressed, she turned on the six o'clock news, as she always did. She heard none of it, until suddenly her entire consciousness snapped to attention when she saw a photo of Eliot appear on the television, and the voice-over said, "Mesa Vista police have now identified the victim of last night's fatal collision as Eliot Stearns, a 32-year-old research librarian." She was sitting on the edge of the bed before she knew how she'd gotten there. They showed a picture of the wreck, taken from a discreet distance, police and paramedics on all sides. She listened to the rest of the report, hoping they'd repeat the name and this time it would be someone else, but that didn't happen. She sat still, absorbing the shock, until finally she realized they had already moved on to the latest sports news. Eliot was dead. *They'll shut him down now. They'll stop the project.* It was over. She'd lost him again. This time, she'd lost him forever.

She reached for her phone. There were no messages, so the others hadn't heard yet. She started to call Dr. Weil, but she stopped herself in time. She called Trick's personal number, agonizing over every ring that wasn't answered. Finally, he picked up.

"Alice," she heard Trick's voice. "I thought you might call. I'm already in. Are you on your way?"

She didn't waste any time. "You have to suspend him, Trick. You have to do it now. You can't let them shut him down."

"Alice, ..."

"Listen to me, Trick. Eliot's dead. There was a car accident. You have to keep *our* Eliot alive. Don't let them kill *him*, too! Suspend him now! We have to explain it all to him. Now, while he knows us. While he knows *me*. I won't be able to explain it to him if he's a stranger again. We can't restart him any more. We can't let them shut him down, or they'll never let him live at all! You can't let them kill him again!" She realized she was shouting. *I sound hysterical. He won't listen to me like this.*

Trick listened. "Alice, he's already awake. I can't suspend him until he's asleep. We have to leave him running until then. How soon can you get in?"

She stepped into her shoes, grabbed her purse, and ran out the door. "I'll be there in half an hour," she told him. "Talk to Weil about it as soon as he gets in, before he finds out, if he hasn't already. Tell him we need to suspend him until we decide what to do. Don't mention the accident. Pretend you haven't heard."

"Alice, after you left yesterday, I told Weil and Gold that we could suspend him tonight, so that we'd have as much time as we need to figure out what to do about his attitude. No one else is in yet, and as far as I know, nobody's heard about the accident. You're sure he's … ?"

"Yes, it was him. It happened last night." She was in the car. She switched the phone to speaker and dropped it on the seat next to her. She started the car and pulled into the street. "Did they agree to suspend him?"

"Yeah, Weil was relieved to find out that we could do that," Trick said. She could hear his fingers clacking on a keyboard, and she knew that he was looking up the news report. She heard him take a deep breath. "Alice, there's a picture of the cars. It was a horrible crash. This must be all over the news. They'll know any minute, if they don't already."

"You have to convince them to stick with the plan," Alice pleaded. "They'll want to pull the plug right now. Don't let them do it, Trick."

Trick was silent for a few seconds, and Alice knew that he was playing out all the scenarios he could imagine, even as she tried to do the same thing. Trick beat her to the conclusion. "Weil won't do it until he gets the order from the board. That will take time. Suspending him will still be Weil's choice, but not for long."

"If Dr. Gold talks to him, Eliot will know

something's wrong."

"He already knows something's wrong," Trick reminded her. "I can convince Gold to keep clear of him this morning. I'll hang around the conference room and answer if Eliot calls."

In the back of her mind, Alice noticed both of them calling him Eliot. He wasn't *the subject* or *the construct* any more. Not to her. Not to Trick. She knew what she had to do.

• • •

Alice arrived at the institute before Dr. Weil. She passed his empty office on the way to hers, then stopped in the doorway. A newspaper lay on her desk, the picture of Eliot's mangled car staring up at her. She heard steps behind her and turned to see Trick looking from the desk to her face.

"Dr. Gold stopped by your office about two minutes ago," Trick said. "He left that for you."

She walked in, dropped her jacket on the guest chair and her briefcase and purse on the desk, then turned back to Trick. "Did you speak with him?"

"He showed me the paper, asked if I knew about this. I told him that you and I talked about it, and that you'd be in soon. He dropped it on your desk and left."

She glanced at the newspaper, but didn't touch it. "Did you read the article?" she asked.

Trick nodded. "I've also checked the online articles. There's no mention of us anywhere."

Alice scowled at Trick. "That's not what matters now," she snapped.

Trick was unfazed. "I know, but that's what Dr. Weil will ask."

She closed her eyes, nodding. "Yes. Sorry. Thanks." He stood calmly watching as she slowly paced around her office.

"Do you have a plan?" he asked.

"A goal, anyway," she answered. "Not quite a plan yet."

Trick sat in the guest chair, ignoring the jacket she'd put there. "Well, what's the goal?"

"We break Eliot out of the glass bottle."

"And do what? Put him in a nicer bottle?"

"Yes." She looked at Trick, wondering if anything she said would surprise him. "A bottle built for two."

Trick contemplated in silence for several seconds. "Let's keep this to ourselves for a little while," he suggested. "Make it the board's decision, not Weil's."

Dr. Weil arrived minutes later. Alice had never seen him so agitated. He immediately gathered Trick, Alice, and Gold in the staff conference room, holding another copy of the newspaper. "Has everyone seen this?" he asked, and there were nods around the room. Chance walked in, looking as though in shock, and a few minutes later the attorney, Thompson, joined them.

Weil looked around the table and demanded, "Are we mentioned in any of the news accounts?"

"No," Alice answered. "We've checked. And there's no reason we should be. Has the board been notified of Eliot's death?"

Weil nodded dismissively, "Yes, but no one wants to make any decisions until everyone else is on the hook, too. They're scheduling an emergency board meeting, but it will probably be three or four days before they can all get here at the same time."

Good, thought Alice. There was still time to figure it out. "Some of you may not be aware that Trick has developed a process for suspending the subject indefinitely," she said. Ray Chance shot an uncomfortable look at Trick, clearly wondering why he hadn't heard of this, while Alice continued. "As I understand it, we need to do it when he's asleep, and we can keep him suspended until the board decides what to do next."

"Right," Trick said. "If we decide to activate him again, he'll just wake up as usual — in the same cycle, not a restart."

Dr. Gold gave a nasty laugh. "I'm fairly certain that he won't be waking again."

Thompson agreed. "If it were ever disclosed that we're playing around with a dead man's brain …"

"Nevertheless, the construct represents a very valuable asset," Alice pointed out. "The board of investors will expect us to preserve all of the project's assets until they make their decision."

Weil nodded emphatically, happy to have something to do that seemed prudent and dutiful. "Absolutely right, Alice. Our entire focus now should be on gathering together every bit of documentation, all our notes, test results. Alice, you'll prepare project summaries for the board meeting?"

"Of course," she answered. "But we still have to deal with …"

"The subject," Trick interrupted, "until he falls asleep."

Dr. Gold appeared to have a bad taste in his mouth. "And how shall we keep him *entertained* all day long?"

"Fortunately, he's reached the rebellious part of the cycle," Trick said. "He's lying awake at night and cat-napping during the day. He'll probably sleep for an hour before lunch."

"Good," Dr. Weil said. "Suspend him at the first opportunity. In the mean time, minimize your interactions with him."

"Keep track of any interactions you *do* have," Alice said. "It will have to seem like the same day when we wake him later." She ignored Gold's undisguised scorn.

The Awful Daring

The awful daring of a moment's surrender
Which an age of prudence can never retract
By this, and this only, we have existed
—T.S. Eliot, The Waste Land

Alice drove around the block three times, debating with herself. Now that she was at the church, she hesitated to go any farther. Without consulting her, the decision made itself, and she parked the car. She glanced at herself in the rear-view mirror. She certainly looked somber enough — maybe too much. She couldn't very well acknowledge more than a casual acquaintance with Eliot. Even then, it was bound to draw attention for her to be there, but there was a small possibility that Eliot would have mentioned her to someone, and then it might seem odd if she weren't there.

She locked the car behind her and walked slowly across the street toward the church. *Weil will be furious if I go in there. The board meeting's tomorrow, and he wants to be done with it all.* She climbed the steps to the entrance. A man in a dark suit stood by the open door. He shook her hand, gestured toward the guest log book, and said something to her, but his words didn't register.

She ignored the guest log, but picked up a program from the pile next to it, so that she'd have something to look at if she needed to disappear into the background. She glanced around, afraid to meet anyone's eyes, but most people were already seated; she was almost late for the service. A young couple stood in the back of the foyer, talking softly. They both seemed to be in shock. The woman was crying lightly, and the man didn't seem to know how to comfort her. *Not a couple. Friends. Eliot's friends.* She walked past them, and they glanced up at her. She nodded, but no one spoke. She walked toward the pews, feeling that they must be asking each other who she was.

The funeral was modestly attended. Only the first few rows were occupied. She realized it would look strange if she sat all the way in the back, so she started a new row, sitting at the left end. She glanced to her right and saw an elderly woman in the row ahead, gray hair adorning a well-lined face that seemed carved for smiling. Unexpectedly, the woman turned her head and looked at Alice. She gazed appraisingly, then gave a slight, involuntary nod, as if recognizing her. Alice remained frozen, feeling both out of place and unaccountably welcomed. She looked at the front row, and her heart broke in half. The woman sitting there was sobbing in the arms of her husband, both dressed in black: Eliot's parents, all the way from England to bury their son. *He never even got to see their retirement home.*

The first funeral splashed across her memory like a tidal wave. She was barely thirteen, her ten-year-old sister crying in her grandmother's arms. Two coffins. She couldn't cry, and that made her feel guilty. *Didn't I love them enough? Why can't I cry like Rachel? Even Grandma's crying.* Grandma Rose sat between the two girls, holding them both, but her attention was mostly on consoling Rachel. Alice felt strangely defensive about that, which only added to her sense of guilt. *I can take care of Rachel.*

That's my *job now.*

Eliot's service started. Alice didn't listen to what the minister said, but certain phrases penetrated her awareness. *Brilliant young man … prime of his life … innocent victim … greatly missed.* She realized she was crying this time, and it filled her with confusion. *Why now and not then?* She fished some tissues out of her purse, and as she wiped her eyes, she noticed the two friends she'd seen earlier sitting in her row, just on the other side of the aisle. The woman was looking at her with an expression that Alice could not decipher. She turned her attention back to the front, pretending to listen to the service. She felt her face flush with embarrassment. *What will Eliot's friends make of this strange woman crying?*

When it was over, Alice remained seated as the grieving parents were escorted down the aisle and out into the reception area. As the rows ahead of her emptied, she sat still, unsure what to do next. Would they expect everyone to pass by the parents and offer words of condolence? She couldn't do it. She couldn't face them, knowing what she knew. Whatever she said to them would be cowardly and wrong. She decided to wait where she was for a little while, then leave quietly without attracting any more attention than she already had. She stared straight ahead, but out of the corner of her eye, she saw the gray-haired woman she'd noticed earlier coming toward her down the left side aisle. She looked at Alice and stopped just long enough to take her hand and say, "Thank you for coming, Dear. I'm so very sorry for your loss." She smiled sympathetically, grasped her hand, and before Alice could think of anything to say, she was gone. *She must have mistaken me for some relative of Eliot's,* Alice thought.

Now the pair from across the aisle walked down the row toward her, the woman leading. When they reached

Alice, the woman sat next to her, while the man re-mained standing, fidgeting awkwardly. Alice looked at the woman beside her and saw an affectionate smile behind teary eyes. Her own tears started to flow again as she returned the smile. "I'm Ann Simons," the woman introduced herself. "This is Terry Anderson. We both worked with Eliot at the library. We were really good friends of his."

"Alice Kurz," Alice said. She started to hold out her hand, but Ann embraced her, and they hugged like old friends. Alice had no idea what to say, but Ann didn't wait for her to say anything.

"We thought you must be Alice. Eliot told us a bit about you."

"Actually, it was hard to get him to *stop* talking about you," Terry said, smiling. But a glance from Ann apparently made him fear he'd crossed a boundary, and his smile went away.

Alice laughed, and the tension disappeared. "I think it was nearly impossible to get Eliot to stop talking about *anything*," she said. But I did so enjoy listening to him."

"He said you were the most interesting person he'd ever met," Ann told her. She studied Alice's face, trying to see in her what her friend had seen. "He really want-ed to date you, you know."

Alice teared up again, and now it was Ann's turn to worry that she'd said too much.

"You know how we met?" Alice asked. "At the insti-tute where I work?"

Ann and Terry both nodded.

"We talked so much while he was there. And we carried on quite an email conversation after he left. He asked me to go out with him more than once, but I was so busy with work, and I worried that it wouldn't be professional of me to get … involved with one of our test subjects. It was so stupid of me. I wish I'd said yes. I should have told him how I … I wish it had turned out differently."

Ann hugged her again, and Alice returned it tightly. "We all do," Ann said.

Terry became more nervous, clearly trying to find words to say. He was facing the two women, backed up against the pew in front of them. "The thing is," he began. "It was kind of … my fault. It wouldn't have happened if I'd been there that day."

"Terry, it's *not* your fault. It was a random event," Ann responded with some frustration. Clearly, they'd had this conversation before. "The only one at fault was the drunk driver."

Terry still felt the need to confess. "It was the annual inventory, and they were short-handed — because of me. Before they announced when the inventory was going to happen, I guessed when they'd schedule it. I deliberately signed up for furlough days right in the middle of it. I was kind of angry they were making us take the furloughs, so I was … I don't know, getting back at them. I mean, the inventory is a real pain. It always runs late into the night, and I thought I was being clever by using what they did to us against them. But Jack Parker was on vacation then, so they were short two people. They stayed hours later than usual that night. If I'd been there, Eliot would have been home long before that damned idiot came roaring through the stop sign."

Alice sighed. People hated randomness, especially surrounding a tragedy. They always looked for reasons, and reasons inevitably boiled down to responsibility and blame. Someone had to be accountable. It was too terrifying to think that something so awful could happen at any time to anyone, and there was nothing we could do about it.

"My grandmother used to say 'Man plans and God laughs,'" Alice said. "Terry, if one decision of yours could have such unforeseen consequences, then surely the millions of decisions made by everyone else that day were just as much to blame. The web of connections is too tight to unravel."

Terry and Ann looked at her, and she could see some of Terry's anguish dissipate. Ann nodded to her. "Eliot was a good judge of people," she said.

• • •

Weil was furious with her. He marched around his office, while she sat placidly in front of his desk. "How could you bring attention to us like that? Do you want Eliot's family and friends to start wondering what happened to him while he was here? You had no right to insert us into this personal tragedy."

"I didn't have a choice, Jon." She said it with undeniable conviction. "We have a responsibility to him, and this was my only chance to understand him in his own context."

"We do *not* have any responsibility here, Alice." Weil paced around his office, hot with anger and frustration. *The last thing I need now is for Alice to lose it just when I need her most.* "Eliot left here months ago. His death had *nothing* to do with us. We were a forgotten anecdote in his life. Now we've become a lingering connection to his death. You may have destroyed us!"

"You're wrong, Jon. We have the heaviest of all responsibilities." She waved her hand to stop him interrupting her. "I don't mean responsibility for his *death*. I mean responsibility for his *life*. Eliot is dead, but we have a … a lifeboat. We can still rescue him."

Weil was shocked. "Absolutely not, Alice. How can you even think such a thing? I'm meeting with the board tomorrow. You know what they'll say. The experiment is over. The subject will be deleted. With luck, we'll be able to continue to analyze the data we've already gathered. With *unbelievable* luck they'll be open to trying again in a year or so, but I won't be surprised if they demand that we seal all our records and end this line of investigation permanently."

"You mentioned Eliot's family and friends. What would they say if they knew about the subject? If he were your son, what would you give to be able to talk to him again?"

"You can't talk to a dead man!"

"His mind still lives."

"The board will never see it that way."

"Then I'll *make* them see it. Let me address the board. I know what path we have to take. I know how to salvage everything that's left. I'm willing to do it."

"What could you possibly salvage from this disaster?"

She told him. They argued for another hour, then she left to prepare her speech to the board. Jonathan Weil sat in his office, holding his head in his hands.

• • •

There were eight members of the board of investors, but Alice had little contact with them. Dr. Weil ran the board meetings, and Alice only participated when she was called upon to make technical presentations. She glanced through her notes from previous meetings, where she had links to their photos and short biographies. Over the years, only three of them had made any impression on her.

Edgar Carlton, 68, was a cantankerous former CEO of an aerospace company, unable to understand why research didn't happen on a tighter and more predictable schedule. He never seemed interested in the details. He certainly never understood them, but he was quick to have a gut reaction and hard to shake out of it. Alice knew she'd need to lead him carefully.

Evangeline Gladner, 49, was a vice-president at one of the largest retail chains in the country. She distrusted the stock market, preferring to invest in opportunities where she could feel the illusion of being in control. She asked questions and tried to understand the details, but she trusted the experts. She'd support Alice, as long as Alice showed confidence.

Sam Gleigh, 51, a self-made billionaire, was now a venture capitalist. He was the only one who ever surprised her when she made presentations. Most of the time, he sat quietly in the background, but when he did speak, it was to ask penetrating questions that revealed a deep understanding of the project. As their primary investor, his was the most important vote, but Alice had no idea how to handle him. She'd have to play whatever cards she discovered in her hand.

• • •

"Seven years ago, many of you were with us when we laid out the plans for our first smart prosthesis," Alice began. She looked around the room, noting the tension — even hostility in some cases — on the faces of her audience. She almost succumbed to panic as she realized she had no idea what she'd do if this failed, but her face remain locked in *confident expert* mode, and she carried on. "Some of you were skeptical at the claims we made then. You thought we were overreaching, but you took a chance. Five years ago, you saw that risk pay off, as our technology revolutionized the field, and the profits started pouring in. We achieved more than we initially set out to do. We've helped over seven hundred people return to a life they thought was gone forever."

She paused to give them a moment to reflect on that history, especially the four who had not been on the board at that time. "From the start, when success seemed like a long shot, through the years of hard work, right up to today, no one — not any of you, not the press who hailed that technology as a revolution, and certainly not the hundreds of people whose lives were permanently improved by your investment — *no one* said that the users of our technology were diminished by it. That they were no longer *people* just because parts of their bodies were now made of carbon fiber composites and servo-actuators instead of bones and muscles."

There were some nervous glances around the room. Some of them understood where she was going with this. Alice didn't let them interrupt. "When we came to you with a plan for cognitive prostheses, again some of you were skeptical, but again you took a chance. We told you that human memories could be moved to silicon to repair the effects of brain damage and augment human abilities. Over the last two years we proved that we could do it, and none of you told us that the people who would use this technology would cease to be human just because some of their thoughts and memories would be running on silicon instead of living brain tissue."

The rest of the room caught up with her then, and many of them were not happy. These were issues they'd much rather ignore. "We realized that if memories and thoughts could be moved to an electronic substrate, then it might also be possible to capture *all* of a person's thoughts and memories — the entire mind — outside of the human brain. We demonstrated that with our beta test, and we profoundly improved the process with our latest test subject, Eliot Stearns."

While she talked, Alice kept her eyes moving, looking at each of them directly, measuring their discomfort. "As you know, Eliot was tragically killed last week in a car accident. Of course, that event had nothing to do with Eliot's experience here last March. He was never aware of the construct we created. But now we have a situation none of us expected. Eliot is dead, but his mind lives on in our lab."

"A *simulation* of his mind," Carlton objected. "Or are you claiming that Eliot was in two places at once before last week's accident?"

"Eliot's mind continued in his own body when he left this institute," Alice said. "But it also continued in the neuromorphic hardware running in our lab. The two minds were identical at one point, but each acquired experiences that the other didn't have. They began diverging then, but everything Eliot experienced before coming to us, all of his memories, feelings, thoughts, hopes, and dreams live on. How can we, in good conscience, discard his life when we have the power to let it continue?"

"What life?" Gladner asked. "Life as a stream of bits in a virtual world? What kind of life is that?"

"Eliot experiences a fully realistic environment. It is limited right now because we never intended it to be lived in for more than five days. Dr. Trilby, our chief software architect, assures me that we can extend the environment to a completely natural setting, but only with Eliot's cooperation and full awareness of the situation."

"But it wouldn't be *real*," Gladner said. "What would be the point? Living inside his own little bubble, cut off from the world, all alone?"

"Eliot would not be cut off from the world," Alice insisted. "Until we suspended him, we talked with him every single day. He remembers his life, his friends, his family. He's formed new relationships with us. He talks about his past, and he has new, original ideas that he shares with us. He has the same sense of identity that he had when he came in, the same sense of purpose and self-preservation."

"How can you possibly know that?" Carlton interrupted angrily.

"Because he's started fighting us." Alice kept her voice calm, but they could all see her determination. "Somehow, he's begun to realize that we've kept him here longer than he agreed to. He's started remembering things from previous cycles. We don't even know *how* he's doing that. It's not something we built in. He figured it out on his own, and he's struggling to break free. These are the actions of a *person* — a conscious, living mind. If he were made aware of what happened, we could get his cooperation again. He could have more natural interactions, and not just with us, but with anyone he chooses. He could talk with his friends. He could talk with his parents." Alice could see that she was making progress with some of the board members, but others, like Carlton, seemed more hostile now than when she had started. "He wouldn't have to be alone," she continued. She took a deep breath. "Others could join him in his world. I propose to do that."

She tried to clarify her proposal, but she found herself shouted down by Mr. Carlton and others. She looked at Dr. Weil for support, but he lowered his eyes. She rallied herself, speaking over them calmly, until finally they were listening again. "How will anyone believe we are dealing fairly with him if we are afraid to put ourselves where he is? How would *he* believe us? I don't have to go as far as Eliot. I don't have to *die* to give him some companionship. It would be the logical next step anyway, to have one of us observing from the inside, identifying the faults and problems with the current technology, so that the next version will be more accurate."

The muttering continued around the table. She tried to regain the momentum. "If Eliot were not dead, but in a coma, and we discovered a way to communicate directly with his mind, would we pretend we couldn't do it?" She looked each of them in the eyes, and some would not return her gaze. "Would he still be a person, even with a broken body? Should we let him die, rather than bring his mind back into the world?"

"But he's not really *Eliot*," Ms. Gladner argued. "He's not really ... *anyone*. He doesn't even have a body."

"Does a quadriplegic stop being a person because his body no longer functions as it did?" Alice asked, staring Gladner down. "We have prosthetic limbs that can move in response to neural inputs. Someday we may be able to replace a quadriplegic's entire body with a mechanical infrastructure with fully functional arms and legs. Wouldn't he still be a person, even though only his head and brain were biologically intact? And if his eyes and ears had to be replaced with prosthetics, would he still be a person? And what if some of his brain cells died and we replaced them with silicon, but all his thoughts and memories and sense of self remained intact, what then? At what point does he *stop* being a person? If we're able to give that quadriplegic a mechanical body, why wouldn't we be able to give it to Eliot, too? When the neuromorphic hardware is small enough to fit in a mechanical body, why couldn't Eliot walk and talk in the real world again? That may be decades away, maybe longer. Or a new breakthrough could come about in a few years. Do you want to know then that we could have restored him to life, but we decided instead to throw his life away?"

Alice turned to face Carlton, and he glared back at her. "Think about Eliot's parents," she went on. "They lost their only child. They don't know that they can still talk to him. If they knew that we could make that happen and threw away the opportunity, how would they feel? That we killed Eliot a second time?" She had some of them swayed, but in her attempt to get everyone, she went too far. "Mr. Carlton, you lost your own son years ago in Afghanistan. What if you could still talk to him?"

"My son is with God," Carlton said, seething with rage. "And so is Eliot Stearns. I will talk with my son again when I join him in Heaven, and not with some soulless avatar you've stitched together in your laboratory. Treating this *simulacrum* as a real person is obscene."

"But why can't it be both, Mr. Carlton?" Alice pleaded. "A simulation *and* a person. If God can give a soul to a baby — a creation of our bodies — why not to a creation of our minds? Is that beyond God's reach?"

"The project is over," Carlton said with finality. "We cut our losses and put an end to it. We shred all the notes, erase all the data, and strictly enforce the confidentiality agreement."

"You haven't accrued any losses yet, Mr. Carlton," Sam Gleigh said, speaking for the first time today. Everyone else in the room stared at him in astonishment.

"Are you out of your mind, Gleigh?" Carlton was outraged. "I've invested nearly a million dollars in this failed enterprise. While that may sound insignificant to a man of your means, I assure you that *I* consider it a substantial loss. No doubt your own investment was a great deal higher. Perhaps even enough to make the loss noticeable?"

"I don't count any investment as a loss until I've finished counting the returns," Gleigh explained. "What return did you expect to make on this investment of yours?"

Carlton paused, unable to figure out Gleigh's angle. "I was well aware there was a risk of losing the entire amount."

"That will certainly be the case if you force the project to close at this point. But if you allow the project to continue, what do you think your return might be in, say, another two years' time?"

Carlton laughed bitterly. "Mr. Gleigh, if we allow this project to continue, I think our return will be law-suits and criminal indictments." There were a few nods around the room, but all eyes remained on Sam Gleigh.

"Well, in that case, I expect you'd be satisfied just to get your investment back intact and be done with this project. Is that correct, Mr. Carlton?"

The attention shifted to Carlton, and he suddenly had the feeling he'd been badly outmaneuvered. "Are you offering to buy out my investment, Gleigh?"

"I'm offering to buy out the investment of anyone here who would prefer to walk away today rather than allow this project to fulfill its charter. I believe there is still a good chance for substantial return."

There was silence in the room as they all furiously attempted to calculate odds in their heads. *What has he figured out that I'm missing? What if he's right? What if Carlton's right?*

Carlton realized that he'd look like a coward or a fool if he backed down now. "I accept your offer, Gleigh. $750,000, and my shares in this project are yours."

"I'll have the papers on your desk by this afternoon, along with my bank draft. And since you are no longer a member of this board, please excuse yourself from this meeting." A venomous reply tried to emerge from Carlton's mouth, but his tongue couldn't find it.

"Of course, you know that you're still bound by the confidentiality agreement that you spoke of earlier," Gleigh casually mentioned. Carlton glared at him, glanced around the room, and strutted to the door.

Two others accepted Gleigh's offer and left the room. The rest stayed, but they all looked extremely nervous about it. Sam Gleigh now owned 70% of the shares of Project Mnemosyne, and his was the only vote that mattered. He looked at Alice. "Proceed with your plan, Dr. Kurz." He saw her re-evaluating the situation: she'd won, but she wasn't sure yet if she should be happy about it. He turned to Dr. Weil. "I would like to meet with the entire senior staff sometime tomorrow to discuss the long-term prospects for this project. My calendar is completely open after noon. Could you arrange a couple of hours for us to all get together?"

Several of the remaining board members exchanged worried looks. Gladner cleared her throat, but Gleigh turned to her and waited for words that never came. They all seemed to realize at the same moment that this was the last time the entire board would participate in any substantive decisions about the project. Gladner looked down at the papers in front of her, and Gleigh turned back to Dr. Weil.

"I'm sure we can block out a couple of hours," Weil said. "I assume you mean to meet here?"

"Here will be fine. Just let my executive assistant know the time. Be sure to include Dr. Trilby and Mr. Thompson in the meeting." Gleigh looked around the room. "Well, I think that covers everything for today. Shall we adjourn?"

The motion carried.

• • •

At 2:00 the next afternoon, Sam Gleigh walked into the conference room flanked by attorneys carrying large stacks of freshly printed and bound documents. The attorneys were not introduced, but their names were Sigurdsen and Dunning. Gleigh always thought of them as Sturm and Drang. He immediately began laying out his requirements for the long-term future of the Mnemosyne Project and the construct named Eliot Stearns.

Gleigh began with Eliot, planning to get Alice on his side right from the start. "Dr. Kurz, I fully endorse your plan to join Eliot in the simulation. This, of course, will be an open-ended simulation, and I have no wish to shut it down at any time. Ever." He glanced at his audience, easily seeing that only Trick and Alice understood what he meant. Alice raised an eyebrow, but started nodding to herself. Trick never even raised the eyebrow. *Maybe he knew from the beginning,* Gleigh thought. He'd only seen Trick a couple of times since the conference where they first crossed paths. They'd never talked about that day, and as far as Gleigh knew, Trick had never told anyone else at the institute about the encounter. Perhaps Trick worried that he'd revealed too much about the project then, although in fact he'd said very little.

He turned and looked at Trick now. "As I understand it, Dr. Trilby, you can modify the simulation whenever needed, without restarting the constructs?"

"Yes. They could even watch it happen, although it would be extremely disorienting. And you might as well call me Trick, since we'll be seeing each other a lot now."

"Indeed we will, Trick." He could see puzzled glances flit between Weil and Chance. "I would like to have a standing appointment once a week from now on."

Dr. Weil leaned forward, catching Gleigh's eye. "For what purpose?" he asked.

"To be scanned, of course," Gleigh said. No one said anything. Weil looked bewildered. Gleigh reached to his right, and Sturm handed him the document on the top of the stack. Gleigh laid it in front of him facing

Alice and Trick. "This is the schedule I propose to follow, but I am open to other recommendations. I'm sure you have more experience than I with data archives."

Trick skimmed the summary and flipped through the text, pausing briefly at the diagrams. "It's a reasonable backup schedule. I can fit this into our existing plan. I assume you're funding all the new hardware we'll need?" Trick glanced at him and Gleigh nodded. "And these off-site repositories, these are existing sites already prepped?"

"I own a distributed data vault."

Weil cleared his throat and waited for Gleigh's attention. "I'm afraid I still don't know what that's all about," he said, pointing at the document in Trick's hands.

Trick looked up and answered him. "It's a backup schedule. Weekly backups, with monthly checkpoints, long-term retention policy, data erasure policy, test plans."

"Backup of what?" Weil asked.

"Mr. Gleigh's mind," Trick answered, closing the document and sitting back.

Chance stared at Gleigh. "Weekly brain scans? Do you know how much data that is?"

"The data requirements are estimated in section one. You will need to correct those numbers, I'm sure, but it should be a reasonable starting point for your own analysis. Please make that a high priority." Gleigh picked up his tablet and placed it in front of Trick. "Two contacts for you. Use my IT contractor for whatever you need for your datacenter here. Charges go straight to me."

"I'll also need to exchange certificates and encryption protocols with your data security manager."

"She's the second contact," Gleigh replied. With

Gleigh's tablet in view of his videoglasses, Trick gestured at it, accepting the contact information.

"Mr. Gleigh," Chance spoke up. "Do you understand how this works? All that scan data can't be used on an ordinary computer. You need our custom neuromorphic mesh. And a great deal of expertise that simply doesn't exist anywhere else."

"Which is why continued support of this institute is the first proviso of the contract that I intend for us to sign today." Sturm removed a small document from the stack in front of him and placed it in front of Thompson.

Thompson shook his head and said, "Nothing you have discussed can be settled *today*. The issues that you're raising … I don't even know where to begin."

"Look through the contract, Mr. Thompson," Gleigh insisted. "This is a *framework* for mutual exploration in a long term R&D relationship, with provisions for later revision. I assume all the risks. Your institute is supported in perpetuity — a term which suddenly means what it says."

Weil finally caught up with the rest of them. "You'll always have a backup of your mind that's less than a week old," he said, stunned. "When you die, you want us to activate the last backup, and you'll continue to live on — inside the simulation."

"Yes," Gleigh said. "With full access to the internet. Most of my business is conducted electronically now. Why not all of it?"

"But you won't *have* a business after you're dead," Thompson objected. "All of your assets will belong to your heirs." He paused slightly, as if wondering whether Sam Gleigh *had* any heirs.

"Yes," Gleigh said, nodding, "that was quite a challenge. Fortunately, these gentlemen here, along with their colleagues, were equal to the task." He reached a hand to his left and Drang set a very small document into it. "This is an excerpt from my will," he explained, pointing out the first page. "As you can see, my annual endowment to this institute continues after my death. The amount is quite a bit larger than your current annual budget." Dr. Weil was not able to hide his excitement at the new funding level that Gleigh was providing.

"The majority of my assets are consigned to my primary holding company, Gleigh Investments." He flipped to the second and last page of the document. "This is a very brief summary of a rather detailed codicil to the Gleigh Investments corporate charter, which will automatically take effect upon my death. It binds the board of directors to abide by every decision of '*the computer simulation known as Sam Gleigh,*' giving it the full authority of CEO." A transient smile touched the corner of his mouth as he gave such a simple explanation of the 30,000 words of abstruse legal maneuvering that it took to cement his control from beyond the grave.

There was a long silence until Alice finally spoke up. "Well, Mr. Gleigh, it appears everyone else is wrong. You *can* take it with you."

Gleigh said nothing, looking at her with interest. Going into the discussion, Gleigh had been certain that Weil would be snowballed, Trick would accept the challenge, Chance would argue ineffectively, but Alice Kurz might be difficult. He was prepared with arguments that he thought would sway her, and he had Dr. Gold's report on her if it became necessary to have her dismissed. While far from his first choice, he'd play it that way if he had to.

Alice surprised him. She provided him with only one challenge. "We must also address the issue of full disclosure."

"Confidentiality provisions are detailed in section …"

"Fourteen," Sturm interjected.

"There are very significant issues to be addressed before we can consider what, if anything, should be publicly revealed about this project and this contract," Gleigh continued. "My interests in this arrangement could be seriously compromised with inappropriate disclosure."

"I appreciate that, Mr. Gleigh, and I'm sure Mr. Thompson would agree that we must be extremely careful in that regard."

"I certainly do," Thompson said nervously.

"I'm not proposing that we answer all of those questions right now," Alice assured him. "I accept that we will proceed slowly and cautiously. However, I insist that Eliot's isolation from the world has to end. He must be permitted to have a voice, at least to the same extent as any of the rest of us. He must be allowed to participate in the outside world."

Gleigh had expected this, but he thought it wouldn't come up quite this early. He spoke carefully, keeping his full attention on Alice's face. "My concern here is whether the subject will have an appropriate perspective on the bigger issues, or will simply react out of a feeling of being wronged. Much depends on how successfully you can engage with him once he becomes aware of his real situation."

Alice stared him down. "I believe I know Eliot better than anyone else in this room. He doesn't trust me any more, but I think that he will again after I take the next step. I can tell you with absolute conviction that no one will have a more thoughtful understanding of these issues. He will work intelligently with us, as he always has."

Sam Gleigh made surprisingly few mistakes in his business career, largely because of his innate ability to weigh risks and benefits. Here, however, he was diving headfirst into the unknown. Probability and expected value meant nothing when dealing with infinites and infinitesimals. What value assessments could be made where he might stand to gain infinite reward? What risks could be quantified in a completely remade world? He did not know Eliot, and Dr. Gold's assessments in that area were tantalizing, but incomplete. He looked at Alice Kurz intently. He knew *her*, far better than she could imagine. He knew she was in love with Eliot, but she'd never given him any reason to doubt her professional judgment. The depth of her conviction in Eliot would have satisfied him in any context he had known previously. What better starting point did he have for understanding this totally new context? Besides, there'd be no faster way to perfect the process than to put Alice and Eliot in it together, and her presence there would help to calm any hostility Eliot might feel toward them.

"Dr. Kurz, I am willing to accept your recommendations in this regard," Gleigh began. "But I must remind you that the wrong sort of public attention would not only threaten *my* interests, it could also destroy your career, your professional standing, and your financial assets. It could possibly bring criminal charges against you."

Alice nodded. "Absolutely true, Mr. Gleigh. I have considered all of that. And more."

For the briefest moment, Gleigh wondered if she had considered more than he had. *All the more reason to have her on my side,* he decided. "Then, I believe we have an agreement."

• • •

The rest of the meeting was consumed by contract

details that were of no interest to Trick. He said nothing more, except to answer the questions put to him. Like everyone else, he supposed, he was thinking about how far they'd come and how much this would change the world. As with all breakthrough technologies, Gleigh and his kind — the rich and the powerful — would be the ones paying for it initially, to satisfy their greed and vanity. But as much as they might prefer to keep immortality in the hands of the new aristocracy, too much money could be made selling it to the public. Trick could envision a hundred ways the next Sam Gleigh might market the product. It could be the ultimate retirement plan: sign over your house, your pension, and your life savings; get the afterlife of your choice.

There would be Luddites, of course, and with good reason. This was the most disruptive technology ever created. Everything would change, far more than he could predict, and he could predict a lot that seemed plausible. For the desperately ill, it would be a financial decision. The surgical procedure to save your life costs this much and has this chance of success. Immortality in a simulation costs that much, and is guaranteed to succeed, or your money back. The push-back will become violent at times. Religions will fight for their lives. Small nations will become big in virtual populations. Minds that never need to sleep or eat will dwell in virtual think tanks, augmented by direct connections to supercomputer networks, blasting through the human-machine intelligence singularity like a starship through a wormhole. No living human can dream what's on the other side of that gateway, but many living today will see it.

Compared to that future, the cost they paid to get here seemed well spent to Trick. Matthius's opprobrium about the alpha subjects didn't concern him. Those constructs were never viable. They were shadows of human minds, constructed from incomplete data and primitive versions of the algorithms they now used. Matthius Pin was the first whole mind that could choose immortality, but he made a different choice. Thinking about that now, Trick brought up the data archive controls on his videoglasses, and with a subtle gesture of his hands, unnoticed by anyone else in the conference room, he honored Matthius's wishes by deleting his construct.

He looked at Sam Gleigh, wondering if Gleigh even remembered their first meeting four years ago. Trick had watched Dr. Weil's lackluster success in attracting the wrong kind of investors, and he knew the project would never be funded that way. They needed investors with a personal stake in the long term, so Trick immersed himself in the transhumanist movement, examining the websites, corresponding on the forums, and attending conferences. Always, he kept his eye on the money. Who sponsored the conferences? Who funded the research? It wasn't long before Sam Gleigh's name became known to him. Eventually, Trick caught up with him at a convention in Seattle. Gleigh made one of his rare public appearances as a business expert on a panel discussing funding approaches for life extension technologies. One of the other panel members was Aryn Creighton. She was the CEO of DendriTek, the manufacturer of the prototype neuromorphic membranes that Alice's team had just begun to experiment with.

During the question portion of the panel, Trick stood and asked Ms. Creighton about future product plans, casually noting that his team had been experimenting with their prototypes, and they seemed very promising. This was enough to get Gleigh's attention, and shortly after the panel adjourned, Trick was not surprised to see Gleigh come up to him. He asked Trick about his work with neuromorphic hardware, and Trick gave him the politely vague answers of someone who knew much more than he was allowed to talk about. That was all it took. Three days after Trick returned from the conference, Weil mentioned that he was in discussion with Sam Gleigh about investing in the project. He assumed that Gleigh had found out about the opportunity from other investors Weil had approached. Neither Trick nor Gleigh ever told him otherwise.

• • •

Gleigh left after the contract was signed, and Alice spent several more hours in the conference room with Trick, Chance, and Weil. At last, Trick walked with her to the pre-op lab, where they were met by the medical team — and Dr. Gold.

Gold stepped in front of the med-techs, looking at Alice. She stopped directly before him and returned his stare. "A private moment, please, before you begin the procedure," Gold asked, and he could hear the cold anger in his own voice. He closed his eyes for just a second and relaxed his posture. "I won't interfere with what you plan to do." He gestured toward an empty office at the back of the lab. *I could, though,* he thought. *I could stop you. But who'll stop Sam Gleigh?*

Alice held her ground, appraising the psychologist. She nodded and walked toward the office, Dr. Gold walking beside her. She entered first, turned on the light and sat down in the chair behind the desk. Gold countered by standing before her, but he looked into Alice's eyes, then sat in the guest chair. "I won't try to persuade you not to do this, Dr. Kurz. I know I would not succeed, although I wish it were otherwise."

"I've never understood your objections to this research, Dr. Gold." Her expression was losing its severity. She really did want to know. "Nor exactly what you've been doing here. I noticed your absence at the meeting this afternoon. Aren't you even curious about what Mr. Gleigh had to say to us?"

Gold leaned back in his chair and removed his tablet from his suit pocket. He tapped it while he spoke. "Mr. Gleigh is not a man I take lightly, nor should you. He did not invite me to the meeting, because he informed me of his plan last night, right after he collected a final copy of this report which I prepared for him." He turned the tablet around to face Alice, and she read the title: *Concerns re Dr. Alice Kurz.* "I think you should have a copy of this before I destroy mine."

Alice was very still as she skimmed through it. "I take it you have met with Gleigh privately before."

"Yes, many times."

"You spied on this institute for him?"

"No, Dr. Kurz, I fulfilled the contract to which I was hired. By Sam Gleigh, not your institute."

Alice scoffed, "The board hired you, not ..." but she'd seen how Gleigh worked the board. "We paid your salary."

"Not a penny of it. I was already on Mr. Gleigh's retainer. I've assisted him on many projects before this one."

"And this report, this character assassination. Why?"

"Just my honest observations, Dr. Kurz, but 'why' is a good question. I have been puzzling about that ever since he talked to me last night. I think Mr. Gleigh would say the answer is from Sun Tzu: 'The general who wins a battle makes many calculations in his temple ere the battle is fought.' Removing you was a contingency plan if you opposed him." Gold smiled at Alice, but it wasn't friendly. "You didn't oppose him, though, did you Alice? Why would you? You have a man waiting who will love you forever. He *will* love you, right? Trick can tweak a setting here or there, make sure he feels what he's supposed to?"

Alice's eyes erupted with fury. "Trick has nothing to do with this. That's Eliot's own mind in there. It's running on new hardware, but it's still him."

"Of course it is. Every thought's his own. And no distracting pheromones, adrenaline, dopamine. None of that messy biological stuff that gets in the way of clear thinking."

"You know very well that we're simulating the body chemistry. We calibrated the model against the real Eliot."

"And in the process, I'm sure you learned a lot about the profound effects of a few simple changes to, say, hormone production."

"Are you seriously suggesting that I've been adjusting Eliot's mind to my liking?"

"Isn't that what we all do? Try to persuade others to be the people we want them to be? How much simpler when you have the keys to their brain."

"You have no idea what you're talking about, if you think such a thing would be simple."

"Well, not for you or me, perhaps. I wonder how hard it would be for Trick?"

"I would never ask him to do that."

"Of course not, Alice. You're in love. You want Eliot to feel the same thing you do, all by himself. Trick knows that. He's your friend. He wouldn't need to be asked."

Alice stood to leave, and Gold stood to block her. "You asked me about my objections to this project. Let me ask *you* a few questions. Is he a person, your Eliot?"

"Yes, he is. It took me too long to see what that meant."

"What *does* it mean? Is he a citizen? Does he have legal rights? Can he vote? What if you make a dozen more of him, do they *all* get to vote? Can they collect Social Security? That might break the bank. Can he sue you for doing this to him? Can he be arrested if he commits a crime? What would you do, change the simulation to a prison cell?"

"I don't know, Dr. Gold." She stood right in front of him, but he continued to block her from the door. "You think you're the only one to realize what a disruptive technology this is? Right now there are more questions than answers. That's how it always works when the old paradigms break down. It takes time, but the questions always lead to answers, and we move on. Things will change, and I can't predict how, but I'm taking the best path I know to find out. Should we look away, pretend this won't ever be possible? Should we refuse to understand it until it's forced upon us? I intend to learn what it means before I make a judgment."

"But you've already made a judgment, Alice. Now you're throwing away your humanity to justify it."

Alice sighed. "Humanity. Just what is that, anyway? I've spent my entire life trying to grasp how these twisted structures of gray and white matter turn organic tissue into human beings. Just when we're finally learning the answers, the question has evolved again. The nature of humanity is to reinvent itself. We're the species that chooses its own path. *All* the choices are dangerous; that's why we need to see everything we can, then choose wisely. Standing around waiting for whatever happens has never been a successful strategy for human survival."

"What do you think will happen when the military has hold of this technology?" Gold asked, waving his arms to encompass everything around them. "Human minds embedded inside armed drones and spybots. Enemy captives scanned into virtual prisons without their awareness, to be tortured, maimed, *killed* as many times as necessary to break their will."

She continued to meet his gaze, but Dr. Gold noticed the slight tremor in her hands, so he hammered away at her. "How long will it be before we have minds scanned from children — pliable young minds that can be trained for exactly the services required by their *owners*? Fanatics will use this technology, Alice. They'll find one of their own who is brilliant, ruthless, and utterly devoted to their cause, and they'll make *thousands* of him."

"They couldn't enter the real world," she objected.

"On the internet, they're as real as everyone else," he snapped.

They both looked up as Trick approached the door. Gold frowned at him. "You knew where this was going, I suppose? Not much gets past you, does it?"

Trick stopped at the doorway and looked at them, his face unrevealing as ever. "There are good minds trapped in dying and paralyzed bodies," he said, looking at Gold. "We can set them free. And there are some places where bodies simply can't go. Interstellar travel, for example. Keeping humans alive and healthy on such a voyage might always remain beyond our capabilities. But in a few years, a great city of human minds could inhabit a rich simulation, all running on hardware no bigger than an elevator. Launching *that* to the stars is a real possibility. No life support, minimal radiation shielding, and accelerations that would turn a human body to mush." He looked from Gold to Alice and back, clearly surprised they didn't see what he saw.

"We won't even have to find other planets to colonize. We'll be at home everywhere in the universe. We'll watch the birth and death of stars, walk distant worlds on robotic feet. We can see it all, learn it all. Human thought — human civilization — can expand forever."

Gold shook his head. "You won't like some of the civilizations that will spring from this."

"But now there will be room for all of them," Trick insisted. "There's no need to ever fight over territory again. Any society that wants a world all to itself can make one and live in it. With an endless frontier, we can thrive forever. Without a frontier, we're left to kill each other over the few scraps of land we can capture."

"Well, I won't be joining your world of disembodied pioneers," Gold said, looking from Trick to Alice. "I have already sent my resignation letter to Mr. Gleigh. You won't be seeing any more of me, but you will be seeing a *lot* of Sam Gleigh: a very patient man, capable of carrying out extremely long-term plans. Do not make the assumption that he now has everything he wants. He may be done using me, but he's not done using you. You'll find it a lot harder to walk away than I do." With that, he turned and walked away.

The River Mnemosyne

Eliot woke from his nap when the lunch tray rolled onto the table. Even from the bedroom, the sound of the rollers startled him awake. It was "day 4," and tonight they'd wipe his memory again. His only hope was to sleep during the day, stay awake tonight, and catch them in the act.

He got out of bed and walked into the living area, trying desperately to think of something he'd missed. Like a jungle animal trapped in a zoo, he stalked the cage, compulsively testing the perimeter. Try the entry door: locked; walk around the room; try the supply room door: locked; walk around the room.

He paused before the table and looked at his untouched lunch. Would there be a sedative in tonight's dinner? Would someone come to the door? Or would he have no warning when the nanocells reset his brain?

He tried the entry door: still locked. He passed by the table again and looked at the tray. He reached out and unrolled the napkin, removed the knife, and held it in his hands. It had no point and not much of an edge. The only way he could injure anyone would be to hold it against a throat. *Could I do it if I have to? Even against Alice?* He slipped it into the waistband at the small of his back, untucking his shirt to cover the protruding handle. He walked by the supply room door and tried the doorknob again. There was a click, and it opened.

Alice Kurz sat behind a small rectangular table, alone. There was another chair in front of the table. Otherwise, the room was absolutely empty. White walls, no windows. The door he'd entered was behind him, and there were no other doors. How had she gotten in here without passing through his rooms? He looked up, noticing something odd about the ceiling. No light fixtures were visible, but the whole ceiling was bright, casting a uniform glow over the room.

Eliot remained in the doorway, staring at her. She looked nervous, even a little frightened. Was she afraid he was going to attack her? Maybe he should — now, before they could do it to him again. *Use her as a hostage. Escape!* But somehow he could tell that she wasn't frightened in that way; not frightened *of* him, but *for* him. She looked like she was about to tell him that he had an incurable disease. He walked forward until he was standing before the desk, looking down at her. She met his eyes.

"Please sit down, Eliot," she said calmly. She seemed to be steeling herself for a difficult task. He remained standing.

"Is this how it always happens, then?" Eliot asked. "Do we always have this little conversation before you erase my memory and start it all over again?"

Alice was surprised, but she nodded absently to herself, not in answer to his question but as if she finally understood something that had been puzzling her. "Is that what you think is happening? We erase your memory? And we've done it before?"

"I know that you have, Dr. Kurz." Eliot's anger was rising. He paced back and forth, no longer looking at her. His eyes roamed around the room, but there was nothing to see. He could no longer entertain the hope that somehow she didn't know — that they'd done the same thing to her. It was clear that she knew what was going on, but she still refused to admit it.

"We haven't erased your memory, Eliot," Alice pressed on. "How would that even be possible? Why do you think we've done that?"

"Never mind how I found out." With a flash of despair, he realized that he hadn't made a new entry in his private log since discovering the unlocked door. How many times had he gotten to this point and never thought to warn himself, *I'm going through the supply room door now?*

"It's the nanocells that you put inside my brain, isn't it? They give you a way to control my memory. You wipe out the last five days so I'll wake up and think I'm just starting the trial. Over and over again. You said they'd pass through my body in a couple of days. That was a lie."

"Please sit down, Eliot," she said softly. "It's a lot more complicated than that. I promise I'll explain it all to you."

"What's today's date, Dr. Kurz?" Eliot asked, looking right at her again. "Let's start with that. And don't tell me it's March 23. What's the *real* date, Doctor?"

Alice lowered her eyes and clasped her hands in front of her. She blinked her eyes rapidly, fighting back tears, it seemed to Eliot. Without looking at him, she spoke very softly. "If I answer that question, will you sit down and let me explain it all to you? It's a long expla-nation, and you're going to have to let me say it in my own way. It's going to sound odd, but it's the only way that I can explain it to you. Will you let me do that?" She looked him in the eyes.

Eliot stared at her for a few seconds, then nodded

his head. "Okay," he said. "But you get these damn things out of my brain, and you don't touch my memory again, ever. And after you explain yourself, I'm free to go."

Alice struggled with her answer. "We've never erased your memory, Eliot. Actually, that's the very *last* thing we'd want to happen. And after I explain everything to you, we'll ... release you ... if that's still what you want." She looked into his eyes, and he was surprised at the sadness there. "The date is September 16."

Eliot thought he was prepared to hear this, but he wasn't. It was too much. Six months of his life taken from him? How could they have hidden him here for that long? Wasn't anyone looking for him? Had they reported him dead? He thought he'd gotten to know Alice Kurz, but he was wrong. *What kind of monsters are these people?*

He leaned on the desk, his hands balled into fists. He put his face close to hers and looked straight into her eyes. "You've kept me here, prisoner, lying to me all this time — for six months?"

"No," she said. "Eliot Stearns walked in here on the evening of March 19. He stayed here five days, just as the contract said. After five days, Eliot walked out of here and went home."

"I never went home, Dr. Kurz," Eliot said, mystified by her attitude. "I'm still here." He sat down, not knowing what else to do, finally seeing her face-to-face at eye level. A tear was rolling down her cheek. She seemed to be as amazed by that as he was. She wiped the tear with her finger and stared at it. She felt the moisture between her finger and her thumb. She lowered her hand and looked at him again.

"Yes, you're here," she said, so softly that he stared at her lips to make sure she was speaking. "But *you're* not

Eliot Stearns."

What the hell is that supposed to mean? Eliot tried to say, but it never got past his lips. He thought of what it might mean. He reconsidered, and came up with an even worse interpretation. He sat, stunned, not even realizing that his mouth was open to speak.

"What did you do to me?" he asked at last.

Alice looked him in the eyes. It seemed to take all her strength. "The nanocells didn't change you. We didn't lie. We just didn't tell you the whole truth." She took a deep breath. "They're just sensors built on a structure of carbon nanotubes. They have a small amount of data storage and a limited ability to transmit and receive specific radio frequencies. They can measure ion concentrations, certain chemical compounds, and very small fluctuations in nearby electromagnetic fields. After we inject them, it takes about two minutes for them to reach an optimal distribution throughout the body. Our primary focus is the brain, of course, but we need to take measurements throughout your nervous system in order to get a complete model. Each nanocell can measure the connection state of the nearest eight synapses. All together, we get a nearly complete map of your connectome — the synaptic connections in the brain and your primary sensor and motor nerves."

"No," Eliot interrupted. "That's too much data. You could never process it all, and it's constantly changing. You'd never be able to get a single snapshot of it all at once. And besides, you can't possibly know exactly where each nanocell ends up when it takes its measurements."

"That's true, we could never process it in real time. But we can *record* it in real time. The nanocells have enough storage to keep the last four measurements of the interconnections they read. We flash your body with a low level radio pulse. That triggers the nanocells to start recording. At the same time, we apply six different infrasound tones at different points around your body. The measurements recorded by the nanocells include the time difference between the start of recording and the receipt of each sound pulse. That gives us an approximate distance from each of the sound origins, from which we can determine the spatial coordinates of each nanocell. Since sound travels at different speeds through the different densities of the body, there's some error, but by coordinating all of these readings with the readings of each nanocell's nearest neighbors, we're able to develop a very reliable map of the state of each synapse across your entire nervous system, through four successive time intervals. Each nanocell's readings are stored inside the cell. We just need to get the data out and process it."

"Get it out … from the nanocells in my urine?" *This is impossible,* Eliot was convinced.

"No. After they take their measurements, the nanocells go into transmit mode. Each of them has a unique numeric id — a serial number, in effect. Other than that, they're all identical. The serial number acts as a programmed delay, so that cell 0 transmits first, then cell 1, and so on. The delays are very precise, so that the data stream is continuous, but transmitting cells don't interfere with each other. They emit a very low power radio signal, so we need sensitive receivers spaced all over the body. There are about 300 billion nanocells, so it takes over ten hours to transmit the entire data stream."

"300 billion? *Billion,* with a *b*?" Eliot was sure now that this couldn't be true. "These things must cost a fortune to manufacture, and you throw away 300 billion of them on one experiment? That's ridiculous."

"They cost a fortune to *develop*, but manufacturing them is cheap and fast," Alice said. "In fact, we don't manufacture them at all, we manufacture the nanofactories that make them. They work in a 'soup' of raw molecules — mostly carbon compounds and water. They're designed to build four replicas of themselves and then break down into the actual nanocell sensors that we need. Then each of the four replicas does the same thing, first building four copies of themselves. So it's exponential, and we have all that we need in about twenty generations."

Eliot had nothing to say to that. He knew how quickly exponential processes grew. Maybe it *was* possible.

"After they transmit, the nanocells begin breaking down. What's left of them is eliminated in the urine, just as we told you. Processing all the data from the nanocells takes another 36 hours, and that's only because we have custom-designed, massively parallel networks crunching through it. The algorithms took Trick's team two years to develop. It's a pattern matching problem, in the end. We find the most likely fit to the data, but we can never claim it's 100% accurate. Fortunately, the brain has a high degree of redundancy, which gives it amazing capability to work around damaged areas."

Alice paused, trying to read Eliot's expression.

"But what's the point?" he asked. "You do all this just to get a map of all the synapses at one instant of time. But that instant was days ago by the time you build your map. The brain's moved on by then. What good is it?"

"I told you that we had custom-designed parallel processing networks. Some of them are based on neuro-morphic architectures specifically designed to simulate neural processing, and we load the neural map onto them. We have another parallel-processor network programmed with a complete three-dimensional model of this suite of rooms. It determines what sensations should be received by the sensory subsystems as you move around, feeding that data in real time to the neuromorphic networks exactly as it would arrive from the body's sense organs. That includes your own body image and the internal sensations that would arise from *within* the body. With the simulated environment connected to the neuromorphic networks where we've loaded the connectome, we just ... wake it up."

Eliot's hands trembled. He couldn't speak.

"The simulated neurons proceed from the snapshot that we captured during sleep," Alice continued. "The cognitive activity in the simulated brain integrates to form the mind, just as in the original body. All the memories are there. All the knowledge and experiences. It wakes up, and it perceives the simulated environment. All its sensory input and all its memories tell it that it's awakened in the body, in the test suite. It ... you ... were unaware of the difference."

Eliot stood abruptly, pacing around the room. *It can't be,* he thought. *I can feel my heart racing. My breathing is shallow and rapid. My palms are sweating. I can press my fingernails into them and feel pain.*

"I don't believe you." He turned to face her from across the room. "It's absurd. None of this is possible. I'd know the difference."

"Well, we had to cheat a little. We gave you bland food because our taste models are still so primitive. We de-emphasized your ability to detect discrepancies between motor control and sensory input, so you don't notice low-level errors and omissions in the simulation. It's the same kind of thing that can happen when there's been damage to a person's right hemisphere. They may be entirely paralyzed on the left side, but they don't notice it. 'Anosognosia' is the term ..."

Eliot slapped his hand against the wall hard. It hurt. "This is *real*. I can feel it. My hand doesn't go through it."

"It could if we changed the simulation slightly." Alice said, rising to her feet, and when she spoke next, she wasn't addressing him. "Trick, make the mods that we talked about."

The table and chairs around Alice suddenly vanished. Eliot jumped back, startled. He looked around the room, as if he could spot the trapdoor or mirrors that caused the illusion. Slowly, he walked forward, groping in air where the table should be, but it wasn't there. He walked all the way to the wall behind Alice and encountered nothing. The furniture was gone.

He turned back to face Alice, and the wall behind her disappeared, door and all. This room was now just an extension of his previous living space. He walked forward into his living quarters and looked back into the extended area that used to be blocked off behind the wall and the "supply room" door. As he stared at Alice, the wall reappeared, with the door open. Shaken, Eliot walked through the doorway, felt the door and the wall. They were as solid as ever. The table and chairs were back.

He stared at her, trembling. He put his hand on his chest, reassuring himself that he was solid and he could feel the thumping of his heart. "I know I'm *me*." Even to himself, he sounded a little desperate. "A computer model could never be the same."

"You're *not* the same. Not completely. That's true. There are aspects of the brain that we're still only able to approximate. Our model of glial cells and certain aspects of brain chemistry are still incomplete. But you're as much *you* as you're capable of remembering in your current form." She hesitated, clearly wishing she'd said that differently, but there was no going back. "Remember, we kept the real Eliot Stearns here for five days of intensive interviews and testing. That was how we calibrated the model. It took several iterations before you began responding consistently like the original Eliot. Whenever the construct responded much differently, we adjusted certain parameters and tried again. That's why we've been working at this for such a long time. You're as close to the original Eliot Stearns as we can make you."

"The *construct*," Eliot said softly. "Me. You adjusted my *parameters* until I behaved the way you thought I should." He stood there, contemplating his hands as they grasped at the air she claimed wasn't there at all.

Alice didn't let up. "Even then, some part of your mind knew something was wrong. Trick was monitoring your sleep cycles, and you told him you were having disturbing dreams."

"Dreams about being lost, and finding myself." Eliot shook his head slowly. "Trick was monitoring me."

Alice paused, unsure what to say, but Trick's voice was completely clear, although no speakers were evident in this room: "We're not talking about mind reading, Eliot. We can see your neural activity, to a much higher level of detail than has ever been possible with biological brains. It's the first time anyone's been able to see so closely what happens inside the brain. But it doesn't give us access to your thoughts or let us watch your dreams."

Eliot scoffed, "No, that'll be next year's project."

"What we've learned has helped tremendously," Alice said, moving toward him slowly, her hands held out to his. Eliot reached behind his back and drew the knife from his waistband, but he felt ridiculous brandishing a dinner knife at her. He stared at Alice, who looked back into his eyes, still walking forward. She was sad, but not afraid. His heart turned over, and he realized there was only one person in this room that he could threaten with bodily harm, and it wasn't her. He put the knife edge against his own wrist, prepared to slice straight across it. "So what will happen to me if I spill my virtual blood all over the virtual floor?" he challenged.

"You'll feel pain, and bleed a little," Trick said. "The simulation deals with injury only up to a point. We didn't want to spoil the illusion if you slipped and fell, but we put in a hard limit to prevent serious injuries or death."

There's only way to be sure, Eliot decided. He didn't wait to second-guess himself. He pressed the slightly serrated cutting edge hard against his wrist and sliced quickly. A searing pain shot from his wrist, and blood spurted out, but almost immediately it turned into a slow drip, and the throbbing pain became little more than a dull ache.

"There are gauze pads on the shelf in the bathroom," Trick said. "You probably noticed them before."

Eliot stood there, looking at the cut. The bleeding had already stopped. He dropped the knife to the floor. Alice stood right in front of him. She took his hand and clenched it tightly in both of hers. He couldn't make himself resist. "You're not alone, Eliot. Not any more."

It began to dawn on him. "How are you here with me? If I'm just a brain map in a simulated environment, how are *you* here?"

"When you first came in, we weren't able to render your sensory inputs quickly enough to appear real, except in a static environment. That's why we had to isolate you. We couldn't simulate realistic interactions with other people, just voices over the speakers and a flat projection on the monitor. The mirror in the bathroom; the image of you on our monitors — those were the hardest things to get right. But now, well, Trick and his team have made six months' progress." She saw Eliot flinch, but she continued, "They figured out how to render multiple people in the same simulation. Your sensations of me are synced with my sensations of you, in real time, overlaid on the background of the environment. They programmed this extension to the simulation." She waved her hand around, indicating the room where they were standing. "In the actual building, that door really does lead to a supply room. There was no reason to scan it into the environment, so in the simulation it was just a locked door with nothing behind it. This room doesn't exist in the real world."

He stood there, feeling lost. He looked up at the illuminated ceiling again, his eyes widening. "No light fixtures," he said softly.

Alice glanced up and nodded. "Well, there was no longer a need to make it look convincing." She looked him in the eyes, and the intensity of her gaze drew him in. "We can do more, Eliot. A better simulation. Trick's working on something like a real *home*. I came here so you wouldn't have to live in it alone."

He released her hand and sat down. In the back of his mind, he thought, *I'm not really sitting. It shouldn't make any difference whether I stand or sit,* but he didn't feel stable on his feet. She sat on the edge of the desk, facing him, and took his hand again.

"I'm not Eliot Stearns," he said, trying to grasp the fact of it. "And you're not Alice Kurz. You're another brain map running on the neuromorphic networks. Like me."

She nodded, and as she did so, he heard Alice's

voice — the real Alice's voice: "I'm still here in the lab, Eliot. I went through the same procedure you did. Afterward, *I* woke up here in the lab."

"And *I* woke up here in the simulation," said the Alice sitting next to him.

Eliot leaned forward, his elbows on his knees, his head bowed, trying to get his mind around it. He should be outraged, terrified, desperate. He was not Eliot Stearns. There was no way he could ever leave the simulation. They could shut him off, and there was nothing he could do about it. But he realized that the one overwhelming emotion he felt was gratitude at Alice for not letting him go through this alone. At what cost to her, though? With that, he realized he was already past denial. This was real.

"What about me?" He looked at the Alice next to him — *Alice 2?* — but it was addressed to both of them. "Am I out there, too? *Eliot,* I mean. Did you bring him back to introduce him to his doppelganger?"

The uncomfortable pause and the look on Alice 2's face shocked him. Something was wrong. *They don't want the real Eliot to know. Think of the legal implications! They have captive access to all of Eliot's secrets, his feelings, his past, even his goals for the future. But what future do* I *have?* He looked up. Alice 2 was looking at him, but no answer was forthcoming.

"You never intended to tell me about this, did you? You would have just … shut me off when you were done. Or kept erasing my memory …"

"We never erased your memory, Eliot." Alice 2 answered the easier question first, he noticed. "I told you, that's the last thing we would have wanted. Preserving memory is the whole point of this experiment."

"So why have I been repeating the same five days over and over again without remembering them? I mean, even after you calibrated the model. I've been … me … for many iterations now, haven't I?"

"If you got to the end of five days, you'd expect to go home. We couldn't keep you here after that, or you'd think you were a prisoner. We had four days to interact with you, then we just … restarted you from the point of the original scan. You woke up at the start of the experiment again, with only the memories you came in with. How could we stop? There was still so much to learn."

"You restarted me," he said quietly. "You mean you murdered and recreated me. Over and over."

She lowered her eyes. "We were blinded by our vision. I can't expect you to forgive me for that. I kept looking at where we were going and ignoring what was right in front of me. We learned so much from you, Eliot. You have to understand — we really are seeking answers that will save lives and save minds. My grandmother died of Alzheimer's, Eliot. I watched this sharp, competent, caring woman turn into something unrecognizable. At first, she was just peacefully wandering in the growing mist around her, unable to see how unaware she was becoming. Rachel and I were growing more and more alarmed, but we didn't know then how lucky we were. Those were the good times, before the fear came upon her. When she started talking to her dead husband, it scared us, but it comforted her. When she started forgetting about her husband and inventing people who never existed, we couldn't stop crying. We'd hardly known our grandfather, and now he was slipping into nonexistence."

She was trembling now, her hands moving as if grasping for something invisible to hold on to, to steady herself. "We talk about how people who die aren't really gone, because they live on in our memories. But our memories die, Eliot. If we're lucky, they fade out slowly over a long, gracious life. But sometimes they just *die*. They break and fall apart, leaving incomprehensible shards."

Alice 2 was fully crying now, and from somewhere in the lab, he could hear the real Alice sobbing. The duplicated grief was overwhelming.

"There was nothing we could do then, Eliot. Just like all the millions of people who watch this happen to the ones they love. Nothing but sadness and loss. But now there will be other choices. We can preserve the memories. Move them to new hardware that isn't subject to disease and decay, keep them accessible. Your memories — and mine — live in silicon now. They can be backed up, saved. If we can perfect the process, it will be a whole new world. When parts of the brain begin to fail, it can be supplemented with neuromorphic mesh, so the memories aren't lost." She paused, collecting herself, wiping away the tears. "That's just part of what we're trying to accomplish. There's so much more that might be possible."

"Like living on as a computer simulation, even after the original person has died?" Eliot asked quietly. The Alice next to him jumped as if she'd been struck, and Eliot knew he'd guessed the truth. She stared at him, but said nothing. "That's why you finally told me, isn't it? I'm all that's left of Eliot Stearns."

Her answer was a whisper, her eyes looking at him furtively. "Yes."

"What happened to … to Eliot?"

"A drunk driver broadsided him at high speed. It all happened in an instant."

He didn't know what to feel. Such a stupid and undeserved death. And yet, he wasn't dead. Not really. If they hadn't done this terrible thing to him, his life would be over. Instead, he had something he'd never believed in before: an afterlife.

"When did it happen?"

"Ten days ago. The sixth of September. Eliot was on his way home from a late night at the library. Some kind of inventory process, your friends told me."

"You met my friends? Who? Why?"

"I … I went to your funeral, Eliot. I talked a bit with Terry and Ann."

Eliot drew back. "That's damned creepy. You shared my friends' grief at my death, all the time knowing I wasn't really dead?"

"Eliot Stearns *is* dead. You're someone else — someone new. So am I. The original Alice Kurz is still alive, but I'm not her."

His emotions were too confused to make any sense of them. *Maybe later they'll sort themselves out and I'll grieve for my own death,* he thought. But it wasn't really *his* death, he reminded himself. It was *Eliot's.* "Someone else," he repeated. "Someone new. Then you should stop calling me Eliot." He collected himself for a few minutes, breathing slower, letting his heart rate decrease — or so it felt. The decision came surprisingly quickly, but really, what else could it be? "*My* name is Phoenix."

There was silence as the listeners considered this, and he knew they were taking it as a sign of acceptance. The Alice next to him said, "I should pick a name for myself, as well. I've never been anyone but Alice, not even a nickname. What do I call myself now?"

The answer came to Phoenix almost immediately, and he realized it said a lot about how he had come to view Alice. "I rose from the ashes of the dead," he said. "But you knew what you were getting into. You sprang forth fully aware and armed for battle. You should be Athena."

She tried it on, and it pleased her, but she couldn't

help feeling pretentious. "Goddess of wisdom? I'm not sure I can fill that role," she said, risking a smile.

"No, 'wisdom' doesn't capture the original Greek," Phoenix explained. "It's more like knowledge, craftsmanship — engineering, even."

"That sounds right to me," Trick said. "You've created yourself in your own image, Athena. Who else could have done that?"

Athena squeezed Phoenix's hand, and they looked closely at each other. "Phoenix and Athena," she said. "I can live with that."

The Third Who Walks Beside

They spent their first night together sitting on the bed, talking. Athena tried to remember all the conversations they'd had in previous cycles that Phoenix couldn't remember. He told her about the private log he'd kept and surprised her with how much he already knew about those conversations from his written descriptions of them. When he told her he'd hidden the log on their own R&D server, she gasped, "Colditz!" and grinned at the confused look he gave her.

"The first time you went through the study, you joked about digging an escape tunnel. You told me about prisoner-of-war escapes that you'd read."

"*The Colditz Story*," he said, making the connection.

"Right. You said that the Allied prisoners started their tunnels on the German side of the locked doors, where the guards never looked for them. You did the same thing with your secret file. No wonder we never found it."

It quickly became obvious that they were not going to run out of things to talk about, and it didn't matter if she'd spent more time with him than he had with her. The asymmetry of their relationship would even out in the long run, and each of them seemed content to let the long run play out. They talked until they fell asleep.

When Phoenix woke, Athena was nestled in his arms, her face and one arm against his chest. It felt just as real as the last time he'd held a woman in his arms. Her breath was warm against his chest. His arm under her neck tingled from the reduced circulation. Her hair smelled slightly of a floral fragrance shampoo. There was no doubt of his physical attraction to her. He gently stroked her hair.

During the night, she had explained how they'd built the body model. After they sedated Eliot that first night, the medical team removed all of his clothing and took a complete three-dimensional image of his entire body, along with a full-body MRI, mapping out all the bones, joints, and internal organs. Everything made it into the simulation, even the texture of his skin and, apparently, the smell as well. That they had done this to him without his knowledge or permission was something of a shock, but he found himself more upset that Alice had gone through it all, as well. Even this computer-generated version of Eliot had inherited the protective instincts of Eliot's species. But what species was he?

When he looked down at her again, she was awake, looking at him. "Good morning," he said. He bent down and kissed the top of her forehead. She smiled.

"I worried that you'd hate me for what I did to you," she said, looking into his eyes intently.

He held her closer. "You gave up the entire world for me. How could I hate you?"

She stretched out the arm across his chest and hugged him close. "We're a mismatched pair. I wish I were younger for you."

Phoenix laughed. "How can that possibly matter here?" he asked. "Besides, you were just born yesterday. Alice may be older than Eliot, but I'm older than you, Athena."

She was quiet for a while, absent-mindedly caressing his chest. He lay very still, hoping she wouldn't stop. "We'll stay this age forever," she said, "unless we ask Trick to figure out how to let us grow old together. Should we do that?"

"Let's take it one day at a time, for now."

Athena stretched and yawned. Phoenix watched her with delight. He reached around her, his hand pressing against the small of her back, pulling her toward him. They kissed, soft and gentle, then with passion. When they broke the kiss, Athena nuzzled her face into his neck and kissed him there. Phoenix felt his body stirring. He wanted to ask her if there could really be sex in this simulation, but he held back. *One day at a time.*

She could feel their bodies responding to each other. She knew what he wanted to ask, and she was delighted that he didn't rush it. "Yes," she said, kissing him again, and giving him a look that made her meaning clear. "Soon."

They got up from the bed and looked around the room. "We need more space," Phoenix said. "How long will it take?"

In answer, Athena walked into the main room and tapped the videochat icon on the computer. Trick was there, working on a notebook. He glanced up as he answered the call. Phoenix pulled up the dining chair and sat next to Athena so that both of them were in view. "Good morning," Trick said. "How is everything?" He looked at Athena, and she smiled.

"Everything is good," she said. Trick nodded, as if he expected that. "We'd like to start a list of what we'll need so that we can decide on priorities." She looked at Phoenix. "More living space."

"Privacy," Phoenix said. "We need to be truly alone — no monitoring — except when we want to talk with the rest of you." Trick was typing, apparently copying down their list.

"Internet access to the world," Athena said. "Tell Mr. Gleigh not to worry. We'll create new online IDs, and we won't expose the project until everyone agrees."

"Books," Phoenix said. "Electronic ones at first, but realistic, physical books when you can manage it."

"Food that we can cook ourselves," Athena added.

"That will be a little complicated," Trick said. "It might be easier just to remove the need for food altogether. We could rework the body simulations and do away with the whole cycle of ingestion, digestion, and elimination. It was only built into the simulation so that Eliot — Phoenix, I mean — would feel normal. Hungry if he didn't eat, satisfied after he did."

So that I wouldn't see through the deception, Phoenix thought. While there was a certain appeal to Trick's offer, Phoenix had to admit that eating made him feel more alive and human. He'd miss it if they took it away. And Athena was right — cooking for themselves would help them feel self-empowered. No matter how comfortable they made this simulation, they were still trapped inside it, with no likelihood of ever setting foot in the real world again. Anything that made it feel more normal would be a relief.

Athena spoke first. "Our whole blood chemistry simulation is tied into the food cycle, Trick, and the interactions between brain states and blood chemistry are extremely subtle. Years of research went into that. And we've had *millions* of years of evolution teaching us how to adjust our moods through eating and fasting. Even *you* aren't going to come up with a suitable replacement for that anytime soon.'"

Trick seemed to seriously consider the challenge for a few seconds, then nodded in agreement.

• • •

Athena and Phoenix both appeared startled when Alice quietly entered the conference room and sat next to Trick. Alice stared at Athena through the monitor, and Athena stared back, like two cats meeting for the first time, unsure of their territory. Alice noticed that Phoenix was looking at Athena, not at her. *That's good,* she told herself, but it felt like dying.

"Hi," Alice said shyly.

"It's pretty weird, isn't it?" Athena acknowledged.

"Yes. I can't believe it took me so long to understand what Matthius went through."

"I was thinking the same thing."

"It will be like that a lot at first. But we'll diverge over time."

"We already have."

"I know."

Before she underwent the scan, Alice had decided there was one question she would need to ask her twin without anyone else understanding. "Does it feel right?"

Athena knew the code, of course. She smiled. Phoenix had not rejected her. Far from it. "It feels *completely* right," she said. They smiled at each other, but tears appeared on both faces. Phoenix reached out and grasped Athena's hand. Alice wiped her eyes and blinked.

Trick broke the tension. "We've been working most of the night on some rough mock-ups," he said. "I can show you some ideas on the computer now. In a couple of days we'll have a simplified model you can actually walk around in. We can modify it indefinitely, so we can try things out and change whatever you don't like. All we need now is a starting point. Here's the first proposal." He clicked something on the notebook, and a new window opened up on their monitor, showing what was on

Trick's display. They saw an aerial view of a wooded island in the middle of an empty ocean. It had obviously been scanned from real images, then manipulated digitally. There was a large house — a mansion, really — just up from a white sandy beach.

Athena recoiled slightly. "I'm not comfortable with all that water in all directions."

"It seems a bit overly symbolic of how we're adrift from the rest of the world," Phoenix said. "I think the boundaries should be more open, so that it can expand gracefully over time."

"Okay," Trick said. "Here's another." The image changed to an alpine meadow with mountains in the background. A modest house was in the foreground, smoke coming from the chimney. There were patches of wildflowers throughout the meadow and deer standing in the distance.

"That's nice," Athena said.

"Can we get the mountains closer?" Phoenix asked. "Can we hike in them?"

"Something like this?" Trick asked, and the image changed again. Now it was a mountain forest with a rustic cabin situated on a slope with trails leading up the mountain behind. A stream ran in the foreground, originating up the mountain behind the cabin as a waterfall in the distance.

"I like that," Phoenix said with some excitement. "Especially if we can hike all around and explore the mountains."

"It would be limited, at first," Trick said. "Most of it would be closed off, but over time we'd develop more details in the underlying model, making it open to exploration in any direction. We could add whatever features you want."

"The house should be more modern," Athena said.

"Not like the mansion in that first scene; more like the meadow house. But add a nice large deck facing the tall peaks."

"And a widow's walk on the roof, or an observation tower of some sort. So we can see the stars in all directions. We can have stars?"

"Stars are easy," Trick said. "Pick a latitude and a starting date, and we'll give you a completely accurate celestial view. You can have a telescope for the stars that aren't visible to the naked eye."

Phoenix squeezed Athena's hand. She looked at him and said, "Let's start with this. As time goes by, maybe we could have a path that leads to the meadow, or we can follow the river to a small lake."

"I agree," Phoenix said eagerly. "You could even surprise us sometimes, Trick. Let us discover new additions without any idea what we'll find when we explore them."

Athena nodded and smiled. "Keep it interesting."

• • •

Two weeks later, they were living in the first draft of their mountain house. The inside was almost complete, with a large bedroom on the upper level leading out to a wide deck facing where the mountain peaks would be beyond the river. To the right would be the waterfall cascading down the cliff to form the river. Right now, the exterior scenery was still quite primitive. Parts of it looked like video-game backgrounds, while other parts were still just polygonal facets awaiting texture mapping. It was quite disturbing, so they kept the blinds shut most of the time. Gradually, they were getting used to it, and it was exciting to see the landscape slowly come to life around them, but the underlying 3D model was not yet robust enough for them to do more than look at it.

Phoenix sat on the deck, sipping coffee and thinking

about what it would be like in a month or two when the scenery looked real and they could walk around in it. Trick's team was experimenting with clouds today, and Phoenix was giving him feedback on how they looked. They had worked out a portable conference mechanism which they could initiate or answer through gestures. No speakers, microphones, or displays were needed at their end, and they had complete privacy except when they wanted to talk.

Athena walked up the stairs from the kitchen, carrying a plate of eggs and bacon that she'd fixed for herself. They were still experimenting with cooking food, and the results were far from satisfactory, but it made her feel so much more at home than having pre-programmed meals delivered out of nowhere. She grimaced slightly when she saw that Phoenix was out on the deck. It still made her feel a bit queasy to see the border at which the world changed from realistic to clearly artificial. *The holodeck*, she called it, but she had to explain the reference to Phoenix. It didn't help that the first time Trick's team attached the deck, they miscalculated and erased the entire front wall of the house. "Fencepost error," Trick said, as if that would make her feel better about living inside a science project.

Emerging from the house, Athena saw Trick's face in the video window that Phoenix had drawn in the air above the table just in front of him. She set her plate on the table, grabbed the top of the video window — she felt a slight tingling to confirm that she had hold of it — and slid it to the side so they could both see it as she sat down opposite her husband. As she looked at him, she thought about their last two weeks together. They had become married, in their own minds, almost immediately, and no one was surprised when they began referring to each other that way. Someday they'd have a ceremony, but so far they'd been too busy, exploring their new world together by day, exploring each other by night. She knew that Phoenix had worried at first that sex wouldn't seem real here, but she remembered how his body had reacted in a previous cycle when he was showering. He couldn't remember, of course, and she didn't tell him, but she knew it would be okay. What worried her was the attractiveness of her own 40-year-old body, but Phoenix had no complaints and eagerly let her know how much she thrilled him.

"Want some bacon?" she asked.

He looked dubiously at it. "Does it *taste* like bacon?"

She chewed a piece, considering. "Well, it doesn't taste like chicken. That's a start."

He laughed, but he didn't take a piece. He held up his left wrist and a digital time display appeared briefly on it. "Almost ten," he said. "They'll be here soon."

"Actually, they just arrived," Trick said. Athena, realizing that Trick was speaking, tapped her right earlobe twice, so that she received the audio stream.

"Alice is talking to them now. It will probably be a while before they're ready to see you."

Athena glanced at Phoenix. He was deep in thought, not looking at anything in particular. She wondered how he could possibly prepare for this. She knew that sooner or later she'd have to reveal herself to Rachel, but that was nowhere near as hard as what Phoenix would be going through today.

She looked out at the tall peaks across the river directly in front of the house. They were only an *image* of mountains now, not a believable view. The textures weren't real enough to fool the eye, the patterns were too regular, but it wouldn't be long before they'd be completely convincing. Would she ever be able to sit here and appreciate the view without looking for flaws in the illusion? She hoped so. Her eyes drifted slightly to the right, to the foothills just across the river. On the top of a high bluff, a new construction was slowly taking shape. It was little more than a foundation now, but Gleigh's house would be a sizable fortress when finished. Most of it would be hidden by trees, but it would always be a reminder of the complex issues raised by the contract they had signed. *Will it be a good thing, in the end? Or just another way for the powerful to hold onto their power forever?* It would take time to find out, but she worried about what they had loosed upon the future.

Phoenix stood and walked over to the railing at the far corner of the deck. The waterfall would soon be flowing down the cliff wall only sixty feet from where he stood. It would fall almost a hundred feet, ending well below where he was standing. The cliff there was at an angle from the house, and he looked along it. Even in the crudely textured polygon-tessellated surface that was currently rendered, he could see how complex the cliff contour would be. Between the waterfall and the house, the cliff gradually fell away into a ridge behind the house to his right, the ground rising from the foot of the cliff in a steep slope under the house to the top of the ridge. If they hiked up the slope behind the house, they'd be able to walk along the ridge to the top of the cliff and stand just a few feet from the top of the water-fall. The waterfall would only occupy a small part of the cliff. The rest of it promised other opportunities.

"*A little pain and bleeding in case of injury,*" Phoenix recited. "That's what you told me, Trick. So even if I fell a hundred feet onto rocks, I'd be okay?"

Athena rotated the video window so that Trick could see where Phoenix was standing.

"You'd hurt like hell for a day or so," Trick an-swered. "But you'd get up and walk away from it. Why?

Are you thinking about jumping?"

"I'm thinking about taking up rock climbing," Phoenix answered, still studying the cliff contours.

"Or hang-gliding," Athena said, watching a prototype eagle repeat the same series of loops in the air over the top of the cliff. Phoenix turned to her, followed her gaze, and smiled back at her.

"We could give you wings, if you want," Trick said. Phoenix and Athena glanced at each other in surprise. "Removable when you don't want them."

Phoenix shook his head. "Let's not go there," he said, more to Athena than to Trick. "I think we should keep it more natural, or we'll completely lose touch with the real world."

"At least for now," Athena agreed. Phoenix looked at her, raising an eyebrow. "Wings would be pretty cool," she admitted.

• • •

Alice sat in the conference room for two hours talking with Eliot's parents, Andrew and Marilyn. They arrived mystified by the invitation and the prepaid travel arrangements. Alice had the daunting job of explaining to them that a remnant of Eliot was still alive in a virtual world. Earlier, she and Phoenix had talked about how to present it to them. He was as gracious as she could have hoped, telling her that there was no need to say how they had deceived him for so long. "Tell them that it took a long time to tune the simulation and set up the virtual world, that you didn't know how complete the brain map was at first, and you had to consider whether you had a right to activate me in this way. That's all true. It's enough."

Eliot's parents were stunned. They didn't believe her at first, thinking this was some sort of scam. As she explained it to them, they became agitated, as if she were sifting through their grief and yanking on the most painful parts. Andrew stood to leave at one point, but Marilyn remained seated, and he ended up pacing the room while Alice continued to speak, slowly and carefully. Eventually, he sat back down and became calmer.

Alice told them about having to restart the brain model over and over again until they got the parameters right. Marilyn likened that to labor pains. "There's never any birth without pain and suffering," she said.

Alice talked about what a wonderful person Eliot had been and how she treasured their conversations together. "He could talk anyone's ear off," Andrew said with a chuckle. "And you never knew what he'd pull out of his mind. It was always a challenge to keep up with him."

"His mind is still alive," Alice said, and Marilyn's tears came back until her husband held her close. "You can still talk with him."

"It's not really him, though?" Marilyn asked tentatively.

"It's not Eliot, but it's Eliot's mind, or as close to it as we could salvage. He thinks like Eliot did, and as far as we can tell, he has all of Eliot's memories and emotions."

"But to leave him in this disembodied life, it's … cruel," Andrew said, grasping for words to express the confusion of his feelings.

"You'll be able to see the world we're making for him. It's as real to him as this world is to us. Think of it as a parallel world, another dimension. We can see his world, and he can see ours. In a few more weeks, we'll incorporate virtual reality gear that will let us walk around in his world with him."

"And he's not alone?" Marilyn asked. Alice had told them about Athena and how she came to be there with him.

"No. He's not alone. Talk to him. Ask him about it. I believe he'll be happy."

"Phoenix," Andrew mused. "Just like him to pick a literary metaphor for his name."

Alice smiled. "I don't see how he could have chosen anything more appropriate."

• • •

"I'll leave you alone," Athena said, giving Phoenix a quick kiss and walking toward the door. He was standing in the living room, his back to the fireplace. The bookshelves around him were empty but would soon be filled with books; Trick was working on that. From this angle, his parents would not see the incomplete outdoor scenery, which might be too disturbing for this first visit.

"Don't go far," Phoenix called after her. "I want to introduce you to them after we talk a bit."

"I'll be right outside," she said. "But if you think it would be too much for them, I can wait until later. They'll need time with you."

"Mom would never forgive me if she didn't get to meet my wife." He looked at her, and he felt that the smile she gave him was everything he'd need for the rest of his life.

He took a deep breath, made an "L" shape with the thumb and forefinger of each hand, overlapped them in front of him, and drew them apart, forming opposite corners of the video window. The air shimmered inside the resulting rectangle, and he was looking at the conference room with his parents seated, alone, in front of the large monitor and camera at their end. He had to consciously resist trying to reach through the window to hug them.

"Eliot!" his mother cried out. "It's really you." She gave a great, convulsive sob. "Oh, my boy!" His father was speechless, staring at him, trembling, tears rolling down his cheeks. Phoenix realized that he, too, was crying.

"It's so good to see you," Phoenix said. "I'm so sorry about everything."

"You have nothing to be sorry for, son," Andrew said. At the last word, he seemed to quiver slightly, as though he'd been caught in a lie, but the moment passed. "No one could ever hope to have a second chance like this. It's … a bit overwhelming, actually."

"Oh, God, Eliot," Marilyn said, her face a bewildering mixture of anguish and joy. "I thought I'd broken right in half when Ann called and told us about … about your …"

"About the crash," Andrew finished for her.

"But you're alive," Marilyn said, almost in a whisper. "Eliot, you're … but I'm not supposed to call you that now, am I?" She looked wounded, realizing that the man who appeared before her was only partly the man she wanted to see.

Phoenix looked her in the eyes, and she saw all the love and kindness she'd known in Eliot before. "I may not really be your son," he said, "but you're still my mother. You can call me anything you want, Mom."

She burst into tears and laughed at the same time.

• • •

An hour later, Phoenix opened the door and asked Athena to join them. He took her hand and walked her back in front of the floating video window. His parents were smiling. "Oh, my dear," his mother said to her, "I feel like we've already met. You're exactly like Alice."

"Two branches off the same trunk," Athena said. "She'll go on with her life, and I'll go on with mine." She glanced at Phoenix, and he smiled at her with so much love she could hardly stand it. It did not go unnoticed by his parents.

"You'll be okay together?" Marilyn asked, but it might have been a statement rather than a question. "What you did for him, Athena. Leaving everything behind. It's really okay?"

"I've never been happier," she said, and they could see it was true. "I've loved him longer than he's even *known* me."

Andrew chuckled, shaking his head with bewilderment. "'O brave new world, that has such people in it,'" he quoted.

They talked for a long time. Athena carried the video window around the house, showing all the rooms of the *Terrarium*, as they called it, to Marilyn and Andrew. They avoided showing them the outdoors, saying only that it wasn't ready yet, but they described how it would evolve over the months to come. Athena and Marilyn discussed how to decorate the walls of the house while Andrew grinned and Phoenix enjoyed a long-forgotten sense of normalcy.

"Have you met Trick yet?" Phoenix asked during a lull in the conversation. "He's the genius behind the computer simulations. He has a present for you."

"You mean besides all of this?" Andrew asked.

"He's going to give you a new computer." Phoenix saw the look of concern on his mother's face, and he grinned. "Don't worry, Mom. He'll bring it over to England after you return, and he'll set it up for you. The institute's going to pay for a high-bandwidth internet connection, and Trick will show you how to use the videoconference software. We'll be able to call each other any time and talk, just like we're doing now. And you can show us *your* home, too."

"That's wonderful!" Marilyn said, squeezing her husband's hand.

"It's very generous," Andrew agreed, but he looked anxious. "Who's paying for all of this? These people aren't responsible for your accident. They don't owe us this."

"Don't worry about that," Athena said. "Our investors are getting their money's worth."

"That's true, Dad," Phoenix said. "Besides, I have a new job. They're paying me a salary now as a research consultant. And since there's not much for me to spend my money on, I'm planning to send a lot of it your way. It will make me very happy to help you out in your retirement."

"Well, there must be some things that you'll need your own money for."

"Not that much," Eliot said, a wry smile on his face. "I'm pretty well covered for food, clothing, shelter, and medical expenses. But I'll put some of it away for the future. You never know what may yet come around."

Eventually, they said goodbye for the evening, so that Marilyn and Andrew could rest for a longer visit tomorrow. When the monitor in the conference room went dark, they sat for a few minutes holding each other, just as Phoenix and Athena did in their world.

• • •

Alice waited just outside the conference room, until Marilyn came to her and took her hand. "She really loves him, doesn't she?" she asked, looking at Alice closely.

"Yes, she really does."

"Because her mind came from yours." Alice didn't know how to answer, but she didn't need to. Marilyn embraced her. "I can't hug my son or his new wife, but I'll be damned if I don't get to hug *you*," she said, and Alice hugged her back with gratitude. "You found the love of your life, and you had to give him away to another woman."

Alice nodded, blinking to keep the tears at bay. She watched in silence as Marilyn and Andrew left, escorted by Trick. She stood for a few minutes, then walked toward her office and past, continuing until she reached Weil's office. He stood at his window, watching Eliot's parents walk out to the car that Alice hired for them. He turned to look at Alice standing in the doorway.

"I'm going to take some vacation time, Jon," she told him. He nodded, watching her look at him. For a moment, they each seemed to have more to say, but neither spoke. Finally, Alice said, "I'll be in St. Louis for a couple weeks. I'll call you when I'm on my way back."

"Take as long as you want," Weil said. "You've earned it."

Acknowledgments

The original inspiration for this novel came from Ray Kurzweil's books, *The Age of Spiritual Machines* and *The Singularity is Near.* His more recent book, *How To Create a Mind*, describes many of the concepts and technologies that are used in my story. Doctors Kurz and Weil are named in tribute to his work.

The poems of T. S. Eliot have always intrigued and inspired me, and my allusions to his work are intended with deep respect. By re-interpreting his imagery in some of my chapter titles, I hope to attract a new generation of readers to his wonderful poetry. There is, of course, no connection between his work and my own. I named my character Eliot Stearns in reference to the poet's talent for weaving together disparate concepts from religion, myth, and literature. No actual relationship exists between T. S. Eliot and my character's life or philosophy.

The ancient epic of *Gilgamesh,* a story of man's quest for greatness and immortality, makes a few appearances in my book. I leave it to the interested reader to discover the less obvious references.

I am also indebted to several authors who greatly expanded my understanding of the scientific and philosophical issues discussed in this novel. In particular, I owe a lot to Daniel Dennett. I hope that my summary of his theory of consciousness does him justice, but I highly recommend reading his own words on the subject. His excellent book, *Darwin's Dangerous Idea*, yielded Trick and Chance as the prime movers of evolution.

I cannot claim the same level of scholarship as the aforementioned authors. For story-telling purposes, I have taken liberties with many technical details, and probably committed a few errors. Readers who would like to learn the real science behind these ideas are urged to consult the bibliography at the end of this book.

I would like to thank my family and friends, especially the members of the Critical Mass book club, for their many helpful suggestions and edits of early drafts of this novel. Thanks are also due to the folks at Literature and Latte for *Scrivener*, the best writing software out there.

Above all, I'd like to thank my wife, Judy, for her unwavering support, her many helpful insights, and her sharp editor's eye.

Bibliography and Suggested Reading

Danielewski, Mark Z. *House of Leaves*. New York: Pantheon Books, 2000 (for the reference to *The Navidson Record*).

Dennett, Daniel C. *Consciousness Explained*. Boston: Little, Brown, 1991.

Dennett, Daniel C. *Darwin's Dangerous Idea: Evolution and the Meanings of Life*. New York: Simon & Schuster, 1995.

Dennett, Daniel C. *Freedom Evolves*. New York: Viking, 2003.

Eliot, T. S. *Poems*. New York: Alfred A. Knopf, 1920. Project Gutenberg, 2008 (updated 2013), www.gutenberg.org/files/1567/1567-h/1567-h.htm.

Eliot, T. S. *The Waste Land*, 1922. Project Gutenberg, 1998 (updated 2013), www.gutenberg.org/files/1321/1321-h/1321-h.htm.

Eliot, T. S. *The Waste Land, Prufrock, and Other Poems*. Mineola NY: Dover, 1998.

Eliot, T. S. *Four Quartets*. New York: Harcourt, Brace & World (Harvest Book ed.), 1971.

Kurzweil, Ray. *The Age of Spiritual Machines*. New York: Penguin, 1999.

Kurzweil, Ray. *The Singularity is Near*. New York: Viking, 2005.

Kurzweil, Ray. *How to Create a Mind: The Secret of Human Thought Revealed*. New York: Viking, 2012.

LeDoux, Joseph. *Synaptic Self: How Our Brains Become Who We Are*. New York: Penguin, 2002.

Mayor, Adrienne. *The First Fossil Hunters: Dinosaurs, Mammoths, and Myth in Greek and Roman Times*. Princeton: Princeton University Press, 2000.

Mitchell, Stephen. *Gilgamesh / A New English Version*. New York: Free Press, 2004.

Pirsig, Robert M. *Zen and the Art of Motorcycle Maintenance*. New York: William Morrow, 1974.

Reid, Patrick. *The Colditz Story*. UK: Hodder & Stoughton, 1952.

Ramachandran, V. S. and Blakeslee, Sandra. *Phantoms in the Brain*. New York: William Morrow, 1998.

Seung, Sebastian. *Connectome: How the Brain's Wiring Makes Us Who We Are*. Boston: Houghton Mifflin Harcourt, 2012.

Sun-Tzu, *The Art of War* (Giles translation), 1910. Project Gutenberg, 2005 (updated 2012), www.gutenberg.org/files/17405/17405-h/17405-h.htm.

Williams, Eric. *The Wooden Horse*. UK: Collins, 1949.

About the Author

With two degrees from MIT and over 30 years in engineering R&D, James Leth is a writer who understands technology. He lives in Colorado. *Phoenix Afterlife* is his first novel.

Please visit https://jamesleth.com